VOLUME THREE OF THE

YALE EDITION OF THE

UNPUBLISHED WRITINGS

OF GERTRUDE STEIN

under the general editorship

of Carl Van Vechten

with an advisory committee

of Donald C. Gallup, Donald

Sutherland, and Thornton Wilder

THE YALE EDITION OF THE

UNPUBLISHED WRITINGS OF GERTRUDE STEIN

Two: Gertrude Stein and Her Brother

Mrs. Reynolds and Five Earlier Novelettes

Bee Time Vine and Other Pieces (1913–1927)

BEE TIME VINE

AND OTHER PIECES [1913–1927]

BY GERTRUDE STEIN

with a Preface and Notes by Virgil Thomson

NEW HAVEN: YALE UNIVERSITY PRESS

London: Geoffrey Cumberlege, Oxford University Press

1953

PREFACE

Some of the writing included in this volume, "The Work" for instance, is easy to understand. Other poems, such as "A Sonatina Followed by Another" and "Lifting Belly," reveal their content to persons acquainted with the regions they describe or with their author's domestic life. Still others, however, like "Bee Time Vine" and "Patriarchal Poetry," are genuinely hermetic, by which I mean that the words mean what they mean in the poem by contrast with their common sense rather than by any easily discernible parallel to it.

The first kind is as clear as Kipling. The second kind invites annotation in the way that the writings of Joyce, T. S. Eliot, Pound, and Valéry do. The third kind, which is extremely resistant to exegesis, it is legitimate to consider, I think, as abstract composition. Indeed, that is the way Gertrude Stein always referred to it—as "narration" or "description" or "paragraphs" or "sentences," never in terms of its meaning.

This does not mean that it had no meaning for her or that the reader is advised against searching for one. There is every reason to suppose that she used her subjects as a painter does his models, sometimes revealing them for recognition and at other times concealing them under such an elaboration of contrasts, puns, private associations, and rhythmic patterns that their resistance to exposure is well-nigh complete.

In my notes to the present volume I have not attempted the full explanation of any text. I have merely shared with the reader such information as I have about each one. Much of this informa-

tion has been given me by Miss Alice B. Toklas, Gertrude Stein's secretary.* The ideas expressed about "Patriarchal Poetry," the only text included that was composed during my acquaintance with Miss Stein, are wholly mine.

I have also abstained, for the most part, from expressing opinions. The high esteem in which I have long held the writings of Gertrude Stein is a matter of public knowledge. That esteem antedates by a good many years my friendship with her. Its basis, like that of all artistic admirations, is instinctive. If it required defense, however, I might offer this: that the greatness of the great poets has never been measurable by the amount of clear thought expressed in their works. It is far more a matter of their ability to compose unforgettable lines. Judged by this standard Gertrude Stein ranks very high indeed. And clarity has nothing to do with the matter. "Rose is a rose is a rose is a rose" obviously needs no bush. Neither does the compact summation, quoted from Disraeli, "What do we live for. Climate and the affections. Jews quote that." "Toasted Susie is my ice cream," though plenty obscure, is equally memorable, explained or unexplained. The second paragraph of "Patriarchal Poetry" has also its solidity, a specific gravity rare in literature, though I have not the slightest idea what it means.

Perhaps one day I may find the meaning in it. Gertrude Stein's lines do sometimes give up their secrets over the years. In Four Saints in Three Acts *there occurs the following dialogue:*

> Ste. Therese: Might with widow.
> Ste. Therese: Might.

I had put this to music in 1927–28, coached and conducted it many times. In 1952 Maurice Grosser, who had known it almost as long as I, surprised me (and himself) with the discovery that it must refer (and how could one have missed it?) to the "widow's

---

* Phrases in quotation marks, unless cited from Gertrude Stein's own text, are quoted from this source.

mite" and, as the spelling indicates, to any widow's might, morally speaking.

Further layers of meaning may be involved also, since I do remember that in 1927, when the Four Saints libretto was being written, Miss Stein was seeing a certain rich and powerful American widow. This woman wore her might as visibly as she did her widowhood. She may well have come into the composition, as did Miss Stein's cook. The latter, a woman named Hélène, had worked for Miss Stein before 1914. In the middle 1920's she returned for about a year and a half. Miss Stein's gratification at the event, mixed with anxiety lest this excellent servant leave again (for she was uncompromising as she was efficient), entered the play in a long sentence beginning "To have to have have Helen." What relation in meaning this passage bears to Spain and to the saintly life I have never known for sure, but I suspect that both women reminded Gertrude Stein of Saint Teresa. Or vice versa.

The present volume has in it landscape and love poetry and much mention of people and a great deal about the War, the first World War. It also contains every kind of writing from the plainest to the virtually impenetrable. The only kind that is not here is the kind Miss Stein never wrote, the kind that people forget. As I said before, she must be one of the great, for she sticks in the mind.

VIRGIL THOMSON

CONTENTS

ALPHABETICAL LIST OF INDIVIDUAL TITLES

A SONATINA FOLLOWED BY ANOTHER

DEDICATED BY REQUEST TO D.D.

A SONATINA FOLLOWED BY ANOTHER *was written during the spring of 1921 in Vence, where Gertrude Stein had been loaned a house by an American friend. The dedication "to D.D." is, according to my chief informant, "one of Gertrude's fantasies. There was no D.D." The title refers to Miss Stein's custom of improvising "every evening" on the pianoforte.*

Miss Stein was no pianist. Even as a listener her musical pleasures were largely limited to an appreciation of music's rhetoric. Nevertheless, during the time she lived at Vence, where there was a piano in the house and where the evenings were quiet, she did like to "improvise," using only the white keys.

That season she always referred to what she played as "sonatinas." She would even announce in advance their content, saying, "I'm going to play a march in my sonatina." And at her companion's look of surprise she would reassure, "Oh! Not a Turkish march."

Ten years later, at Bilignin, where there was also a piano, Miss Stein spoke to me of "improvising on the white keys"; but I never heard her do it. I did, however, write her a sonata on the white keys "to improvise on the pianoforte." This direction, of course, was purely dedicatory, since she did not read music at all fluently.

The subject matter of the present poem is the region around Vence and its personal associations. Everything in it refers to the daily life. The local palm trees, for instance, reminded the author of Tubb's Hotel in Oakland, California, where she had acquired in her early years so firm an association regarding palms and eucalyptus that palms, wherever seen and whether growing in terrains or in tubs, always meant to her Tubb's Hotel. Godiva was Miss Stein's pet name for her Ford car. The poem is not hermetic, however obscure some references in it may seem. It is a picture of Vence and its environs and of Miss Stein living there.

V.T.

I

Thank you very much, how often I have thanked you, how often I have cause to thank you. How often I do thank you.

Thank you very much.

And what would you have me do.

I would have you sing songs to your little Jew.

Not in the form of games not in the way of repetitions. Repetitions are in your first manner and now we are in the South and the South is not in the North. In the North we resist even when we are kissed and in the South we are kissed on the mouth. No sonatina can make me frown.

I love my love with a g because she is so faithful. I love her with a p because she is my pearl.

Can you subsist on butter, oil and edibles and rosebuds and weddings. Can you have weddings in many countries. How do each how does each mountain have a hill a steep hill, and I, I am always good.

Coo-coo, Mona. Plan away.

Have you seen a mixed dream. I dreamed of dances and guesses and cooing. How did you guess that.

Eighty pages of love and blandishment and small hand writing. And now a poem a conversation an address and a dialogue and a rebuttal.

Birds are fat and roses are yellow.

Tea is a color and tileul a drink.

Politics is a subject and obedience is necessary.

Blandishments are long and the buds are budded.

Who budded the buds.

I do love Tubbs hotel very well with Eucalyptus and palms and Godiva and a mistress.

A little hand writing is precious.

And now a conversation.

Let me neglect you. Do not let me neglect you. I do not let you neglect me. I am reproachful.

I have been reading. What. The book about Russia. And you

have loaned it to me. No I was personal. In the french sense. In the french sense. Do not be elusive and remember the last sign of the Moor. We walked far for that. I forgot that it was a conversation. That it is a conversation.

And now an address.

Address me to number thirteen rue San Severin and St. Anthony, address Saint Anthony too. And building blocks. Address building blocks and the can for the oil, address the can for the oil. Address it to all.

A dialogue.

I love you, I know it, how do you know it, I know it by my feeling.

And a rebuttal.

We do not use coal, we burn wood, we find it more economical and pleasanter. Before the war we used to wish that we could afford to burn wood instead of coal, now that we are no richer and wood is dearer we find it more economical to burn wood. Can you reason with me. I do not wish to.

And now as to cooing.

Coo away.

I miss the Mistral.

And the wood.

The wood misses the mistral.

And misses. Misses does not miss the mistral. Eighty pages are not eighty leaves, there are forty leaves, forty leaves make eighty pages.

And thunder.

The thunder comes from the door.

What can roses do, they can grow red without being seen.

How faithful is Caroline.

I can tell you a story about the North west.

Northwest from here is a hill and above the or rather near the top is a village. They grow orange blossoms, olives and winter grapes. The olive crop has been a failure for two years, the orange trees have been frozen, and the vines which are now just budding have been affected by the fog. In spite of all this the village is extremely prosperous. This is owing to the constant visits of artists and tourists. Thank you very much.

Pussy said that I was to wake her in an hour and a half if it didn't rain. It is still raining what should I do. Should I wake her or should I let her sleep longer.

Coo, coo.

The coo coo bird is sitting on the coo coo tree, budding the roses for me.

Why is pussy like the great American Army. Because she buds so many buddies.

And now I want to explain again the difference between the South of France and Brittany. In Brittany they have early potatoes. In the South they have early vegetables. In Brittany there is a great deal of fish caught. In the South they catch a great deal of fish. There are trout in the streams in some streams of Brittany and in some streams in the South. They grow camellias in some places in Brittany. They also grow camellias in the South.

I am very pleased to be in the South.

I address my caress, my caresses to the one who blesses who blesses me.

I usually say it for each separately.

I am going to say it for all of them altogether.

White yellow and pink roses, single ones.

Pink roses. Single ones.

White red and yellow roses.

An elephant.

Pink roses, single ones.

White roses.

Lilacs white roses and red roses and tea roses.

I need not mention the others.

How can gaiters cover old shoes.

How can rubber heels come off.

How can oil be thick and thin.

How can olives flower.

And why don't figs.

If Napoleon had a son, we could see Corsica in the morning. We have not seen Corsica yet. Everybody has mentioned it.

Why can butter be yellow or white.

She is so political.

And Mrs. Johnson is so afraid.

Coo, coo, I mention it. Coo coo I hear it. Coo coo let us be moderate. We are personal. We have a personal husband.

How can you read a book how can you read a book and look. I have no book.

I look.

Coo coo don't listen to me.

Do you know how to say buggy wagon riding. Do you know how to go slow. Go slowly. I go very slowly. Coo-coo I love but you.

This is old fashioned stuff. Now we say, Coo coo, I am all to you.

Cover up roses scratches, with what with black oil, and what else frog's noises.

I can understand copying gallo romaine pottery but I do not care to spend much money buying original ones. You can buy them for almost nothing.

Egg shells. Who sells egg shells and oranges and green peas. Who does. Answer me.

Eight out of eighty is how much. It isn't out of eighty, it's out of forty. Eight out of eighty is how much.

I said hastily that I was very rich.

I can think of everything to say.

Call to me with frogs and birds and moons and stars. Call me with noises. Mechanical noises.

I do not disturb you unnecessarily. Oh yes, you do.

I aspire to acquire every virtue and the allied armies. They will ride and we will see them. At a distance perhaps. And she sneezed. I am quite sure that it did not portend a chill. No indeed brilliant sunshine.

Gladys Deacon is so brilliant and so is Chicago. I do not mention either of them here.

Coo coo a message to you.

And she did not make cheese very well.

We see no necessity for reductions.

I please myself and I please Mrs. Johnson. I pay her. Who payed her. You payed her. Why certainly you payed her.

Let me tell you about yesterday. Yesterday I was Lindoed and you you were so gracious. And to-day. To-day I was still lindoed and you were even more gracious. You are extraordinarily gracious and I am very contentedly grateful. In this way we are adjusted. Pinions are adjusted. They are not like a bird. They do not fly.

I spy a fly.

It was a bee.

You are my honey honey suckle.

I am your bee.

You are my honey honey suckle.

I am your bee.

We saw a blacksmith making springs and we waited in the dust and were content not content to wait but content with the springs. We hope we have cause to be content with the three springs.

Two weeks are less than three weeks. We will see everything.

Olives for wood, butter for cheese, milk for honey, and wind for sunny sunny weather and clouds. How can you distress me. You can't. You can please me. And an apprentice. You can please me as an apprentice. Apprentisage.

A nice library a very nice library, she mentions it as a very nice library.

Coo coo come dirty me, coo coo. I am for thee.

Do we like corn bread.

Here is an interesting story. In visiting churches we find many little colored images pretty renaissance altars and late colored glass chandeliers and flowers and we said what we liked best were the colored glass and after that the little colored images on the ceiling and after that the flowers. We sent our servant to see these treasures. She walked 5 miles and enjoyed them very much. So had we.

We have a multitude of roses and mountains of lilac. We pick everything as it shows. We are a model to every one. We are wonderfully productive.

This is another interesting story. We found ourselves suddenly without eggs for supper. We were quite near an Italians and we bought some very good sausages. We also bought some anchovies and cakes and then we came home at a very rapid pace.

We came home so rapidly that we were able to go down hill slowly. We always prefer going down hill slowly. When we had finished supper we were very certain that we were not hurried. We always linger in a chair. To-morrow in a fashion of speaking is the Holy Sabbath.

How can you think of everything when roses smell the most and tea pots lean on elephants and a spring is lost. How can you mention orange wear when orange blossoms last how can you laugh at me all day when all day has been passed, splendidly with an Englishman a negro and a Pole who might have had a Russian name.

How can you easily please me you can do so very well and how can you laugh as asparagrass when peas will do as well, and gloves. How we appreciate doves. Gloves and palms, please take care. Take care of what. Take care of electricity. Electricity takes care of itself.

A reform for two is not to stew.

A red poppy is for decoration and a daisy is a humble expression of a husband's love. Together they make a bouquet. Joined to nasturtiums and pansies they show unexpected tenderness.

If the South is cold and the North is colder, if the wind is strong and the palms are stronger, if there are no palms in the North only lilacs what emotion do canticles express. Canticles are religious.

Can we still be a necessity.

Counting horses, a large horse is named butterfly.

Relieve me relieve me from the Turk. He was not a Turk he was partly Negro. His father came from New Orleans in Louisiana.

Can you prefer one who is not Italian can you prefer cooking that is not Italian. Can you prefer rice that is Italian. Can you be selected to look through the window. And what do I see. I see you.

Can a cow keep sweet. Yes if it has a blessing. Can a cow keep its retreat. No not if it has a blessing. Can a cow have feet. Yes if it has a blessing. Can a cow be perfect. Yes if it has a blessing.

I bless the cow. It is formed, it is pressed, it is large it is crowded. It is out. Cow come out. Cow come out and shout.

Have Caesars a duty. Yes their duty is to a cow. Will they do their duty by the cow. Yes now and with pleasure. Mock oranges do not mock me.

We have the true orange the orange blossom. And do perfumes smell. Yes in the grass.

How can I welcome you. I do.

Now there is a case in point.

I arouse, you arouse we arouse and Godiva arouses me. This should not be. We should tranquilly think of the remedy. I arouse the sympathy of Grasse. Why is grass white. Because it is covered with white hail. How pleasantly we back out.

And now mountains, and now mountains, do not cloud, over. Let us wash our hair and stare stare at mountain ranges. How sweet are suns and suns. And the season. The sea or the season, and the roads. Roads are often neglected.

How can you feel so reasonably.

And what were the pages.

And why were there men who had hurry as their reason. Not now. They were not in a hurry now. How precious you are.

A poppy, need I say a red poppy. A poppy by its color is a symbol of the decoration a grateful country gives you in recognition of your devotion to duty and the daisies are a humble expression of a husband's love. Now take it.

Can we count a nightingale. Can we escort one another. Can we feed on artichokes and olives and may we sell anchovies. No we may buy eggs. And now often do you say, I argue often about words and houses. How are houses entered. By the determination to be well and happy. How kindly you smile. How sweetly you smile on me. How tenderly you reward me and how beautifully you utter your words. We have no use for botanically painted plates.

How can I thank you enough for holding me on the ladder for allowing me to pick roses, for enjoying my fireside and for recollecting stars. How can I thank you enough for all your kindness to me. How can I thank you enough.

If I could I would make this arrangement.

Here donkey and he brays, so does not my mistress.

Here donkey. Just a minute. Monte Carlo. Just a minute.

Here donkey. We crave sweets.

Not because we like honey or landscapes but just because we have ancient habitations. We are placed under a torn sky, and the Romans were lenient and paused on the road. How nicely we go up hill.

When I was wishous, when I had wishes. When I wished I wished to be remembered to you.

How can you silently think of me. Rest easily on the terrace look out on the blue sea and think of me.

How can rows of roses spare matches. How can matches strike. How can images be blue, temples are blue and how are brooches red. Fish come in summer. They need rain and warm weather.

I can lean over a parapet, you can lean over a parapet, we can lean over a parapet, she can lean over a parapet, they can all stand as if they were waiting for their king. There are no kings there are nothing but princesses. Princes and princesses.

And where have I seen you before.

In a way a honey moon is not treated to hail. It is not treated to rain, it is not treated to mischief, it is not treated to threats. It is treated to pleasure and prophecy. I prophesy good weather.

How do I care for hair. I care for hair by cutting it.

That is an excellent method.

And how long does an inventory take.

It takes all day. Not every day. No not every other day. I leave mine behind me. You are so wise.

Do you despise decorations.

Do you admire gypsies.

Do you really wear a chinese hat.

We do.

Can we eat to-day, to-day is the month of May. Can we eat to-day largely.

And how nicely we sing of the thirteenth of April. The thirteenth of April is the day which is the month of May. On that day we hesitate to sing. Why because we are so happily flourishing.

We make a list, a sauce dish, a saucer, a tile, a gilded cushion, a handkerchief, a glass, two plates and an oratory. And what do we do in the oratory. We tell about our blessings. We bless the day every day. We say gayly the troubadour plays his guitar to his star.

How can we whistle in our bath. By means of oxygen. Oxygen in water makes oxygenated water. Thank you for all you are doing for me. And don't mind the rain. It is not going to rain long.

The song of Alice B.

Little Alice B. is the wife for me. Little Alice B so tenderly is born so long so she can be born along by a husband strong who has not his hair shorn. And what size is wise. The right size is nice. How can you credit me with wishes. I wish you a very happy birthday.

One two one two I come to you. To-day there is nothing but the humble expression of a husband's love. Take it.

I caught sight of a splendid Misses. She had handkerchiefs and kisses. She had eyes and yellow shoes she had everything to choose and she chose me. In passing through France she wore a Chinese hat and so did I. In looking at the sun she read a map. And so did I. In eating fish and pork she just grew fat. And so did I. In loving a blue sea she had a pain. And so did I. In loving me she of necessity thought first. And so did I. How prettily we swim. Not in water. Not on land. But in love. How often do we need trees and hills. Not often. And how often do we need mountains. Not very often. And how often do we need birds. Not often. And how often do we need wishes. Not often. And how often do we need glasses not often. We drink wine and we make, well we have not made it yet. How often do we need a kiss. Very often and we add when tenderness overwhelms us we speedily eat veal. And what else, ham and a little pork and raw artichokes and ripe olives and chester cheese and cakes and caramels and all the melon. We still have a great deal of it left. I wonder where it is. Conserved melon. Let me offer it to you.

How can you sleep so sweetly, how can you be so very well. Very well.

How can you measure measures I measure measures very well.

To be a roman and Julius Caesar and a bridge and a column and a pillar and pure how singularly refreshing.

We know of a great many things we are not to do. We are not to laugh or be sarcastic or harsh or loud or sudden or neglectful or preoccupied or attacked or rebukeful.

He is so generous with the towels. He leaves her two fresh clean ones.

How can you worship extras. I find it exceedingly simple to do so. I have but to see.

I see the sea and it is a river not a murmuring river nor a roaring river nor a great river nor a callous river. I see Saint Anthony in the river. Saint Anthony the fruit of the olive, the crown of the orange the strength of the cork. Saint Anthony, pray for us.

I feel nearly everything.

How often the wind how often the wind resists iron. How often it manages to show. We have tall walls and so have palaces.

I can be seen to be a queen. I can be seen declaring that wine how can wine be so cheap. It will be cheaper. And is there a providence in Provence. There is no comfort in a home, because they are not as reasonable in their hopes as they are in their fears. Wine makes no water. Water makes wine. The wine, the vine needs water and we we wish to eat our lunch in the department of Vaucluse. And we will we will arrange the department to be willing. Napoleon, why did they declare their purpose. Napoleon listened to music in Avignon, he felt the strength of the violin and the composition. We were not inimical to women nor to men, nor even to educated strangers. We liked best of all the soldiers and the salt. How many leaves have pitchers. And what is the difference between white and yellow. And how many lions are golden. All dogs seen at a distance, run.

Willy nilly with a roasted kid, how can you be so delicious and give it to the cat. I gave to the cat because we were uncomfortable. We are not naturally uncomfortable, we are a little nervous. I took a piece of pork and I stuck it on a fork and I gave it to a curly headed jew jew jew. I want my little jew to be round like a pork, a young round pork with a cork for his tail.

A young round pork. I want my little jew to be round like a young round pork. I do.

A special name for careless is caress. A special name for answers is tenderness a special name for Master is Mrs. C. A special name for an enormous hotel is very well I will not answer back.

When the swallows fly so high you mustn't cry because when the swallows fly so high the sun will shine out by and by.

I never answer back.

Back there.

How can the mother of a priest see through your glasses.

The times, the times is a rose, the rose is a nose, in time the nose arose. To arise means to clean, to wash out. Thank you so much.

What have little museums in them. They have dutch British English and austrian things in them and when we see them we say they are copies of French and when we see them and we see them when we see of them we read of them. We know we will like them. And we are not mistaken.

We did not stay where St. Stephen was to pray we did not stay we did not play we saw the guns and what did they say, they said that it was not necessary to be protected, it was only necessary to be firm and numerous, it was only necessary to be stoned it was only necessary. A great many people hesitate about St. Stephen. We didn't.

When we came away we came away to stay we came away steadily. And where are we. We are in the land of sky larks not in the land of nightingales. We do not mention robins swallows, quails and peacocks. We do not mix them. We murmur to each other, nightingales, we please each other with fruit trees we allow each other melons and we throw each other shoes. And pork. What do we think about pork and asparagus. What do we think about everything. It is necessary for us to know what we think. We think very well of butter and church cheese. We think very well of cracked church bells.

How many is four times two. Eight. And seven plus one. Eight. And six and two. Eight. And how much is seven. Seven is five and two and four and three. We are free. We are free to have false smiles. I smile falsely and I do not hesitate to give pleasure I speak sharply and I hear the sound of falling water. I linger and I kiss a rose. How often do I kiss a rose. Everytime. I approach the wonder. I wonder why I have so many wishes. I wish to please and to be repeated. This is in my first manner. Thank you so much for your first manner. That is most kind of you.

Misses meet Mister.

Is that what you were doing.

I quit early. So does every one who works eight hours a day.

Georgie Sand is in my hand and what are omelettes made of, of oranges and lemonade and how did you see the new moon. It was not the new moon it was the first quarter.

Don't make fun of me.

How sweet to tickle little sweet and how prettily little pigs eat, and how interesting to collect treasures and how admirable to celebrate pleasures. Napoleon was a great pleasure.

A sonatina followed by another. The public is not invited to laugh. Who brought the turkeys to France. A Jesuit father brought the turkeys to France and ate them and then they grew and then we ate them and then we grew. Let me see the cups. How often do we say let me learn to stay. I stay all day and all night too.

How can I be relished by lunches. How can I be stolen for tea. I cannot. How can I be earnest in churches how can I be wise in a chateau. We say so.

False smiles are wiles to make one's styles realise the difference between a tone and a tone. I atone with smiles and miles.

How many forests believe in Carpentier and will he win on a foul. How many times have I asked this and how often has a fowl replied. Oh the dear dear fowl oh the sweet false smile oh the tender tender while, we while the time away so pleasantly and she, she is my nature's daily food and she is wooed and chewed. Respect me.

I see the moon and the moon sees me god bless the moon and god bless me which is she.

II

A sonatina followed by another. This ought to be the other. And it is.

A sonatina song is just this long. A sonatina long is just this song.

Come along and sit to me sit with me sit by me, come along and sit with me all the next day too. Come along and sit with me sit by me sit for me, come along and sit by me sit by me and see.

Seneca said that he loved to be wed. And he said that was what he said.

Carefully meddle with me.

If you think, if you think much, if you reflect if you reflect me, I reflect that I have not been serviceable. But you are very serviceable.

Do not be plaintive and sing, meddle with me, meddle with me, medal, who has the medal.

Sing reasonably.

How happy we are on the fourth of July.

There is more short hair than long hair here. Hear me. I will be clerical. And researches. Researches rhyme with churches!

Rachel says Rachel says she is my aunt. I do not deny her. Nor do I blaspheme the saints. I am always to see Saint Anthony thought of.

Please be very still. And repeat, let us lead it by ourselves. And we did. Godiva did. And happily.

What can Beauvais say, Beauvais can say come away. And we did. We will go to Brussels. Brussels rhymes with muscles.

I look very pretty in sculpture.

Make a new way to say, how do you do. I can write to there. And how will you do it. By measuring from there to there. France is french.

A sonatina caressed. I like that best.

I have a fancy for reconciliation. How can you reconcile beets and strawberries. By knowing they both are red.

How easily we release images. And why do we worry the blacks. Black and blue all out but you.

I reason, we reason we reason for a reason. How prettily I shimmer. We have assisted ourselves. And sunshine. We brought rain, in our train, Godiva Godiva Godiva.

Let us and let us and let us say. We go away and absolutely we reason in this way. Why are pages open and why are we not disappointed. Why do we moisten our hands. Because it is hot. I breathe freely.

Birds and pages and Brussels. Lobster will be cheaper. Lobsters will be cheaper after a bit. And how often do we intend to go a mile.

Summaries are precious to me. Left over every where is precious to me.

Continue to purse your lips and remember that fruit is not abundant this year.

And how much patience is there in singing.

All the mouths are near and all the mouths are here and all the mouths have that.

I am still satisfied.

Wedding jelly.

Have that colored white.

The reason is not far to seek.

The honey honey honey suckle. I am the bee.

Words and sizes. There are surprises. Can you quote speeches. Can you quote speeches. Words and sizes there are surprises. And little screens. How literally we screen her. We have barricades and weaponless sisters and all sorts of repeated curtains. Curtains let us take advantage of repetitions. She tells a story so brightly. And a hero has patience. He leans this way.

How can so many sonatinas be followed by another. Everybody smiles.

How can you press me to you.

All the rest of the bale is filled with down. We find it very compressible.

Can you thank me for so much.

A great many numbers indicate the number of places to which we can go. A great many numbers have this to say. Go this way. A great many numbers have special sizes and under them there is a large F. Be so pleased to see for tea.

We are going to remember this very soon. And recall her. And recall her call her.

Now no motion is so fast as hurling.

She is immovable.

Have a chance repeatedly for the use of this have a chance repeatedly collect me.

I have been useful to her.

ANNEX TO NO. 2

SONATINA FOLLOWED BY ANOTHER

NOT YET SAT BUT WALKING

I can but think I can but think, and what do you stare at. Cultivation.

In the forest by the sea in feathers, two white feathers have decorated Normandy. They have been placed there by the girl who came by sea from Barbery. Casablanca is now entirely a french city.

We are spending our honeymoon in Normandy. We are following in the footsteps of our brother who found that the inhabitants singularly flattered his wife. He has been married a long time and has a son twenty five years old.

How old are brave women. We find that a disrupter we find that a disrupter is singularly useful in an emergency but entirely impractical when used too continuously. We have returned to our normal footing. We love the hand. The hand that forbids collisions. The french avoid a crisis and the Americans arise to it.

Do not think that we are safe.

We are safe in a safe deposit that is in a hotel found for us by our brother.

And now gently guide us up hill.

Uphill and down dale.

How is it that the English do not mind remembering that they once possessed Normandy. How is that they do not mind noticing that all their civilisation resembles the civilisation of Normandy. How is it that they do not mind me. I love to mind to remind to remind them and they remind me of everything.

Why is there a certitude in recreation. Why is there feeling in antithesis.

Leaves cabbage grass, apples trees gold cream oaks and ears, now many people need me.

I need her, she needs me, she needs me, I need that she is splendidly robust. Please me by thinking at ease.

Good-night now.

Sincerely yours,
Augustus Wren.

Flaubert have a care. Have a care Flaubert. Flaubert don't be hurt don't be hurt Flaubert.

When we were traveling we saw cunning, we saw cunning in women, we saw cunning in men, we saw cunning in children, when we were traveling we hesitated before wishing and then in the evening we saw a star and we start wishing. I wish I was a fish with a great big tail, a polly wolly doodle a lobster or a whale. This was not what I wished. I never tell my wish.

Earnestly we notice that a pharmacy has a green light that a railroad has a red light and a green light, that an automobile has a white light, that a ship has a green light and also a white light. We also notice that distances are not deceptive.

Please recall to me everything that you have thought of.

And now for squares. It is astonishing that it has never been observed that squares are frequently expressive of ignorance on the part of the inhabitants. They inevitably consider those who come to them as strangers, they certainly feel lonely in their inter-course with another. Some are too young to marry and others never will be of service. Some appear at windows and again others say we have joined a circus. In France it is not easy to join a circus. Barges have a boat to lead them. How do you do. I forgive you everything and there is nothing to forgive. Some prefer going up hill quickly and down hill slowly and some really prefer go-ing up hill practically all the time. I myself am to be remembered among the number of these. I understand what she says. Peas and beans and barley grows. You nor I nor nobody knows. And yet flowers are very pretty.

The fruit that falls from the tree and is picked up from the ground is often sound.

I am always glad when I please you.

Around the world around the world there is a square. How can I forget the square. It is very large and the town is small.

We have been very pleased to hear him say that he likes to be where they play all day in the Casino.

The apple marks a day, the day when in the evening we heard of the ocean. Water does not resemble water at all. I am not worried about breadth.

Let me tell you about museums. When glass was made and there was no shade, and buildings were necessary for symmetry, then objects which of which many are beautiful were collected together. They were placed so that they might be seen. They give pleasure. As for me I prefer purchase. I even prefer that the seller breaks his treasure. The buyer of course does not. Thank you so much. We are sincerely remembered wherever we have been. She said that she regretted but the staff had already been sent away and the inventory had been begun.

Sixes and sevens oh heavens oh heavens.

A fig an apple and some grapes makes a cow. How. The Caesars know how. Now. The Caesars know how and they know how now. The Caesars know how. How can you be able to obey a whim. Whine and shine is not the same as whim and vim. How can you be stout. By eschewing reminiscences. And how can you be on time. How can you be left to serve me. An Italian has not gone yet. We are very pleased to see that a woman wears the medal of Eighteen seventy of Alsace and Lorraine. We wear the medal of the Reconnaissance Française. Thank you so very much. We sign ourselves respectfully yours, Mrs. Herbert Howard. We like Breton names such as Patty Requets. I do not smell nicely. Seasons are upon us. And the snow threatens. And the sea is soft. Please me.

Back, we do not go back, but by a back we go across, we Godiva and Saint Christopher.

Back and over, how well I remember that song. Back and over and is he a good father. Back and over over there, we and Godiva and Saint Christopher and the pair, the pair and the pair. Father and son, and one another. Over there. When there is no bridge there is a river. I might have said this in another way.

This is a list of my experiences. I cannot describe beauty. I cannot describe a square, I cannot describe strangeness. I cannot describe rivers, I cannot describe lands. I can describe milk, and women and resemblances and elaboration and cider. I can also describe weather and counters and water. I can also describe bursts of melody.

I was reasonably gratified that we did not lose that.

How often have I said, what do you wish.

The question is is the broom a broom and I cannot mention this. I cannot mention the half of a honeymoon which was finished too soon but there are always plenty of them shining in the sunshine. I am your honey honeysuckle you are my bee, I am your honey honey suckle you are my bee I am your honey honey suckle you are my bee.

Treasure measure pleasure, whether it is a pleasure, whether it is a pleasure. Treasure measure, whether we consider the placing of the treasure, whether we consider that the treasure is whether we consider that the treasure is a pleasure. Measure, whether we consider that the treasure is a measure of a treasure, whether we treasure, whether we measure whether it is a pleasure. I remember with so much pleasure the crossing of the river. I remember with so much pleasure all the pleasure and all of the pleasure we had crossing the river. I remember the pleasure we had in looking at all the treasure that was made of steel and had to do with instruments that measure. I remember very well the pleasure when I recollect, when I recollect the treasure and can we place that treasure, can we replace that treasure can we place that treasure, whether we can place that treasure. I have decided to be sunburnt.

Thank you so much.

Augustus Lyon.

Can you sit can you sit can you sit easily. How valiantly Florence says I find it astonishing.

And how often is there a republic. Very often and very tenderly. I feel the republican.

A honeymoon so soon again, when, why now.

Some have a honey moon with a husband too soon, some have a honeymoon with a husband soon enough. And we have a honeymoon at noon, every noon, we have a honey moon, a honey honey-moon at noon and in the afternoon and before noon and between the afternoon and the forenoon which is not noon. You understand me. I understand you very well.

I can sign myself sincerely yours.

And the old woman. The old woman is enjoying the best of health. She is annoyed with the American who detained her.

Brown thread and white thread, it is a pity that we do not find what we want and that I am such a nuisance to you. It is a great pity that I bother you but it is best so. How do you do I forgive you everything and there is nothing to forgive. How do you do I adore you.

Sincerely yours,

Augustus Merryweather.

Forty francs for a pencil. So Emil says. He says the pencil is worth forty francs. Please finish eating.

I gave seen something delightful. The cathedral rising to the stars the band practicing, the dark figures laughing and saying good night and we going away. I have seen something delightful. Sincerely yours,

Augustus Caesar.

How can you have been so thoughtless as to have brought this book and the melon. We have brought both. I have seen something really delightful, I have been mistaken for whom, for no one. I have just been mistaken. You have been mistaken for the benefit of flowers. That is exactly what I mean. And how often do we not mean we do not mean this.

Instead of that this. Tenderly little Miss, tenderly little Misses.

Instead of that this and we would miss the honey and the money but we do not because we have the money and the honey.

I do not astonish you at all, you are my ball and what do you do sitting, you sit there. And why are you not anxious to please because flowers come to you with ease and you are pleased with the flowers and all.

Thank you very much, Mrs. James Allen Augustus. Mrs. James Allen. Mrs. Augustus Allen. Thank you very much Mrs. Augustus Allen.

How can you cherish husbands. Husbands and husbands.

Thank you very much.

I am trying so hard to get to bed that is what she said that is what she said. I am trying so hard to get to bed is what she said.

We have been very wise to enjoy ourselves so much and we hope to enjoy ourselves very much more.

Thank you so very much.

Sincerely yours,

Augustus Ruine.

We have eaten heartily of food well salted and in consequence have found it necessary to eat a great deal of sweet to stimulate our thirst.

We have had all of these experiences in this climate and really the moon and the earth have reason to deal politely with one another. Columbus and the egg, Columbus or the egg or my darling with her eye glasses.

We have been nervous and now we are better, we pray every evening that we may the next day be a good husband.

When they are patriotic they do know the difference.

Kindly drink water again.

They have mentioned being Asiatic and Northern. They have mentioned having farmed their loving. They have mentioned being in earnest about sunshine and for moon-light. They have been in earnest more together. And did he buy a trailer. Did he buy their trailer. Did he buy their trailers.

I certainly think that automobiles suit cathedrals very well.

I am very much [in] earnest Mr. James Raymond.

And what became of their inhabitants.

I can do it from there by just pulling. How can you do it from there by just pulling.

There were a great many windows not broken and there were a great many windows not broken.

What do you say to gathering together a good woman and a strong man. What do you say to river scenery. What do you say to spending this day to spending a day to devoting a day to this journey. We have been mistaken and I have been mistaken. We have not mistaken one thing for another thing. Godiva speaks earnestly and says that. So does many another saint.

A honeymoon, so soon, again, yes it pleases when it comes

so soon and again. Yet or again, and some times when there is need of honey for the moon again.

Now let us say pussy. When did I say pussy. You are so full of a cow factory. You manufacture cows by vows. The cows produce reduce reduce they reduce the produce. Cows are necessary after feeding. We are needing what we have after feeding. After feeding we find cows out. How are cows multiplied. By proper treatment. Thank you so much for being so explicit.

She is gentle and considerate. She can do no more than be gentle and considerate and we find that to be quite enough to satisfy and not rebuff.

And now we hear her sentences. She says that as to inequality she is reminded of most things by their cautiousness. Do not be afraid to be of an early religion. And as to that dominion, what are dominion rights. Honey moons do not get startling information. And cows come out.

Little singing charm can never do no harm, little baby sweet can always be a treat. And are sonatinas in music boxes and do they follow one after the other and are music boxes grind organs yes or no. I believe it and I told her so and she believed it as I very well know. I tell her so so.

A belly band is made strand by strand a belly band can stand being knit by hand. And sewed together. And sewed together then. We know how to build a fire. Can tickle can tickle can tickle her for sin is said by writing on the wall with lead with lead penciling. We have two pen holders for which we have cared for which we have cared very much. We do not know this about these.

He ate she ate they ate there, she ate he ate and they are there, he ate she ate and they do care, they ate and we mate and we are there.

Oh no I love you so oh no.

I have often heard it said that a sky-lark never goes to bed. I have often heard it said that they sing. I have often heard it said that they are suddenly ahead and I have often heard it said that they sing.

When we were listening they were attending and when they

heard it said that they were frightening we wondered if they had heard.

I believe almost immediately in a soft egg. And so do I. I believe almost immediately in a pleasant surprise.

I see the moon and the moon sees me, God bless the moon and God bless me.

I did not know that the south wind brought the moon.

We are in their way I can see that plainly.

Yes now we will go.

When we say beg we say I beg you to do so. When I say beg I say I beg you to believe me. And when I say I beg you I beg it of you I mean I know you are all well and happy. This is the meaning of exclamation. He is led he is led he is gently led to morality. I understand the difference between bathing and bath tubs between elegance in a dentist's chair and elegance in a pair. I understand the difference between accounts and recounting and I understand the difference between rose and white. I also understand the difference between able and to be able. She is able she is said to be able, she is said to be able to receive me.

Sweet affection.

They say that they say woods are made that way. They are made altogether. And we gave them away. We gave them away to-day. So we say. Now can you tell me the rest.

This is the rest.

Thank you for the rest.

And now how earnestly we say it is the wrong color. But not this anyway.

And further flowers.

We sleep on the seat and we stay near the bench and we mount the electricity and we gather no indignation.

We sign what do we sign.

Fine fine.

I said it.

We said it.

We saw it.

And the choppers chop it.

And all alike we find the wood is woolen.

So is knitting.

I am not quitting.

Sitting.

I sit.

And you sat.

What does cover a hat.

Underneath it I have reason to need hawthorne.

Hawthorne for me.

A flower an open flower, a sensible extra flower, a seasonable and so-called flower.

I shall re-adjust my solution.

I solve, I resolve, I absolve, I fasten it with a tassel. I do know that church.

I suddenly see the scene. And the scene sees me. God bless the scene and God bless me.

Then we will go on so as not to get there too late.

Is there anything we hate.

I'll say so.

Then we'll go on.

In different countries ploughed fields are softer than in others. In different countries in different countries can you guess by the F.

Can you explain to me about the sparrows, the song sparrows and the Seine.

The Seine is a river which we can see.

It is very clear it is very clear when we hear and now shall we get ourselves ready. Yes.

We do not call a wind break a Robinson tree, nor do we call a hawthorne a thorn, we find it not at all useful when there are leaves on it. Useful enough for that much. Do you remember that a pump can pump other things than water. For this search the land. Yes tenderness grows and it grows where it grows. And do you like it. Yes you do. And does it fill a cow full of filling. Yes. And where does it come out of. It comes out of the way of the Caesars. Caesars are rich in thought and in deed. Indeed.

Coming in at the door.

Shut the door.

Yes.

What do you want to-day. Just the same as yesterday. Now do you. Yes I do.

Just a minute and you can have it. I don't want to wait. You are not waiting. I am not.

We read indeed and an Italian.

Would you drink with him for him or to him. Would you drink anything.

At her request I did suggest that the primroses were not all for the best. Oh no indeed, I have a creed. I have decreed that we consider speed. And what did we spend. We didn't spend any of it to-day.

We will call it so we will call it a celebration, because we had them and we have them and we will have them and we handled them and we handle them and we will handle them. I call it a celebration because we handled them and we will handle. I call it a substantial celebration because we increased hearing them and we settled them and we settled for them. I call it a celebration and so do they. She says she is really full of tenderness.

LAST PART

ONE SONATINA FOLLOWED BY ANOTHER DIVIDED
BY A PLAY

Distinguished by there being no moat there at all. We have settled this by asking again and again about it.

The Black hand of the Porte Maillot. She says that a summer day can come in early spring. What is the difference between an early spring and a late spring.

The Black Hand of the Porte Maillot.

A PLAY

Those prominent in what is necessary to the automobile and dreaming in dusting.

She dreams of me in not that capacity. This is said to be erroneously referred to by themselves.

Allan and the best.

She with her mind attuned to cows.

They undertaking elements of pears. And he well he was the

third tenant of a large and really friendly house but it was not taken in his name.

Windows are prominently open and there are a great many monetary advantages. Do you know that Ripolin is the name of a certain kind of paint. I take a deep interest in invented names for universal industries. There is Kodak, there is Ripolin there is the recitative and there is the fact that a Lord Derby can not count.

Now we plunge into that play. I play you play and they play. Play and play and play away. I have already said this. Now I said this is the way I make a play. Play it if you please play it, I say play it, I say if you please play it and do you know I am perplexed and respected for having had an indicator of the slant of roads twice smashed in the same town and once when it was guarded.

A PLAY

Not the dears.

But dears.

Dears are the dears.

I look at my own and I see them.

We gain on them.

The first black hand dining.

We stayed home to sit and we did.

How can you think for money how can you think for me how can you think my honey how can you my busy bee. When I have time I will blow my nose.

What was a nice idea, to have my wife hear, hear what. It was a nice idea to have my wife here. Hear me. It was a nice idea to have my wife hear hear what. It was a nice idea to have my wifey hear. Hear. Hear.

A PLAY

I play for baby I play she is baby and I play that baby and Vincent Astor builds a home. Do you believe what I say.

I often say it so that you can know it, when this you see remember me and now I am a poet and I know it and I say to the Caesars all the four shut the door. Caesars all the four open the door and I adore not only a treasure but now I find that a cow is a treasure it is a treasure and loved without measure as it comes out through the door. And the floor. Yes and the floor. It comes out behind and the door before the door there are four four Caesars and I will show them the door. They know of the door. And the cow comes out of the door. Do you adore me. When this you see remember me.

Y.D.

Are you resting nicely. Oh charmingly. Are you pleased with everything. Oh so very pleased. Do you feel satisfied. Oh so satisfied. Have you pleasure in your point of view! Oh a great deal of pleasure.

There where they were pleased there where they were longer, there where they were there. Where. Everywhere. You please me you do please me.

Instance in this instance that flattery succeeds with Caesars but they do not really feel it because it is not flattery it is adequate representation.

I have thanked them privately, I now thank them publicly and to-morrow we will gratify them with fruit.

Middle man. Middle man. Middle of middle woman, middle of middle man, middle man when you can middle woman middle of middle woman. Caesars do not stray they stay.

Caesars stay they do not stray.

Caesars stay they do not stray. Stretch away not into the distance but close to and successfully separating they permit indeed they insist indeed they cause indeed they aid they do not pause they cause and we register with a smile and a nod that there is no need of a prod indeed we register that satisfaction has been obtained.

We have been told that telegrams are sold and we do not buy them. We have been told that rooms can be sold but we do not buy them. We have been told that chairs can be sold but we do not buy them.

What we buy is this and with it we satisfy the longing for a solitude à deux.

When we see women we say do you inhabit this hotel. When they see us they say we can very easily tell all that we wish to state.

I would indeed wish to wed. Would you indeed. When all is said it is very pleasant to be wedded.

Yes indeed and it is a pleasure that we can enjoy.

When we say did they we say they did. When we say did they we say they didn't. When we say they did, they did. When we say they didn't, they didn't. I think the thing to do is to telephone to the hotel if we can on Sundays to the hotel this evening.

I smoke a little pipe.

And who has given it to me.

We were we were.

They applaud. And them the electricity disappointed them. This was so unnecessary.

A beauty is known to be beautiful. How beautiful you are I see.

A reason why I see this is this.

Prettily prettily me she is all the world prettily.

They knew all that you know.

In this way I mention what she will say. In this way I will say what she will say. In this way. I take it literally.

Pleasure for her and pleasure for him it is a pleasure to her and it is a pleasure to him.

Pleasure.

Please.

To please.

He pleases me pleasurably. She pleases me pleasurably.

Pleasurably.

Eyes please

Yes.

Eyes please.

Bright at night not too bright at night.

I read to you and you read to me and we both read intently. And I waited for you and you waited for me and we both waited attentively.

I find knitting to be a continuous occupation and I am full of gratitude because I realise how much I am indebted to the hands that wield the needles.

I have been most pleasantly engaged in saying so.

I practice caution.

And delight in his treasure. And then we will measure our ears and their ears and we will know that we told them so and so and so we know and we feel about a fountain of joy and a well and all well. Very well.

Very well indeed very well indeed. And how are you. Very well indeed.

I have been pleased to hear that you have been pleased to hear what has pleased you to hear.

What do you hear.

I hear you say what you say.

Well you can hear it all day. Good day.

And what is his reward. His reward is the reward of the ages. A cow. All of us worship a cow. How. By introducing and producing and extension.

How.

You know about pipes. A shepherd has pipes. So he has. And so have I.

I do mention this and that, it is true of a pussy and a cat, that this is that and that is this and you are sleepy with a kiss. Who miss, us.

Why misses us, who dismisses us.

We kiss us.

Very well.

She is very well.

And as to cow which is mentioned anyhow. A cow is mentioned anyhow.

Thank you Romans Caesars and all.

I say it to you and I say it to you I say it to you how I love my little jew. I say it to you and I say it to you. I say it to you and I say it to you. I say it to you.

How I can I have the air of here and there and I say it to you I say it to you I love my own little jew. How can I have the air and I do care I care for her hair and there for the rest of her too my little jew. I love her too my little jew. And she will have endured the cold that is cured, it is cured it is cured and a cow how can a cow follow now a cow can follow now because I have a cow. I had a cow you have a cow, you have a cow now.

She is that kind of a wife. She can see.

And a credit to me.

And a credit to me she is sleepily a credit to me and what do I credit her with I credit her with a kiss.

1. Always sweet.
2. Always right.
3. Always welcome.
4. Always wife.
5. Always blessed.
6. Always a successful druggist of the second class and we know what that means. Who credits her with all this a husband with a kiss and what is he to be always more lovingly his missus' help and hero. And when is he heroic, well we know when.

Win on a foul pretty as an owl pretty as an owl win on a fowl. And the fowl is me and she is pretty as an owl. Battling Siki and Capridinks capridinks is pretty and winks, winks of sleep and winks of love. Capridinks. Capridinks is my love and my Coney.

SHORT POEMS, 1913

BEE TIME VINE (*1913*) *is highly hermetic. As in* Tender Buttons, *the aim is "to describe a thing without mentioning it." The subject is Spain, probably Granada; and it is a landscape.* Four Saints in Three Acts (*1927*), *also a Spanish landscape piece, contains a recall of this poem in the Saints' Procession:* *

> With be there all their all their time there be there
> vine there be vine time there be there time there all their
> time there.

This second version is not hermetic at all or even obscure. It is simply a hymn about the future life.

V.T.

BEE TIME VINE

Bee time vine be vine truth devine truth.

Be vine be vine be vine truth, be vine be vine be vine.

Class grass not so mange not a linen starch not emblem. not in blend blemish and a tooth. Love callous kidding with little lozenges and a mouth and moist neglected pens pens full of under standing bold ess with leases and below, below whites, glaze and exchange water with sooth for soot and lower for a cat which is a goat. It was so fine.

Response. Responder to a sofa with and measles four and coolidge paint and neathless which never bless and more colloose with it. Please bet.

Go gout.

A cook makes cake and never less never less grating which be when. This noon.

A lass which moists the beat wax so and it was a ring it was a necessary trim. Alright.

No taste in two.

No twine in two and a best set.

Coal hole.

If coal oil means water and a memory and fine.

* *Interpreting this passage as a procession was Gertrude Stein's own wish.*
V.T.

35

Which pen.

Leaves in, no boat.

This is a talk.

Plain grease in covers.
Covers, covers, little lamb.

No poe, coop ham.
Leaf as not.
Ixtact, lime.
Co hie.

Wee nus, poodle nut, all bow with cut hup. Leave len. A go lash. Lips tip. No pie. Rest.

We tight, Nigger. Nasal, noseite. Not we when. Butt, but set. All that, cold. nigh jigger.

Pea sells. All.
Way mouth, soph, chive, bee, so, it, any, muse, in, lee, vie.

MIGUEL (COLLUSION) *is also about something in Spain but is "not a landscape." It is more probably a still life, like those in* Tender Buttons. *Its purpose of making a description by "getting away from the object" is more completely accomplished here than in the preceding piece. It is a "real abstraction." I am inclined to think, as a matter of fact, that Miss Stein never produced landscapes or narratives or arguments, and rarely the portraits of persons, with that complete removal from common-sense meaning she so frequently achieved in description. We shall see later, in "Patriarchal Poetry," a similar achievement in "emotional" writing.*

V.T.

MIGUEL (COLLUSION). GUIMPE. CANDLE.

Collection of eggs white, white as know excellent.
Are the holds extra skinned.
A bland is curtain grease with a fine tart. A field might a field might. Blame cross extermination. Please porouses. Please porouses contumely. A glass plate. A glass white is a shadow in the

bun. A shadow in the begun oar box. Or not pleasing. Or not white. In read old lozenges. Instead. In that bread. In that bred and a lower a real old heard, a real cold curry able to be at it with a crush in without, with out all ox holds at neither best.

A clinging fancy, clinging lightly in astrakhan and silver and a sweet tooth surely swelling. A sigh in distributed add in dresses and a little lounge a clean piece of murder girder to seem high long. And yet coloratura in the beef.

Nicely.

Cold in, cold in, why not a servant wedding. Why not peak pillow with a peck. So creek.

Out on pledges and a intwine, out occasional. Out in occasion to be sold gracious goodness, it in, it in seen.

Bay win. Bay cake.

Be cake saddle and mud or a can be so much. More mew. More clever stroked beside the lead of liver cake in shake. In shake.

Miguel, migall in all to lend a stand to lend it bender to lend an upright circle an upright circle beam, beam in loads, why are knees feet.

A lamb a white long loan and an ostrich and a tin bin a real cold cake with season and a little blind oak, a coon is sooner.

Cup up, Cube in, Cube in a sand curl.

Cheese and a dirty weight.

My dear sir. The left place which shows a signer, the left place which shows a signer and please please be a mercy, pertain to more clothes than older and a little twinkle almost a shouter and a study, almost that blind.

Could not a bee line a coat with guimpes and tin peas and a cold ice. The rest of the funnel is nice and strong and relieved all went.

Cooled queue, glass, a guile which is toes in cuts more angels. Let us say, let us say girls, let us say furls, let us select haughty bowls and a little towels and leaves wild stolen leaves and sleeves, combined sleeves. A little tun is likely to mean a standing step. The rest is deep. Cold, mingle.

Just let me say that there is a little tall thing to catch, just listen to it and say more spanish, more spanish finish, more finish that just manage and a little thing a little thing means a light steady, not so steady as flowers and any way there are twenty counting, not likely that there should.

A second better.

A wilderness causes stirrups, a cool pet is native.

Chimera.

Woods long, to let a branch of cases and please, see the tea and cold. A best chance is with the tool and long bedrooms are divided really divided uttering the tune. Best low, best quite too painful with little cut tigers where there are transoms. The less best flower is white with roses and a team a whole team is scarce it runs on the hill. Who would know that donkey, who would cherish houses and little paints and clear white beans with more pressings. Just the same the gold is blue. A chance bow with a piece of strewn heel so that anyway there is a dam factory. The like white is steak. So long meal.

Guimpe.

Consider the kind call, make it show, make it beady make it please the name of called pieces.

If a change comes to pay darlings, if it seizes the plain chill of the told price and a little ladder is brightly, a little light has no seam no solid bounce.

Then the purse then the tiled rubber roof is collision and really what is fur, fur is summer.

A little date pretty a little date pretty with a log, a little date pretty with a horse and cow and cheese real cheese that repeats the call the call of the untamed harbor and legs and everything.

Please pay that, please pay a kind of succeeding peaches and little curls.

Will wild rubbers single out paces, will they ease cold hares and little sturgeons will they rarely be soluble.

A beet in the foundry is likely to be sat forward, it is naturally suggested that long tall pinches are pleasant.

I am clad in sweet syrup and odors.

A way to build collars with little cs and heights, the way to build collars with a two old boat, a way to build cellars with coins and shadows and real old bouts.

Too soon a vacation, two pieces and another, a ran old cut

with a juice with juice, could bursts shower, could a clean boat move politely. Egg off egg off the leader, egg and a persuasion. Little told, little too collared with a sodden beam. Is it final is it so bellowing, is it not that three names are singular only two are audacious the third is contrasting that is to say they are three together. Black, black sill, black still will frill, frill calm, frill in a bother in a bother together, the noise is boiled.

Miguel, Miguel is not boweled by a little water founting away behind a table center. Not there harry no night nice in peep, nuts and sound shades put in the place of upright and tunes piano tunes.

A Mother.

Cool with the spring of a dark respectable lantern question.

Calling.

Calling in that exercises walking so that if there is a night there is long excuse with a shade of a piece of labor, much labor if tables are waiting so that they need washing and window cleaning.

A little pull perplexed shows a result in.

Continue so that when a regular base ball is put there is no choice in blots and anyway there is no hesitation in not biting. The least best is naughty. Cold bowls mean somewhere.

Why should waking be old. A little waiter naturally peeps and lets a bag sigh and meddles with rocks. A little wedding shows intelligence and calm and slices and all the reason why bites are black. Leave kindly saloon leave kindly saloon in white slices and little onions. A church is colored. It shows papers. Papers are so many.

Really big special willows.

Pack waist in dog. A case short, laugh lump of wood pieces lessly.

Two between cold and hot entirely turned to change silence to a lung which makes rash seals.

The right of a case and the back of a deal a deal square short with lazy thorns. The best ungainly little rasp which makes tall not twins twins are a bloom two four and this makes a lawn biter with lapse of little angles which means nails hand nails and length.

A class a class is beaten, it has necklaces and spy glasses and measures and slats and little ferns and bugs and nice paws and a pine a pine rabbit and even a bell a long bell.

Certainly a clamor means a steak a steak to push. And really a little language means a dog a dog to sober. Naturally pans are sweet and neighborly and almost a blind a really blind call, a sweet long tall towel which hums hums by the day. A little of seize a clam a billow a rack a lantern settler and a pall a pell mell shoulder.

Petunia Wilmington.

Such is sucking when there is a pack of sound which is goats which is lamb last lambling. Loaf. A hole is in seen and likely is to pudding when color is to buds. Buds when in seen solid, no coats, no black necessaries. A real kind is dew real cue act one.

A bed, suppose hair pleats in easy canisters so that in again have check to a blossom. My house. A land to call water.

A little please to pay, a time to choose figs and baled asses and nearly all the cooks and little pieces and more oil puddings. There is no use.

A blame to little gutter and ruin all ruin to a choice mind a mind chosen to burnish little asters and big golds entirely and leave plates leaves plates with sugar and extra almost extra.

A single ruin a return a lively dog a lively dog to sit, to place collections in little blouse in cold and so called arch change. Really it is no use. The best day is complete with hoes. All hoes and all places.

A cow shapes leaves and salt and flesh behind. More ice more catching of the pills that sigh. The rest is meat and cold grapes and a sad a sole sad chase.

Leave little tones to blink with a constitution.

Sad board. Negligible undertaking. Leading mattresses. Celebrate. Collect class. Be so.

The best pealing, necessitate more oiled opera glasses which show such nice, such near bolts and shoes.

Paul paul.

Unheld bore bore what water wine eye glass and summer rain. Gnats little flies and coffee not cups. Not nearly good enough to exchange for places. I exchange more next day than before.

Leave little wheels so that the whole case is this. Beg more and say that chick chicken is rested. The best way is not to say anything, press it in a flavor and put it in to answer. Really that is an occupation not like the lazy lily.

Please bite, please bite this.

Please bite.

Please bite please bite this.

An awful chance to be a cook's cake.

Little teas are bitten able and the knives are best away. Little miser is in hale brothers to mean a mother and eight children with four twins. Four twins are two. No check. Lest the noise fogs a supple ended plight. Cigarettes are mud. Least is said. Show a correction. More please bananas.

More fat what, bail it, putter white, beady in the fly, hit chat, left more, gale glass no so syrup, joist, joist with, no pretty little seat to fizzle with the summer so.

No next collapse with confusion in a in a taste with lungs taste not taste and little pleasing and oh cans oh cans see. Least is the party vogue and necessary and instant craning with a loud perpendicular neglected coat more.

C A R R Y *and the two pieces following it were also composed in 1913 in Spain and are abstractions.*

                                                                    V.T.

CARRY

Fed in an f e d this makes a color sure.

Fed in fed makes a pleasant shoulder with it.

Cup back, cup back the swing, cup back in swing. To rent. To makes u. To makes u so glass. Rest. less.

Rest less, rest less in stephens regular hand book, rest less that makes a curve a curve has v, v is c that is to say rest has not t, not in tea, not in t. Rest has in s s.

CARNAGE

In the center.

Peals and peals and puts in sugar.

The rest necessity with little likeness. Why does the fly blow. It beggars.

A shame buffet with a sand whole neat and possessing person this made pet. The least need is in the middle and more necessary feeling together. Do they hit jet. Do they pass butter. Do they put in stretches.

A kind blow a kind kindle, single ages and a feather a tail blister with tallow gentle and precious little minister minister to a corner.

This is both.

A loudness is so what the white night calls bloomer, bloomer when, in purgirl, this makes sight, white is big eye.

Suppose it is a dust, suppose it is and knocking, suppose a little food feather is behind, so much sun. This makes a practice. A shove is more more what more flies.

A least see, a least see sought, leave posts leave posts there, brown is simple, The student shows.

Go on in green, go on so white with a little news paper and in between a courier a ruining fuss, a change of mean, a pleasant house. This makes the same everywhere. Flea flies. Show it a trait. The more hurtily. The most so.

In a collision.

There is no entry, a paste a sweet paste makes a pool lack water, a little water is winning. This is pie. Lest we see birds. Lest we go.

Come to heading.

Come to grease, this is a point, needless to say a towel, a clean clanking has a kind of stool.

Then the purpose of little places and no seat and a red cry and moist moist what has a pointed variance, a cheese, a little lemon and aid, aid to all, all best. This is so.

Come to show weight, come to it, come please, be a short, a short weight, be a short reunion and a little honey a near little honey. This does willing.

If a dear rate is what is called then anyway two is in order. It was a little lean, lean on then. It showed put, put into the floor on. It came to a gay, a gay eat, with a climate, a change and a shadow, shadow is straight, it has a window. This is the case.

GO IN GREEN *is obviously a description of some "scene or object."*

V.T.

GO IN GREEN

> Go in green. Go in, case. Go in green.
>> Go in green. go in. in, go in green.
>> Go in green.
>> Go in green.

A LIDE CLOSE. THE STORY OF A SPANISH MORRI-SON (*1913*) *is the portrait of a Spaniard, the son of Miss Stein's landlord in Terreno, near Palma de Mallorca. He reminded her of an English friend named Morrison.*

V.T.

A LIDE CLOSE. THE STORY OF
A SPANISH MORRISON

> Bier. All thee fur.
> A little bit.
> New rice then sick. Sick.

THANK YOU (*1913*) *was probably written in Paris. It refers to the English woman-suffrage leader Sylvia Pankhurst, who when released from arrest on her promise to reappear for trial had said to the magistrate, "Thank you, I'll be there." But she was not there. When questioned about her breach of parole she replied that the word "there" had not, in her mind, as she said it, meant the court-room.*

V.T.

THANK YOU

> Thank you thank you thank you I'll be there. Thank you. I'll be there. Thank you. Thank you. A good time in knee grows hands.

I N (*1913*), *composed in Paris, is a study in vowel contrasts and consonant relationships. It is "definitely 'sound,'" though Gertrude Stein would have denied this, since she regularly denied that sounds and their play were a major consideration to her in writing. The words and letters in the left margin are a structure game not unlike the kind she liked to play in enumerating the scenes of her operas and plays.*

V.T.

IN

(I)

Was is ice
Was is ice
Was is ice
Was is ice
Elastic. Elastic in layed.

Was.

(I)

Was. Cream.
Pear——ery.
Cut——ery
Slice ear——ie
A creamerie.

(I no)

He is says.
He is says he is. says.
He is says
He is says

(B)

Nine Tea
Nine tea times.
Nine tea times four tea.
Nine tea four tea.

(No B)

Colored wading.
Collect will he.
Collect steps.

(I no B)

Because in.
Because in on o.
Because in on o shall.

Because in on o shall low set long.
Because in on o
Because in. Because in on o shall.
Because in on o shall low.
Because in on o shall low say by. Because in on o shall low say be see o. Because in. Because in on o shall low see see o. Because in see see see see o shall see be be be be see o.

(Extra)   Excel lantern and each.
Excel lantern.
Rude in and in. Rude in an an told. Excel lantern.

(Extra M)   Mate and hen, is hen. Mat and is and in, Mat and is and in and in and is and in. and. Mat and.

(Extra M,)   Heat go and back, Heat go and back lea. Heat
(and M)   go and back leak back leak back blister. Heat go and back. Heat go and back leak and blister heat go and back heat and leak and blister. Heat go and heat go and back, and heat go and back, heat, and go, and back, heat.

(B.O.M.)   It is a new lap of a crumble. Guard whole in a no necessity. No necessity.
(B.O.M. not)   A clear ball, a close say eat, a close say eat.

(Be old M)   A close say eat add appease add see o coat, see o coat, add see o coat.
A close say eat, a close say eat o coat, say eat, a coat say eat a close say eat o coat.

A jack and cry see sir, a jack and cry see sir.

(L. P)   Leet, leet ill a rise in eye o yes. Let it be let it boil let it.
(L. P. B.)   Let it bee let it be o soon chew severe, let it

be o soon chew severe. Let it be o soon. Let it be. It is ill in ill in all owe, ill in all owe seen creak, see in creation is a be twist extreme re-syllable.

(N. O.)   Two, two more e. Two more ease. Knee strays.

(I)   Vacation all to resay.
               Variation axe sold but, variation it see well butt.

(III)   Eat in a climb bill eat in a climb bill all a way. Eat ill a climb bill all in a climb bill in a eat in a climb bill, eat in a climb bill in all a way.

(II II)   It so in sear, it so in sere. It so in sere lawn mow it it blame, it shall have, shall have, it in sere shall have bow laps, bow laps and a stern a stern resound, a wound in yes in yes in sere, a wound in yes in sere, in sere. In the be the in the be the and in there there, in there ochre extra, in the ochre extra sake it.

(Bird Bet)   Archie, archie texture, Archie texture seed.

               Cut but in yes.

               Pale well, sigh in. Sigh in then sigh in then no account no account shaving, no account shaving eye dough know, I dough cut it expressly, cut it expressly in soon, in soon a bunch.

(Bird yet)   It is a measure, it is sudden and a not a neg-lectful or precise omit, not a plain pin even it is like a most moist, a real wheel, an e glass, that is likely, that is more stable than harts on end and anyway where is a bunch, it is just like

a bloom stone, it is a tell, it is a tell not beside
not beside specialty and folds. That is the reason. It is a reday any way more close.

(G. N.)   Open. Open wood bits open wood bits of
not in between grease and shies, shies solds,
solds so yes preliminary.

                Cook and Cook and Cook. Capeing.

(B. N.)   Ben, benefice, a please cache met, in a creeche,
crecher, in a create, beach her, in a pea in
stall.

(B L)   A curtain of a curtain of in a hiddle he middle
in a hemidal rest course with hhs with h and s
and a curtain of a curtain of who pin, who pin a
considerable close.

(J)   Join it a creep cross, a cross send which and
a neat a neat m a neat m, join which a neat m.

                Was it in nice, will it in nose, will it in then,
will it in then pour which.
Water cut ccs in seal extras.

$\begin{pmatrix} \text{P. B.} \\ \text{P. B. O.} \end{pmatrix}$ It was a pea with. Shut upper reseem to see
reseparate, resave when, in, older in lean o
dear.

                addle is an alligator.
addle means a rattle snake.
Not bake. bakery.
not burn, not burner, not burning.
Go back her.
Told, told to go eating.
Fell back hymn.
Felt belt on cheery, too.

(A. H. A.)   A brew sue, portal.
Breathe, breathe little plain page with collapse with collapse thick it.

A never in knee needles.

Coal lapse, coal it, will he.
A leave center pill to lent.

It was an example of nearly yearly of nearly
nearly yearly, exercise.
It was a simple wailing peal toe ridicule, ridiculous.
All the organs in and a sober in and a call a
red peal coalter shaker shadow.
Read irons hot regrow shells blue, so far no
kite, not it set.

It remains to ready and ness, it remains to
read and ness, it remains.

Excellent excelling allowing and behaving and
behaving.

(B. U. T. A. N.)   Ray refine but, ray able, able, able, stew, las.
Able able able able white.
Able able able able able plate.
No in need to be cork cork case.
A leg to be scared seal wash.

In beds, in beds there is a regular a regular
believe me a regular a regular, on the store
on the pillar places, nearly the same best, more
of it in, and need less need less and in more
and in more reach rode bowed bowed with
when.

(Eugene)   sympathetic an add liking.
even and a pace.
accidents accidents accidents deep cloth. Come

along button why.
Parallel day but too for.
read Clare read Clare bust.
all the little will he will be all the little shade
in case, in case more money in case more in
money attend shun, in case more money in
shun, in shun blast, cool cool cake, little ccs,
little ccs coo back coo back to stole, coocback
to any old in any old in.
It was a case, it was not especially needed it
was not especially needed by any not so much
tear not so much tear in widows in little hand
sums, in little amusing central repeated repeated old sheds, repeated old sheds with
must, must is the time to say not to say bib,
not to say bib.

A considerable buss neglected.

An egg cold see.

Pardon a shampoo.

(Pale Blow)   Pale blue pale blew utter,
a cheese. Leave it in dress.
new sat new sat took.
Pale blow is it you place is it you shall you ccs.
Pale blow shall collect in relate, pale blow shall
cool arose in relate, pale exceed on shed.

On no on no no, on no on.
On no no. In. In. in. in.

Goal pronounced jell. this is a please.
not sent.
Gale pronounced gill is a weak still sew.

Please night night, not it so not it so so so, not
it so so so so, a couple, couple of so far, a couple
of so far sew.

That is a by, that is a by, that is or run, that is
by that is by in by in or are, that is by in or are
air, that is by in or are air store tea are, that is
by in or are air store tea are on air ear hear
hearer berry.

(By Jo)   By Jo by Jo a k a k to in be.

Believe in a ride oak, a spool bamboo a neck
wear in a case.

If in if. Press. Tons.
Press but tons.

       Leaves of shout in go lest.
(E.M.A. Belle) Wider in weed where in the mean the in
meantime
Coal gate coal gate rose.
In an in gang changer, changer rose.
Rice seat pole repair show set on in, in or rest
show on in in.
Regular remains on in tree.

(G. C.)   Please or bust.
Rest in kisses.
Neither or shaker in see
Lose extreme side by.
It was a big are hair been hymn.
All hear been hymn.
New hills new hills in see here.

(E.)   Eggs ample for.
Four peas a best.
A best not see in.
In so peer random.
Random eye gas,
A near pea a near pea buy it.

(E. E.)   Little pole little pole in three three, in three
                 three Irene, in three three h wards, h wards to
                 cake, cake nuts.

(Miss S.)   Miss S is a regular a regular ccs sir, ccs sir in
                 process, process to do, to do, to do.
                 Knee fur. knee fur cup.

                 It is civil.
                 A remarkable open short in spoon.
                 Ten place, in the poke when, poke seen, in the
                 perceptible research for these set.
                 All along the go so it is there sale lay and nearly
                 neat near that, show it all in the below rate
                 with no and in it, not by the if the land in for
                 the shadow short which and is no in the pale
                 chase, pale chased in for. It was a in the, see
                 here, it was and it show another to be in the
                 for saw. Four.

(t)   In race seen by the low carpet with a sort class
                 a sort class of or it or it bit.
                 Be the can come see by the say so shall couple
                 mere violet violet pour see.
                 Put in the put lit and or bidding next grass.

(T. E. O. Soon- Neither in the see at in to be when in on they
ing.)   see it of by the knee call caller.

                 Example more, a call i and the interesting the
                 next to the soon which has an articulate which
                 means pours which means pours through.
                 Pours through ball receiver.

                 The tread all bed.

                 Nearer a better curl, nearly a cuctom, nearer
                 a towel so will.

Pea so last a cows section.

Out so shade power guess.

Pear in.

No nose printers.

Printers call I cow.

(Eddie.)   Leak in a leak in earn leak in urn eucalyptus new rights new rights pole light lime.

(Eddy)   A steel well the raise colder see waist showed her.
A receptacle more by the whole way so to be so Kate. Kate why. Pole lightly.

(Niece)   Peel o set a hole o absolutely absolutely absolute layer, absolute layer goat, absolute layer goat go, go spit goat.
Bean. Bean neither shudder.
Shut share south two four fore lap.

It is e it is e e eat e eight.

Eight a piece of marble.
Cone under aims.

YET DISH (*1913, Paris*) *is "a portrait of the Jews," its title a transyllabification of the word "Yiddish."*
Later, in the portrait of Jo Davidson, Gertrude Stein rendered the handwriting on the wall, mene, mene, tekel, upharsin, as "Many many tickle you for them" and then explained unmistakably her reference to the Babylonian captivity by adding, "It was written on the stairs but it was not their stairs." Similarly, "bean" means "been" and refers to British pronunciation. A.R. is a

woman Miss Stein once knew. This skit will yield up many amus-
ing, and some barbed, remarks to those who read it with its sub-
ject in mind.

V.T.

YET DISH

I

Put a sun in Sunday, Sunday.
Eleven please ten hoop. Hoop.
Cousin coarse in coarse in soap.
Cousin coarse in soap sew up. soap.
Cousin coarse in sew up soap.

II

A lea ender stow sole lightly.
Not a bet beggar.
Nearer a true set jump hum,
A lamp lander so seen poor lip.

III

Never so round.
A is a guess and a piece.
A is a sweet cent sender.
A is a kiss slow cheese.
A is for age jet.

IV

New deck stairs.
Little in den little in dear den.

V

Polar pole.
Dust winder.
Core see.
A bale a bale o a bale.

VI

Extravagant new or noise peal extravagant.

VII

S a glass.
Roll ups.

VIII

Powder in wails, powder in sails, powder is all next to it is does
wait sack rate all goals like chain in clear.

IX

Negligible old star.
Pour even.
It was a sad per cent.
Does on sun day.
Watch or water.
So soon a moon or a old heavy press.

X

Pearl cat or cat or pill or pour check.
New sit or little.
New sat or little not a wad yet.
Heavy toe heavy sit on head.

XI

Ex, ex, ex.
Bull it bull it bull it bull it.
Ex Ex Ex.

XII

Cousin plates pour a y shawl hood hair.
No see eat.

XIII

They are getting, bad left log lope, should a court say stream, not
a dare long beat a soon port.

XIV

Colored will he.
Calamity.
Colored will he
Is it a soon. Is it a soon. Is it a soon. soon. Is it a soon. soon.

XV

Nobody's ice.
Nobody's ice to be knuckles.
Nobody's nut soon.
Nobody's seven picks.
Picks soap stacks.
Six in set on seven in seven told, to top.

XVI

A spread chin shone.
A set spread chin shone.

XVII

No people so sat.
Not an eider.
Not either. Not either either.

XVIII

Neglect, neglect use such.
Use such a man.
Neglect use such a man.
Such some here.

XIX

Note tie a stem bone single pair so itching.

XX

Little lane in lay in a circular crest.

XXI

Peace while peace while toast.
Paper eight paper eight or, paper eight ore white.

XXII

Coop pour.
Never a single ham.
Charlie. Charlie.

XXIII

Neglect or.
A be wade.

Earnest care lease.
Least ball sup.

XXIV

Meal dread.
Meal dread so or.
Meal dread so or bounce.
Meal dread so or bounce two sales. Meal dread so or bounce two
   sails. Not a rice. No nor a pray seat, not a little muscle, not a
   nor noble, not a cool right more than a song in every period
   of nails and pieces pieces places of places.

XXV

Neat know.
Play in horizontal pet soap.

XXVI

Nice pose.
Supper bell.
Pull a rope pressed.
Color glass.

XXVII

Nice oil pail.
No gold go at.
Nice oil pail.
Near a paper lag sought.
What is an astonishing won door. A please spoon.

XXVIII

Nice knee nick ear.
Not a well pair in day.
Nice knee neck core.
What is a skin pour in day.

XXIX

Climb climb max.
Hundred in wait.
Paper cat or deliver.

XXX

Little drawers of center.
Neighbor of dot light.
Shorter place to make a boom set.
Marches to be bright.

XXXI

Suppose a do sat.
Suppose a negligence.
Suppose a cold character.

XXXII

Suppose a negligence.
Suppose a sell.
Suppose a neck tie.

XXXIII

Suppose a cloth cape.
Suppose letter suppose let a paper.
Suppose soon.

XXXIV

A prim a prim prize.
A sea pin.
A prim a prim prize
A sea pin.

XXXV

Witness a way go.
Witness a way go. Witness a way go. Wetness.
Wetness.

XXXVI

Lessons lettuce.
Let us peer let us polite let us pour, let us polite. Let us polite.

XXXVII

Neither is blessings bean.

XXXVIII

Dew Dew Drops.

Leaves kindly Lasts.
Dew Dew Drops.

XXXIX

A R. nuisance.
Not a regular plate.
Are, not a regular plate.

XL

Lock out sandy.
Lock out sandy boot trees.
Lock out sandy boot trees knit glass.
Lock out sandy boot trees knit glass.

XLI

A R not new since.
New since.
Are new since bows less.

XLII

A jell cake.
A jelly cake.
A jelly cake.

XLIII

Peace say ray comb pomp
Peace say ray comb pump
Peace say ray comb pomp
Peace say ray comb pomp.

XLIV

Lean over not a coat low.
Lean over not a coat low by stand.
Lean over net. Lean over net a coat low hour stemmed
Lean over a coat low a great send. Lean over coat low extra extend.

XLV

Copying Copying it in.

XLVI

Never second scent never second scent in stand. Never second

scent in stand box or show. Or show me sales. Or show me
   sales oak. Oak pet. Oak pet stall.

XLVII
Not a mixed stick or not a mixed stick or glass. Not a mend stone
   bender, not a mend stone bender or stain.

XLVIII
Polish polish is it a hand, polish is it a hand or all, or all poles sick,
   or all poles sick.

XLIX
Rush in rush in slice.

L
Little gem in little gem in an. Extra.

LI
In the between egg in, in the between egg or on.

LII
Leaves of gas, leaves of get a towel louder.

LIII
Not stretch.

LIV
Tea Fulls.
Pit it pit it little saddle pear say.

LV
Let me see wheat air blossom.
Let me see tea.

LVI
Nestle in glass, nestle in walk, nestle in fur a lining.

LVII
Pale eaten best seek.
Pale eaten best seek, neither has met is a glance.

LVIII
Suppose it is a s. Suppose it is a seal. Suppose it is a recognised
   opera.

LIX
Not a sell inch, not a boil not a never seeking cellar.

LX
Little gem in in little gem in an. Extra.

LXI
Catch as catch as coal up.

LXII
Necklaces, neck laces, necklaces, neck laces.

LXIII
Little in in in in.

LXIV
Next or Sunday, next or sunday check.

LXV
Wide in swim, wide in swim pansy.

LXVI
Next to hear next to hear old boat seak, old boat seak next to hear.

LXVII
Ape pail ape pail to glow.

LXVIII
It was in on an each tuck. It was in on an each tuck.

LXIX
Wire lean string, wire lean string excellent miss on one pepper cute. Open so mister soil in to close not a see wind not seat glass.

LIFTING BELLY

LIFTING BELLY *seems to have been written in Mallorca,
Paris, Perpignan, and Nîmes during the years 1915, 1916, and
1917. Like "A Sonatina Followed by Another," it is not a hermetic
composition but a naturalistic recounting of the daily life. Internal
evidence therefore makes possible the dating of its pages, if we ac-
cept, as there is every reason to do, the premise that Gertrude
Stein in her poetic writing dealt constantly with the immediate
present and virtually never with the past.*

*The piece begins in Palma de Mallorca, where Miss Stein went
in 1915 intending to sit out the war. Fires of olive wood, a dog
(his name was Polybe), a man friend (it was an American painter
named Cook), and an English couple (named Penrose) appear in
its first pages. All these give us the year 1915. Later, in the spring
of 1916, there is a reference to the Battle of Verdun and to the
fact that its outcome was no longer a source of anxiety. The title
"Part II" on page 66 is merely rhetorical, for the real Part Two
comes only after page 80 and is entitled "Lifting Belly Is So
Kind, II."*

*Part II also begins in Mallorca, with apricots and decorated
wax candles (bought against accidents to the electric system). By
page 82 it has become "necessary to have a Ford" (for war work
in France). On page 87 appear "platinum knitting needles" (an
idea that Miss Stein entertained for helping out the French war
economy by spending in France the largest possible amount of
American money) and on page 93 "a splendid little table." There
is no doubt that by this point in the work's composition she was
back in Paris, for the "little table," bought through an antique
dealer in the rue Bonaparte, was imported from Spain with sausages packed in it—a device for exporting food illegally from Spain
to France. This incident took place in 1916.*

*On page 96 of the second part occurs the celebrated line
"Rose is a rose is a rose is a rose." This had first appeared in "Sacred
Emily," written in 1913. It was not Gertrude Stein's habit to use
old material in new poems. The reappearance here of this striking
sentence is a unique case to the contrary. Commonplaces of the*

language, like "When this you see remember me," come back in work after work; but this direct quotation of an original phrase violates the principle of spontaneity that she followed so consistently. My only explanation of the reference is that by 1916 the phrase had become for her a household object. It had been engraved in circular form on writing paper as early as 1914; and in 1916, during the very period when the present poem was being composed, fine linen handkerchiefs had been embroidered in Mallorca with the same device. It must by this time have become detached in her mind from its original inspiration and taken on the life of a motto, anybody's motto, like "E Pluribus Unum" or "In God We Trust." Without some such explanation, I find its presence in this poem both illogical and incredible.

Part III may have begun in Paris, where there were wood fires and smoked salmon. But early it starts to travel, as Part II had done; and by page 102 we are at Perpignan in 1917, with references to "a bun" (she liked the local pastries) and, on page 104, to that city's celebrated nightingales.

On page 111 there is mention of photographs and of waiting for them. This refers to Miss Stein's having been photographed with her Ford truck in front of the birthplace of Marshal Joffre, at Rivesaltes, near Perpignan. The photographs were intended for sale in America to aid the American Fund for French Wounded, the organization for which Miss Stein was driving her truck. All this gives us 1917 in Perpignan. The city and its not particularly good strawberries are actually named on page 113. By by page 115, the end of the poem, Miss Stein must have been moved to Nîmes, for it was there and not in Perpignan that she knew Miss Cheatham. Aunt Pauline, I may add, is what she called her Ford truck, as she later called her runabout Godiva.

I do not know the meaning of the title, "Lifting Belly." It may be a pun, and it may be literal. The poem itself is a diary, like the "Sonatina," and a hymn to the domestic affections. The current events that determined the author's movements and whereabouts during the years of its composition gave frequent cause for anguish

*and difficult decisions. And yet the piece is full of gaieties and
lightness of heart. It shows Miss Stein in one of her most winning
aspects, that of the happy woman. Her power of love and her
hilarity are there too, but dominating all is the author's gift for
well-being and for spreading it around her. The sight of her must
have been good for wounded soldiers.*

V.T.

LIFTING BELLY

I have been heavy and had much selecting. I saw a star which
was low. It was so low it twinkled. Breath was in it. Little pieces
are stupid.

I want to tell about fire. Fire is that which we have when we
have olive. Olive is a wood. We like linen. Linen is ordered. We
are going to order linen.

All belly belly well.

Bed of coals made out of wood.

I think this one may be an expression. We can understand
heating and burning composition. Heating with wood.

Sometimes we readily decide upon wind we decide that there
will be stars and perhaps thunder and perhaps rain and perhaps
no moon. Sometimes we decide that there will be a storm and
rain. Sometimes we look at the boats. When we read about a
boat we know that it has been sunk. Not by the waves but by the
sails. Any one knows that rowing is dangerous. Be alright. Be
careful. Be angry. Say what you think. Believe in there being the
same kind of a dog. Jerk. Jerk him away. Answer that you do not
care to think so.

We quarreled with him. We quarreled with him then. Do
not forget that I showed you the road. Do not forget that I
showed you the road. We will forget it because he does not oblige
himself to thank me. Ask him to thank me.

The next time that he came we offered him something to read.
There is a great difference of opinion as to whether cooking in oil
is or is not healthful.

I don't pardon him. I find him objectionable.

What is it when it's upset. It isn't in the room. Moonlight and darkness. Sleep and not sleep. We sleep every night.

What was it.

I said lifting belly.

You didn't say it.

I said it I mean lifting belly.

Don't misunderstand me.

Do you.

Do you lift everybody in that way.

No.

You are to say No.

Lifting belly.

How are you.

Lifting belly how are you lifting belly.

We like a fire and we don't mind if it smokes.

Do you.

How do you do. The Englishmen are coming. Not here. No an Englishwoman. An Englishman and an Englishwoman.

What did you say lifting belly. I did not understand you correctly. It is not well said. For lifting belly. For lifting belly not to lifting belly.

Did you say, oh lifting belly.

What is my another name.

Representative.

Of what.

Of the evils of eating.

What are they then.

They are sweet and figs.

Do not send them.

Yes we will it will be very easy.

PART II

Lifting belly. Are you. Lifting.

Oh dear I said I was tender, fierce and tender.

Do it. What a splendid example of carelessness.

It gives me a great deal of pleasure to say yes.

Why do I always smile.

I don't know.

It pleases me.
You are easily pleased.
I am very pleased.
Thank you I am scarcely sunny.
I wish the sun would come out.
Yes.
Do you lift it.
High.
Yes sir I helped to do it.
Did you.
Yes.
Do you lift it.
We cut strangely.
What.
That's it.
Address it say to it that we will never repent.
A great many people come together.
Come together.
I don't think this has anything to do with it.
What I believe in is what I mean.
Lifting belly and roses.
We get a great many roses.
I always smile.
Yes.
And I am happy.
With what.
With what I said.
This evening.
Not pretty.
Beautiful.
Yes beautiful.
Why don't you prettily bow.
Because it shows thought.
It does.
Lifting belly is so strong.
A great many things are weaknesses. You are pleased to so.
I say because I am so well pleased. With what. With what I said.
There are a great many weaknesses.

Lifting belly.
What was it I said.
I can add that.
It's not an excuse.
I do not like bites.
How lift it.
Not so high.
What a question.
I do not understand about ducks.
Do not you.
I don't mean to close.
No of course not.
Dear me. Lifting belly.
Dear me. Lifting belly.
Oh yes.
Alright.
Sing.
Do you hear.
Yes I hear.
Lifting belly is amiss.
This is not the way.
I see.
Lifting belly is alright.
Is it a name.
Yes it's a name.
We were right.
 So you weren't pleased.
I see that we are pleased.
It is a great way.
To go.
No not to go.
But to lift.
Not light.
Paint.
No not paint.
All the time we are very happy.
All loud voices are seen. By whom. By the best.
Lifting belly is so erroneous.

I don't like to be teased and worried.
Lifting belly is so accurate.
Yes indeed.
She was educated.
And pleased.
Yes indeed.
Lifting belly is so strong.
I said that to mean that I was very glad.
Why are you very glad.
Because that pleased me.
Baby love.
A great many people are in the war.
I will go there and back again.
What did you say about Lifting belly.
I said lifting belly is so strong.
Yes indeed it is and agreeable and grateful.
We have gratitude.
No one can say we haven't.
Lifting belly is so cold. Not in summer. No nor in winter
either.
All of it is a joke.
Lifting belly is no joke. Not after all.
I am so discouraged about it. About lifting belly. I question.
I am so discouraged about lifting belly.
The other day there was a good deal of sunlight.
There often is.
There often is here.
We are very well satisfied at present.
So enthusiastic.
Lifting belly has charm.
Charming.
Alright.
Lifting belly is not very interesting.
To you.
To me.
Say did you see that the wind was from the east.
It usually is from the South.
We like rain.

Sneeze. This is the way to say it.

You meant a pressure.

Indeed yes.

All the time there is a chance to see me. I don't wish it to be said so.

The skirt.

And water.

You mean ocean water.

Not exactly an ocean a sea.

A success.

Was it a success.

Lifting belly is all there.

Lifting belly high.

It is not necessary to repeat the word.

How do you do I forgive you everything and there is nothing to forgive.

Lifting belly is so high.

Do you like lilies.

Do you like lilies.

Use the word lifting belly is so high.

In place of that.

A special case to-day.

Of peaches.

Lifting belly is delightful.

Lifting belly is so high.

To-day.

Yes to-day.

Do you think that said yesterday.

Yes to-day.

Don't be silly.

In that we see that we can please me.

I don't see how you can write on the wall about roses.

Lifting belly a terminus.

What is there to please me.

Alright.

A pocket.

Lifting belly is good.

Rest.

Arrest.

Do you please m.

I do more than that.

When are you most proud of me.

Dare I ask you to be satisfied.

Dear me.

Lifting belly is anxious.

Not about Verdun.

Oh dear no.

The wind whistles that means it whistles just like any one. I thought it was a whistle.

Lifting belly together.

Do you like that there.

There are not mistakes made.

Not here at any rate.

Not here at any rate.

There are no mistakes made. Not here at any rate.

When do I see the lightning. Every night.

Lifting belly again.

It is a credit to me.

There was an instant of lifting belly.

Lifting belly is an occasion. An occasion to please me. Oh yes. Mention it.

Lifting belly is courteous.

Lifting belly is hilarious, gay and favorable.

Oh yes it is.

Indeed it is not a disappointment.

Not to me.

Lifting belly is such an incident. In one's life.

Lifting belly is such an incident in one's life.

I don't mean to be reasonable.

Shall I say thin.

This makes me smile.

Lifting belly is so kind.

A great many clouds for the sun. You mean the sun on high.

Leave me.

See me.

Lifting belly is no joke.

I appreciate that.
Do not show kindness.
Why not.
Because it ruffles me.
Do not say that it is unexpected.
Lifting belly is so scarce.
Not to-day.
Lifting belly is so kind.
To me there are many exceptional cases.
What did you say. I said I had not been disturbed. Neither
had we. Lifting belly is so necessary.
Lifting belly is so kind.
I can't say it too often.
Pleasing me.
Lifting belly.
Extraordinary.
Lifting belly is such exercise.
You mean altogether.
Lifting belly is so kind to me.
Lifting belly is so kind to many.
Don't say that please.
If you please.
Lifting belly is right.
And we were right.
Now I say again. I say now again.
What is a whistle.
Miracle you don't know about the miracle.
You mean a meteor.
No I don't I mean everything away.
Away where.
Away here.
Oh yes.
Lifting belly is so strong.
You said that before.
Lifting belly is so strong and willing.
Lifting belly is so strong and yet waiting.
Lifting belly is so soothing. Yes indeed.
It gives me greater pleasure.

Does it.

It gives me great pleasure.

What do you mean by St. John.

A great many churches are visited.

Lifting belly try again.

I will not say what I think about lifting belly. Oh yes you will.

Well then please have it understood that I can't be responsible
for doubts. Nobody doubts.

Nobody doubts.

I have no use for lifting belly.

Do you say that to me.

No I don't.

Anybody who is wisely urged to go to Inca goes to the hill.

What hill. The hill above lifting belly.

Is it all hill.

Not very well.

Not very well hill.

Lifting belly is so strong.

And clear.

Why do you say feeding.

Lifting belly is such a windmill.

Do you stare.

Lifting belly to me.

What did he say.

He didn't say that he was waiting.

I have been adequately entertained.

Some when they sigh by accident say poor country she is
betrayed.

I didn't say that to-day. No indeed you didn't.

Mixing belly is so kind.

Lifting belly is so a measure of it all.

Lifting belly is a picnic.

On a fine day.

We like the weather it is very beautiful.

Lifting belly is so able.

Lifting belly is so able to be praised.

The act.

The action.

A great many people are excitable.

Mixing belly is so strange.

Lifting belly is so satisfying.

Do not speak to me.

Of it.

Lifting belly is so sweet.

That is the way to separate yourself from the water.

Lifting belly is so kind.

Loud voices discuss pigeons.

Do loud voices discuss pigeons.

Remember me to the hill. What hill. The hill in back of Genova.

Lifting belly is so kind. So very kind.

Lifting belly is so kind.

I never mean to insist to-day.

Lifting belly is so consecutive.

With all of us.

Lifting belly is so clear.

Very clear.

And there is lots of water.

Lifting belly is so impatient.

So impatient to-day.

Lifting belly is all there.

Do I doubt it.

Lifting belly.

What are my plans.

There are some she don't mention.

There are some she doesn't mention. Some others she doesn't mention.

Lifting belly is so careful. Full of care for me. Lifting belly is mean. I see. You mean lifting belly is all right.

Lifting belly is so simple.

Listen to me to-day.

Lifting belly is so warm.

Leave it to me.

Leave what to me.

Lifting belly is such an experiment.

We were thoroughly brilliant.

If I were a postman I would deliver letters. We call them let-
ter carriers.
Lifting belly is so strong. And so judicious.
Lifting belly is an exercise.
Exercise is very good for me.
Lifting belly necessarily pleases the latter.
Lifting belly is necessary.
Do believe me.
Lifting belly quietly.
It is very exciting.
Stand.
Why do you stand.
Did you say you thought it would make any difference.
Lifting belly is not so kind.
Little places to sting.
We used to play star spangled banner.
Lifting belly is so near.
Lifting belly is so dear.
Lifting belly all around.
Lifting belly makes a sound.
Keep still.
Lifting belly is gratifying.
I can't express the hauntingness of Dugny.
I can't express either the obligation I have to say say it.
Lifting belly is so kind.
Dear me lifting belly is so kind.
Am I in it.
That doesn't affect it.
How do you mean.
Lifting belly and a resemblance.
There is no resemblance.
A plain case of misdeed.
Lifting belly is peacable.
The Cataluna has come home.
Lifting belly is a success.
So is tenderness.
Lifting belly is kind and good and beautiful.
Lifting belly is my joy.

Do you believe in singling. Singing do you mean.
Lifting belly is a special pleasure.
Who can be convinced of this measure.
Lifting belly is perfect.
I know what you mean.
Lifting belly was very fatiguing.
Did you make a note of it of the two donkeys and the three
dogs. The smaller one is the mother of the other two.
Lifting belly
Exactly.
Lifting belly all the time.
Do be careful of me.
Remarkably so.
Remarkably a recreation.
Lifting belly is so satisfying.
Lifting belly to me.
Large quantities of it.
Say that you see that you are praised.
Lifting belly.
See that.
You have entertained me.
Hurry up.
Hurry up with it.
Lifting belly does that astonish you.
Excuse me.
Why do you wish to hear me.
I wish to hear you because it pleases me.
Yesterday and to-day.
Yesterday and to-day we managed it altogether.
Lifting belly is so long.
It is an expression of opinion.
Conquistador. James I.
It is exceptional.
Lifting belly is current rolling. Lifting belly is so strong.
Lifting belly is so strong.
That is what I say.
I say it to please me.
Please yourself with thunder.

Lifting belly is famous.
So are many celebrations.
Lifting belly is so.
We mean lifting belly.
We mean it and do we care.
We keep all the letters.
Lifting belly is so seen.
You mean here.
Not with spy glasses.
Lifting belly is an expression.
Explain it explain it to me.
Lifting belly is cautious.
Of course these words are said.
To be strong.
Lifting belly.
Yes orchids.
Lifting belly is so adaptable.
That will amuse my baby.
Lifting belly is a way of sitting.
I don't mean to laugh.
Lifting belly is such a reason.
Lifting belly is such a reason.
Why do I say bench.
Because it is laughable.
Lifting belly is so droll.
We have met to-day with every kind of consideration.
Not very good. Of course it is very good.
Lifting belly is so kind.
Why do you say that.
Bouncing belly.
Did you say bouncing belly.
We asked here for a sister.
Lifting belly is not noisy.
We go to Barcelona to-morrow.
Lifting belly is an acquisition.
I forgot to put in a special cake. Love to be.
Very well.
Lifting belly is the understanding.

Sleepy.

Why do you wake up.

Lifting belly keep it.

We will send it off.

She should.

Nothing pleases me except dinner.

I have done as I wished and I do not feel any responsibility
to you.

Are you there.

Lifting belly.

What do I say.

Pussy how pretty you are.

That goes very quickly unless you have been there too long.

I told him I would send him Mildred's book. He seemed very
pleased at the prospect.

Lifting belly is so strong.

Lifting belly together.

Lifting belly oh yes.

Lifting belly.

Oh yes.

Remember what I say.

I have no occasion to deliberate.

He has no heart but that you can supply.

The fan goes alright.

Lifting belly what is earnest. Expecting an arena to be mon-
umental.

Lifting belly is recognised to be the only spectacle present.
Do you mean that.

Lifting belly is a language. It says island. Island a strata. Lifting belly is a repetition.

Lifting belly means me.

I do love roses and carnations.

A mistake. There can be no mistakes.

I do not say a mother.

Lifting belly.

Lifting belly.

Cry.

Lifting belly.

Lifting belly. Splendid.
Jack Johnson Henry.
Henry is his name sir.
Jack Johnson Henry is an especially eloquent curtain.
We see a splendid force in mirrors.
Angry we are not angry.
Pleasing.
Lifting belly raining.
I am good looking.
A magazine of lifting belly. Excitement sisters.
Did we see the bird jelly I call it. I call it something religious.
You mean beautiful. I do not know that I like large rocks. Sarsen
land we call it. Oh yes. Lifting belly is a persuasion. You are
satisfied. With it. With it and with you. I am satisfied with your
behavior. I call it astonishing. Lifting belly is so exact and audible
and Spanish curses. You know I prefer a bird. What bird. Why
a yellow bird. I saw it first. That was an accident. You mean by
accident. I mean exactly what I said. Lifting belly is a great
luxury. Can you imitate a cow.
Lifting belly is so kind.
And so cold.
Lifting belly is a rare instance. I am fond of it. I am attached to
the accentuation.
Lifting belly is a third.
Did you say third. No I said Avila.
Listen to him sing.
She is so sweet and thrilling.
Listen to me as yet I have no color. Red white and blue all
out but you.
This is the best thing I have ever said. Lifting belly and it, it
is not startling. Lifting belly until to-morrow. Lifting belly to-
morrow.
I would not be surprised surprised if I added that yet.
Lifting belly to me.
I am fondest of all of lifting belly.
Lifting belly careful don't say anything about lifting belly.
I did not change my mind.
Neither did you carefully.

Lifting belly and again lifting belly.

I have changed my mind about the country.

Lifting belly and action and voices and care to be taken.

Does it make any difference if you pay for paper or not.

Listen to me. Using old automobile tires as sandals is singularly interesting. It is done in Avila.

What did I tell. Lifting belly is so kind.

What kind of a noise does it make. Like the man at night. The man that calls out. We hear him.

Lifting belly is so strong. I love cherish idolise adore and worship you. You are so sweet so tender and so perfect.

Did you believe in sandals. When they are made of old automobile tire. I wish I knew the history of it.

Lifting belly is notorious.

A great many people wish to salute. The general does. So does the leader of the battalion. In spanish. I understand that.

I understand everything.

Lifting belly is to jelly.

Holy most is in the sky.

We see it in three.

Yes we see it every night near the hills. This is so natural. Birds do it. We do not know their name.

Lifting belly or all I can never be pleased with this. Listen to me. Lifting belly is so kind.

Lifting belly is so dear.

Lifting belly is here.

Did we not hear and we were walking leave it to me and say come quickly now. He is not sleepy. At last I know why he laughs. Do you.

I will not imitate colors. From the stand point of white yellow is colored. Do you mean bushes. No I mean acacias. Lilacs do fade. What did you say for lifting belly. Extra. Extra thunder. I can so easily be fastidious.

II

Kiss my lips. She did.

Kiss my lips again she did.

Kiss my lips over and over and over again she did.

I have feathers.

Gentle fishes.

Do you think about apricots. We find them very beautiful.
It is not alone their color it is their seeds that charm us. We find
it a change.

Lifting belly is so strange.

I came to speak about it.

Selected raisins well their grapes grapes are good.

Change your name.

Question and garden.

It's raining. Don't speak about it.

My baby is a dumpling. I want to tell her something.

Wax candles. We have bought a great many wax candles.
Some are decorated. They have not been lighted.

I do not mention roses.

Exactly.

Actually.

Question and butter.

I find the butter very good.

Lifting belly is so kind.

Lifting belly fattily.

Doesn't that astonish you.

You did want me.

Say it again.

Strawberry.

Lifting beside belly.

Lifting kindly belly.

Sing to me I say.

Some are wives not heroes.

Lifting belly merely.

Sing to me I say.

Lifting belly. A reflection.

Lifting belly adjoins more prizes.

Fit to be.

I have fit on a hat.

Have you.

What did you say to excuse me. Difficult paper and scattered.

Lifting belly is so kind.

What shall you say about that. Lifting belly is so kind.
What is a veteran.
A veteran is one who has fought.
Who is the best.
The king and the queen and the mistress.
Nobody has a mistress.
Lifting belly is so kind.
To-day we decided to forgive Nellie.
Anybody can describe dresses.
How do you do what is the news.
Lifting belly is so kind.
Lifting belly exactly.
The king and the prince of Montenegro.
Lifting belly is so kind.
Lifting belly to please me.
Excited.
Excited are you.
I can whistle, the train can whistle whistle we can hear the whistle, the boat whistle. The train is not running to-day. Mary whistle whistle for the whim.
Didn't you say you'd write it better.
Mrs. Vettie. It is necessary to have a Ford.
Yes sir.
Dear Mrs. Vettie. Smile to me.
I am.
Dear Mrs. Vettie never better.
Yes indeed so.
Lifting belly is most kind.
What did I say, that I was a great poet like the English only sweeter.
When I think of this afternoon and the garden I see what you mean.
You are not thinking of the pleasure.
Lifting belly again.
What did I mention when I drew a pansy that pansy and petunia both begin with p.
Lifting belly splendidly.
We have wishes.

Let us say we know it.

Did I say anything about it. I know the tittle. We know the title.

Lifting belly is so kind.

We have made no mistake.

The Montenegrin family.

A condition to a wide admiration.

Lifting belly after all.

You don't mean disobedience.

Lifting belly all around.

Eat the little girl I say.

Listen to me. Did you expect it to go back. Why do you do to stop.

What do you do to stop.

What do you do to go on.

I do the same.

Yes wishes. Oh yes wishes.

What do you do to turn a corner.

What do you do to sing.

We don't mention singing.

What do you do to be reformed.

You know.

Yes wishes.

What do you do to measure.

I do it in such a way.

I hope to see them come.

Lifting belly go around.

I was sorry to be blistered.

We were such company.

Did she say jelly.

Jelly my jelly.

Lifting belly is so round.

Big Caesars.

Two Caesars.

Little seize her.

Too.

Did I do my duty.

Did I wet my knife.

No I don't mean whet.
Exactly four teeth.
Little belly is so kind.
What did you say about accepting.
Yes.
Lifting belly another lifting belly.
I question the weather.
It is not necessary.
Lifting belly oh lifting belly in time.
Yes indeed.
Be to me.
Did you say this was this.
Mr. Louis.
Do not mention Mr. Louis.
Little axes.
Yes indeed little axes and rubbers.
This is a description of an automobile.
I understand all about them.
Lifting belly is so kind.
So is whistling.
A great many whistles are shrill.
Lifting belly connects.
Lifting belly again.
Sympathetic blessing.
Not curls.
Plenty of wishes.
All of them fulfilled.
Lifting belly you don't say so.
Climb trees.
Lifting belly has sparks.
Sparks of anger and money.
Lifting belly naturally celebrates
We naturally celebrate.
Connect me in places.
Lifting belly.
No no don't say that.
Lifting belly oh yes.
Tax this.

Running behind a mountain.
I fly to thee.
Lifting belly.
Shall I chat.
I mean pugilists.
Oh yes trainer.
Oh yes yes.
Say it again to study.
It has been perfectly fed.
Oh yes I do.
Belly alright.
Lifting belly very well.
Lifting belly this.
So sweet.
To me.
Say anything a mudding made of Caesars.
Lobster. Baby is so good to baby.
I correct blushes. You mean wishes.
I collect pearls. Yes and colors.
All colors are gods. Oh yes Beddlington.
Now I collect songs.
Lifting belly is so nice.
I wrote about it to him.
I wrote about it to her.
Not likely not very likely that they will seize rubber. Not
very likely that they will seize rubber.
Lifting belly yesterday.
And to-day.
And to-morrow.
A train to-morrow.
Lifting belly is so exciting.
Lifting belly asks any more.
Lifting belly captures.
Seating.
Have a swim.
Lifting belly excuses.
Can you swim.
Lifting belly for me.

When this you see remember me.
Oh yes.
Yes.
Researches and a cab.
A cab right.
Lifting belly phlegmatically.
Bathing bathing in bliss.
I am very well satisfied with meat.
Kindness to my wife.
Lifting belly to a throne.
Search it for me.
Yes wishes.
I say it again I am perfection in behavior and circumstance.
Oh yes alright.
Levelheaded fattuski.
I do not wish to be Polish.
Quite right in singing.
Lifting belly is so recherché.
Lifting belly.
Up.
Correct me.
I believe he makes together of pieces.
Lifting belly.
Not that.
Think of me.
Oh yes.
Lifting belly for me.
Right there.
Not that yesterday.
Fetch missions.
Lifting belly or Dora.
Lifting belly.
Yes Misses.
Lifting belly separately all day.
I say lifting belly.
An example.
A good example.
Cut me a slice.

You see what I wish.
I wish a seat and Caesar.
Caesar is plural.
I can think.
And so can I.
And argue.
Oh yes you see.
What I see.
You see me.
Yes stretches.
Stretches and stretches of happiness.
Should you have put it away.
Yes you should have put it away.
Do not think so much.
I do not.
Have you a new title.
Lifting belly articulately.
It is not a problem.
Kissing and singing.
We have the habit when we wash.
In singing we say how do you do how do you like the war.
Little dumps of it.
Did you hear that man. What did he say close it.
Lifting belly lifting pleasure.
What can we say about wings.
Wings and refinement.
Come to me.
Sleepy.
Sleepily we think.
Wings after lunch.
I don't think.
No don't I regret a silver sugar.
And I platinum knitting needles.
And I sherry glasses.
I do not care for sherry I used to use for castor-oil.
You mean licorice.
He is so fond of coffee.
Let me tell you about kissing. We saw a piece of mistletoe.

We exchanged a pillow. We murmured training and we were asleep.

This is what happened Saturday.

Another day we said sour grass it grows in fields. So do daisies and green flowers.

I have never noticed green flowers.

Lifting belly is my joy.

What did I tell Caesars.

That I recognised them.

It is the custom to answer swimming.

Catch a call.

Does the moonlight make any difference to you.

Lifting belly yes Miss.

I can lean upon a pencil.

Lifting belly yes address me.

I address you.

Lifting belly magnetically.

Did you make a mistake.

Wave to me.

Lifting belly permanently.

What did the Caesars.

What did they all say.

They said that they were not deceived.

Lifting belly such a good example. And is so readily watchful.

What do you think of watches.

Collect lobsters.

And sweetbreads.

And a melon.

And salad.

Do not have a term.

You mean what do you call it.

Yes sir.

Sing to me.

Lifting belly is neglected.

The Caesar.

Oh yes the Caesar.

Oh yes the Caesar.

Lifting belly pencils to me.

And pens.
Lifting belly and the intention.
I particularly like what I know.
Lifting belly sublimely.
We made a fire this evening.
Cooking is cheap.
I do not care for Ethel.
That's a very good one. I say that's a very good one.
Yes and we think.
A rhyme, I understand nectarine. I also understand egg.
A special case you are.
Lifting belly and Caesar.
Did I explain it.
Have I explained it to you.
Have I explained it to you in season. Have I perplexed you.
You have not perplexed me nor mixed me. You have addressed
me as Caesar. This is the answer that I expected. When I said do
not mention any words I meant no indifference. I meant do your
duty and do not forget that I establish myself.
You establish yourself.
When this you see believe me.
Lifting belly etcetera.
Lifting belly and a hand. A hand is black and not by toil. I do
not like fat resemblances. There are none such.
Lifting belly and kind.
This is the pencil for me.
Lifting belly squeezes.
Remember what I said about a rhyme.
Don't call it again.
Say white spots.
Do not mention disappointment in cups.
Oh you are so sweet.
Lifting belly believe me.
Believe it is for pleasure that I do it.
Not foreign pleasure.
Oh no.
My pleasure in Susie.
Lifting belly so kind.

So kindly.
Lifting belly gratuitously.
Lifting belly increase.
Do this to me.
Lifting belly famously.
When did I say I thought it.
When you heard it.
Oh yes.
Bright eyes I make you ties.
No mockings.
This is to say I knit woolen stockings for you. And I understand it and I am very grateful.
Making a spectacle.
Drinking prepared water.
Laughing together.
Asking lifting belly to be particular.
Lifting belly is so kind.
She was like that.
Star spangled banner, story of Savannah.
She left because she was going to have the child with her.
Lifting belly don't think of it.
Believe me in truth and marriage.
Believe that I use the best paper that I can get.
Do you believe me.
Lifting belly is not an invitation.
Call me semblances.
I call you a cab sir.
That's the way she tells it.
Lifting belly is so accurate.
I congratulate you in being respectable and respectably married.
Call me Helen.
Not at all.
You may call me Helen.
That's what we said.
Lifting belly with firmness and pride.
Lifting belly with industry beside.
Heated heated with cold.

Some people are heated with linen.
Lifting belly comes extra.
This is a picture of lifting belly having a cow.
Oh yes you can say it of me.
When this you see remember me.
Lifting belly says pardon.
Pardon for what.
For having made a mistake.
Can you imagine what I say.
I say impossible.
Lifting belly is recognised.
Lifting belly presumably.
Do we run together.
I say do we run together.
I do not like stubbornness.
Come and sing.
Lifting belly.
I sing lifting belly.
I say lifting belly and then I say lifting belly and Caesars. I
say lifting belly gently and Caesars gently. I say lifting belly again
and Caesars again. I say lifting belly and I say Caesars and I say
lifting belly Caesars and cow come out. I say lifting belly and
Caesars and cow come out.
Can you read my print.
Lifting belly say can you see the Caesars. I can see what I kiss.
Of course you can.
Lifting belly high.
That is what I adore always more and more.
Come out cow.
Little connections.
Yes oh yes cow come out.
Lifting belly unerringly.
A wonderful book.
Baby my baby I backhand for thee.
She is a sweet baby and well baby and me.
This is the way I see it.
Lifting belly can you say it.
Lifting belly persuade me.

Lifting belly persuade me.
You'll find it a very easy to sing to me.
What can you say.
Lifting belly set.
I can not pass a door.
You mean odor.
I smell sweetly.
So do you.
Lifting belly plainly.
Can you sing.
Can you sing for me.
Lifting belly settled.
Can you excuse money.
Lifting belly has a dress.
Lifting belly in a mess.
Lifting belly in order.
Complain I don't complain.
She is my sweetheart.
Why doesn't she resemble an other.
This I cannot say here.
Full of love and echoes. Lifting belly is full of love.
Can you.
Can you can you.
Can you buy a Ford.
Did you expect that.
Lifting belly hungrily.
Not lonesomely.
But enthusiastically.
Lifting belly altogether.
Were you wise.
Were you wise to do so.
Can you say winking.
Can you say Francis Ferdinand has gone to the West.
Can you neglect me.
Can you establish the clock.
Yes I can when I am good.
Lifting belly precariously.
Lifting belly is noted.

Are you noted with me.
Come to sing and sit.
This is not the time for discussion.
A splendid table little table.
A splendid little table.
Can you be fortunate.
Yes sir.
What is a man.
What is a woman.
What is a bird.
Lifting belly must please me.
Yes can you think so.
Lifting belly cherished and flattered.
Lifting belly naturally.
Can you extract.
Can you be through so quickly.
No I cannot get through so quickly.
Are you afraid of Negro sculpture.
I have my feelings.
Lifting belly is so exact.
Lifting belly is favored by me.
Lifting belly cautiously.
I lift it in place of the music.
You mean it is the same.
I mean everything.
Can you not whistle.
Call me for that.
And sing.
I sing too.
Lifting belly counts.
My idea is.
Yes I know what your idea is.
Lifting belly knows all about the wind.
Yes indeed Miss.
Yes indeed.
Can you suspect me.
We are glad that we do not deceive.
Lifting belly regular.

Lifted belly behind.

Candidly.

Can you say that there is a mistake.

In the wash.

No in respect to the woman.

Can you say we meant to send her away.

Lifting belly is so orderly.

She makes no mistake.

She does not indeed.

Lifting belly heroically.

Can you think of that.

Can you guess what I mean.

Yes I can.

Lovely sweet.

Calville cow.

And that is it.

Lifting belly resignedly.

Now you laugh.

Lifting belly for me.

When this you see remember me.

Can you be sweet.

You are.

We are so likely.

We are so likely to be sweet.

Lifting belly handy.

Can you mention lifting belly. I can.

Yes indeed I know what I say.

Do you.

Lifting belly is so much.

Lifting belly grandly.

You can be sweet.

We see it.

We are tall.

We are wellbred.

We can say we do like what we have.

Lifting belly is more.

I am more than ever inclined to how do you do. That's the way to wish it.

Lifting belly is so good.
That is natural.
Lifting belly exactly.
Calville cow is all to me.
Don't excite me.
Lifting belly exactly.
That's respectable.
Lifting belly is all to me.
Pretty Caesars yes they do.
Can you spell mixing.
I hear you.
How do you do.
Can you tell me about imposing.
When are you careful to speak.
Lifting belly categorically.
Think of it.
Lifting belly in the mind.
The Honorable Graham Murray.
My honorable Graham Murray.
What can you say.
I can say that I find it most useful and very warm, yet light.
Lifting belly astonishingly.
Can you mention her brother.
Yes.
Her father.
Yes.
A married couple.
Yes.
Lifting belly names it.
Look at that.
Yes that's what I said.
I put down something on lifting belly.
Humph.
Lifting belly bells.
Can you think of singing. In the little while in which I say
stop it you are not spoiled.
Can you be spoiled. I do not think so.
I think not.

I think everything of you.
Lifting belly is rich.
Chickens are rich.
I cannot disguise nice.
Don't you need to.
I think not.
Lifting belly exactly.
Why can lifting belly please me.
Lifting belly can please me because it is an occupation I enjoy.
Rose is a rose is a rose is a rose.
In print on top.
What can you do.
I can answer my question.
Very well answer this.
Who is Mr. Mc Bride.
In the way of laughing.
Lifting belly is an intention.
You are sure you know the meaning of any word.
Leave me to see.
Pink.
My pink.
Hear me to-day.
It is after noon.
I mean that literally.
It is after noon.
Little lifting belly is a quotation.
Frankly what do you say to me.
I say that I need protection.
You shall have it.
After that what do you wish.
I want you to mean a great deal to me.
Exactly.
And then.
And then blandishment.
We can see that very clearly.
Lifting belly is perfect.
Do you stretch farther.
Come eat it.

What did I say.
To whom.
Calville or a cow.
We were in a fashion deceived in Calville but not in a cow.
I understand when they say they mean something by it.
Lifting belly grandly.
Lifting belly sufficiently.
Come and be awake.
Certainly this morning.
Lifting belly very much.
I do not feel that I will be deceived.
Lifting belly fairly.
You mean follow.
I mean I follow.

Need you wish me to say lifting belly is recognised. No it is not necessary lifting belly is not peculiar. It is recognised. Can you recognise it. In a flash.

Thank you for me.
Can you excuse any one for loving its dearest. I said from. That is eaten.

Can you excuse any one from loving its dearest.
No I cannot.
A special fabric.
Can you begin a new thing.
Can I begin.
We have a dress.
You have a dress.
A dress by him.
Feel me.
I feel you.
Then it is fair to me.
Let me sing.
Certainly.
And you too Miss Polly.
What can you say.
I can say that there is no need of regretting a ball.
Mount Fatty.
That is a tremendous way.

Leave me to sing about it to-day.

And then there was a cake. Please give it to me. She did.

When can there be glasses. We are so pleased with it.

Go on to-morrow.

He cannot understand women. I can.

Believe me in this way.

I can understand the woman.

Lifting belly carelessly. I do not lift baby carelessly.

Lifting belly because there is no mistake. I planned to flourish.
Of course you do.

Lifting belly is exacting. You mean exact. I mean exacting.
Lifting belly is exacting.

Can you say see me.

Lifting belly is exciting.

Can you explain a mistake.

There is no mistake.

You have mentioned the flour.

Lifting belly is full of charm.

They are very nice candles.

Lifting belly is resourceful.

What can lifting belly say.

Oh yes I was not mistaken. Were not you indeed.

Lifting belly lifting belly lifting belly oh then lifting belly.

Can you make an expression. Thanks for the cigarette. How
pretty.

How fast. What. How fast the cow comes out.

Lifting belly a permanent caress.

Lifting belly bored.

You don't say so.

Lifting belly now.

Cow.

Lifting belly exactly.

I have often been pleased with this thing.

Lifting belly is necessarily venturesome.

You mean by that that you are collected. I hope I am.

What is an evening dress. What is a cape. What is a suit. What
is a fur collar.

Lifting belly needs to speak.

Land Rising next time.
Lifting belly has no choice.
Lifting belly seems to me to be remarkably kind.
Can you hear me witness that I was wolfish. I can. And that
I do not interfere with you. No I cannot countenance you here.
Countenance what do you mean by that. I mean that it is a pleas-
ure to prepare you. Thank you my dear.
Lifting belly is so kind.
Can you recollect this for me.
Lifting belly naturally.
Can you believe the truth.
Fredericks or Frederica.
Can you give me permission.
The Loves.
I never forget the Caesars.
Or the dears.
Lifting belly casually.
Where the head gets thin.
Lifting belly never mind.
You do please me.
Lifting belly restless.
Not at all.
Lifting belly there.
Expand my chest endlessly.
You did not do so.
Lifting belly is loved.
You know I am always ready to please you.
Lifting belly in a breath.
Lifting belly.
You do speak kindly.
We speak very kindly.
Lifting belly is so bold.

III

Lifting belly in here.
Able to state whimsies.
Can you recollect mistakes.
I hope not.

Bless you.

Lifting belly the best and only seat.

Lifting belly the reminder of present duties.

Lifting belly the charm.

Lifting belly is easy to me.

Lifting belly naturally.

Of course you lift belly naturally.

I lift belly naturally together.

Lifting belly answers.

Can you think for me.

I can.

Lifting belly endears me.

Lifting belly cleanly. With a wood fire. With a good fire.

Say how do you do to the lady. Which lady. The jew lady.
How do you do. She is my wife.

Can you accuse lifting belly of extras.

Salmon is salmon. Smoked and the most nourishing.

Pink salmon is my favorite color.

To be sure.

We are so necessary.

Can you wish for me.

I never mention it.

You need not resemble me.

But you do.

Of course you do.

That is very well said.

And meant.

And explained.

I explain too much.

And then I say.

She knows everything.

And she does.

Lifting belly beneficently.

I can go on with lifting belly forever. And you do.

I said it first. Lifting belly to engage. And then wishes. I wish
to be whimsied. I do that.

A worldly system.

A humorous example.

Lindo see me.
Whimsy see me.
See me.
Lifting belly exaggerates. Lifting belly is reproachful.
Oh can you see.
Yes sir.
Lifting belly mentions the bee.
Can you imagine the noise.
Can you whisper to me.
Lifting belly pronouncedly.
Can you imagine me thinking lifting belly.
Safety first.
That's the trimming.
I hear her snore
On through the door.
I can say that it is my delight.
Lifting belly fairly well.
Lifting belly visibly.
Yes I say visibly.
Lifting belly behind me.
The room is so pretty and clean.
Do you know the rest.
Yes I know the rest.
She knows the rest and will do it.
Lifting belly in eclipse.
There is no such moon for me.
Eclipse indeed can lifting belly be methodical.
In lifting belly yes.
In lifting belly yes.
Can you think of me.
I can and do.
Lifting belly encourages plenty.
Do not speak of San Francisco he is a saint.
Lifting belly shines.
Lifting belly nattily.
Lifting belly to fly.
Not to-day.
Motor.

Lifting belly for wind.
We do not like wind.
We do not mind snow.
Lifting belly partially.
Can you spell for me.
Spell bottle.
Lifting belly remarks.
Can we have the hill.
Of course we can have the hill.
Lifting belly patiently.
Can you see me rise.
Lifting belly says she can.
Lifting belly soundly.
Here is a bun for my bunny.
Every little bun is of honey.
On the little bun is my oney.
My little bun is so funny.
Sweet little bun for my money.
Dear little bun I'm her sunny.
Sweet little bun dear little bun good little bun for my bunny.
Lifting belly merry Christmas.
Lifting belly has wishes.
And then we please her.
What is the name of that pin.
Not a hat pin.
We use elastic.
As garters.
We are never blamed.
Thank you and see me.
How can I swim.
By not being surprised.
Lifting belly is so kind.
Lifting belly is harmonious.
Can you smile to me.
Lifting belly is prepared.
Can you imagine what I say.
Lifting belly can.
To be remarkable.

To be remarkably so.
Lifting belly and emergencies.
Lifting belly in reading.
Can you say effectiveness.
Lifting belly in reserve.
Lifting belly marches.
There is no song.
Lifting belly marry.
Lifting belly can see the condition.
How do you spell Lindo.
Not to displease.
The dears.
When can I.
When can I.
To-morrow if you like.
Thank you so much.
See you.
We were pleased to receive notes.
In there.
To there.
Can you see spelling.
Anybody can see lines.
Lifting belly is arrogant.
Not with oranges.
Lifting belly inclines me.
To see clearly.
Lifting belly is for me.
I can say truthfully never better.
Believe me lifting belly is not nervous.
Lifting belly is a miracle.
I am with her.
Lifting belly to me.
Very nicely done.
Poetry is very nicely done.
Can you say pleasure.
I can easily say please me.
You do.
Lifting belly is precious.

Then you can sing.
We do not encourage a nightingale.
Do you really mean that.
We literally do.
Then it is an intention.
Not the smell.
Lifting baby is a chance.
Certainly sir.
I please myself.
Can we convince Morlet.
We can.
Then see the way.
We can have a pleasant ford.
And we do.
We will.
See my baby cheerily.
I am celebrated by the lady.
Indeed you are.
I can rhyme
In English.
In loving.
In preparing.
Do not be rough.
I can sustain conversation.
Do you like a title for you.
Do you like a title.
Do you like my title.
Can you agree.
We do.
In that way have candles.
And dirt.
Not dirt.
There are two Caesars and there are four Caesars.
Caesars do their duty.
I never make a mistake.
We will be very happy and boastful and we will celebrate
Sunday.
How do you like your Aunt Pauline.

She is worthy of a queen.
Will she go as we do dream.
She will do satisfactorily.
And so will we.
Thank you so much.
Smiling to me.
Then we can see him.
Yes we can.
Can we always go.
I think so.
You will be secure.
We are secure.
Then we see.
We see the way.
This is very good for me.
In this way we play.
Then we are pleasing.
We are pleasing to him.
We have gone together.
We are in our Ford.
Please me please me.
We go then.
We go when.
In a minute.
Next week.
Yes indeed oh yes indeed.
I can tell you she is charming in a coat.
Yes and we are full of her praises.
Yes indeed.
This is the way to worry. Not it.
Can you smile.
Yes indeed oh yes indeed.
And so can I.
Can we think.
Wrist leading.
Wrist leading.
A kind of exercise.
A brilliant station.

Do you remember its name.
Yes Morlet.
Can you say wishes.
I can.
Winning baby.
Theoretically and practically.
Can we explain a season.
We can when we are right.
Two is too many.
To be right.
One is right and so we mount and have what we want.
We will remember.
Can you mix birthdays.
Certainly I can.
Then do so.
I do so.
Do I remember to write.
Can he paint.
Not after he has driven a car.
I can write.
There you are.
Lifting belly with me.
You inquire.
What you do then.
Pushing.
Thank you so much.
And lend a hand.
What is lifting belly now.
My baby.
Always sincerely.
Lifting belly says it there.
Thank you for the cream.
Lifting belly tenderly.
A remarkable piece of intuition.
I have forgotten all about it.
Have you forgotten all about it.
Little nature which is mine.
Fairy ham

Is a clam.
Of chowder
Kiss him Louder.
Can you be especially proud of me.
Lifting belly a queen.
In that way I can think.
Thank you so much.
I have,
Lifting belly for me.
I can not forget the name.
Lifting belly for me.
Lifting belly again.
Can you be proud of me.
I am.
Then we say it.
In miracles.
Can we say it and then sing. You mean drive.
I mean to drive.
We are full of pride.
Lifting belly is proud.
Lifting belly my queen.
Lifting belly happy.
Lifting belly see.
Lifting belly.
Lifting belly address.
Little washers.
Lifting belly how do you do.
Lifting belly is famous for recipes.
You mean Genevieve.
I mean I never ask for potatoes.
But you liked them then.
And now.
Now we know about water.
Lifting belly is a miracle.
And the Caesars.
The Caesars are docile.
Not more docile than is right.
No beautifully right.

And in relation to a cow.
And in relation to a cow.
Do believe me when I incline.
You mean obey.
I mean obey.
Obey me.
Husband obey your wife.
Lifting belly is so dear.
To me.
Lifting belly is smooth,
Tell lifting belly about matches.
Matches can be struck with the thumb.
Not by us.
No indeed.
What is it I say about letters.
Twenty six.
And counted.
And counted deliberately.
This is not as difficult as it seems.
Lifting belly is so strange
And quick.
Lifting belly in a minute.
Lifting belly in a minute now.
In a minute.
Not to-day.
No not to-day.
Can you swim.
Lifting belly can perform aquatics.
Lifting belly is astonishing.
Lifting belly for me.
Come together.
Lifting belly near.
I credit you with repetition.
Believe me I will not say it.
And retirement.
I celebrate something.
Do you.
Lifting belly extraordinarily in haste.

I am so sorry I said it.
Lifting belly is a credit. Do you care about poetry.
Lifting belly in spots.
Do you like ink.
Better than butter.
Better than anything.
Any letter is an alphabet.
When this you see you will kiss me.
Lifting belly is so generous.
Shoes.
Servant.
And Florence.
Then we can sing.
We do among.
I like among.
Lifting belly keeps.
Thank you in lifting belly.
Can you wonder that they don't make preserves.
We ask the question and they answer you give us help.
Lifting belly is so successful.
Is she indeed.
I wish you would not be disobliging.
In that way I am.
But in giving.
In giving you always win.
You mean in effect.
In mean in essence.
Thank you so much we are so much obliged.
This may be a case
Have no fear.
Then we can be indeed.
You are and you must.
Thank you so much.
In kindness you excel.
You have obliged me too.
I have done what is necessary.
Then can I say thank you may I say thank you very much.
Thank you again.

Because lifting belly is about baby.
Three eggs in lifting belly.
Éclair.
Think of it.
Think of that.
We think of that.
We produce music.
And in sleeping.
Noises.
Can that be she.
Lifting belly is so kind
Darling wifie is so good.
Little husband would.
Be as good.
If he could.
This was said.
Now we know how to differ.
From that.
Certainly.
Now we say.
Little hubbie is good.
Every Day.
She did want a photograph.
Lifting belly changed her mind.
Lifting belly changed her mind.
Do I look fat.
Do I look fat and thin.
Blue eyes and windows.
You mean Vera.
Lifting belly can guess.
Quickly.
Lifting belly is so pleased.
Lifting belly seeks pleasure.
And she finds it altogether.
Lifting belly is my love.
Can you say meritorious.
Yes camellia.
Why do you complain.

Postal cards.
And then.
The Louvre.
After that.
After that Francine.
You don't mean by that name.
What is Spain.
Listen lightly.
But you do.
Don't tell me what you call me.
But he is pleased.
But he is pleased.
That is the way it sounds.
In the morning.
By that bright light.
Will you exchange purses.
You know I like to please you.
Lifting belly is so kind.
Then sign.
I sign the bulletin.
Do the boys remember that nicely
To-morrow we go there.
And the photographs
The photographs will come.
When
You will see.
Will it please me.
Not suddenly
But soon
Very soon.
But you will hear first.
That will take some time.
Not very long.
What do you mean by long.
A few days.
How few days.
One or two days.
Thank you for saying so.

Thank you so much.
Lifting belly waits splendidly.
For essence.
For essence too.
Can you assure me.
I can and do.
Very well it will come
And I will be happy.
You are happy.
And I will be
You always will be.
Lifting belly sings nicely.
Not nervously.
No not nervously.
Nicely and forcefully.
Lifting belly is so sweet.
Can you say you say.
In this thought.
I do think lifting belly.
Little love lifting
Little love light.
Little love heavy.
Lifting belly tight.
Thank you.
Can you turn over.
Rapidly.
Lifting belly so meaningly.
Yes indeed the dog.
He watches.
The little boys.
They whistle on their legs,
Little boys have meadows,
Then they are well.
Very well.
Please be the man.
I am the man.
Lifting belly praises.
And she gives

Health.
And fragrance.
And words.
Lifting belly is in bed.
And the bed has been made comfortable.
Lifting belly knows this.
Spain and torn
Whistling.
Can she whistle to me.
Lifting belly in a flash.
You know the word.
Strawberries grown in Perpignan are not particularly good.
These are inferior kinds.
Kind are a kind.
Lifting belly is sugar.
Lifting belly to me.
In this way I can see.
What
Lifting belly dictate.
Daisy dear.
Lifting belly
Lifting belly carelessly.
I didn't.
I see why you are careful
Can you stick a stick. In what In the carpet.
Can you be careful of the corner.
Mrs. the Mrs. indeed yes.
Lifting belly is charming.
Often to-morrow
I'll try again.
This time I will sin
Not by a prophecy.
That is the truth.
Very well.
When will they change.
They have changed.
Then they are coming
Yes.

Soon.
On the way.
I like the smell of gloves.
Lifting belly has money.
Do you mean cuckoo.
A funny noise.
In the meantime there was lots of singing.
And then and then.
We have a new game
Can you fill it.
Alone.
And is it good
And useful
And has it a name
Lifting belly can change to filling petunia.
But not the same.
It is not the same.
It is the same.
Lifting belly.
So high.
And aiming.
Exactly.
And making
A cow
Come out.
Indeed I was not mistaken.
Come do not have a cow.
He has.
Well then.
Dear Daisy.
She is a dish.
A dish of good.
Perfect.
Pleasure.
In the way of dishes.
Willy.
And Milly.
In words.

So loud.
Lifting belly the dear.
Protection.
Protection
Protection
Speculation
Protection
Protection.
Can the furniture shine.
Ask me.
What is my answer.
Beautifully.
Is there a way of being careful
Of what.
Of the South.
By going to it.
We will go.
For them.
For them again.
And is there any likelihood of butter.
We do not need butter.
Lifting belly enormously and with song.
Can you sing about a cow.
Yes.
And about signs.
Yes.
And also about Aunt Pauline.
Yes.
Can you sing at your work.
Yes.
In the meantime listen to Miss Cheatham.
In the midst of writing.
In the midst of writing there is merriment.

SHORT POEMS, 1914–1925

OVAL (*1914*) *is an abstraction, full of rhymes, puns, and other wordplays.*

V.T.

OVAL

Offal slow.
Slowly.
With fern.
Deal term.
Reckless manner.
Naughty spoon.
Murder.
Meal wing meal wing meal wing melody member setter member setter nervous earnest pot where there is season, old a road pay sees with churning runner with a with a stout loud hemstitch.
Spit.
Tender toe binder.
Paper coal gas.
Glass glass ray of certain, sand worth worth of liberal setting setting mover around ridiculous cobbles wade absolute roses.
Shut the coat place so able to see shade with all the observation to be a card when. Let the place call where boats and what may what do you call what do you call coal gas.
Noon.
Noon.
Noon.
Supper.
Able to stand straight stiffly.
Clock a clock.
Water melon.
Tortoise shell.
Spade.
Over a deeper.
Over a deeper deeper.
Over a deeper.
Ray ray or peep.

Ray ray or ram.
Ray ray or ram.
Slippers.
Ray or ram ray.
Ray or ram ray.
Cold ups.
Ray or ram ray ray or ram ray.
Ray or ram ray either.
Ram or ram ray either.
Ram or ram ray either.
Chicken.
Tail.
Disappear.
Nose axe. Sounder.
Leave eye.
Pollute.
Next a grace next a grace white.
Ahead of a thinker ahead of a thinker. Ahead of a thinker.
Pealings.
It was a sum.
Summer.
Summer in mean.
Varnish.
A chance.
Patience.
Vehement.
Necessarily pile.
Pile necessarily.
Paper as weight.
Paper a wait.
Color rices.
Color rices not need it not need it not need it.
If the strange show states that the melons are to be.
Nevertheless.
If he change show states that the wet stress. The wet stress.
Noisily.
Collapse.
Veins.

Bought.
Capable of hair.
Precious center lay lips.
Old shavings.
Put a cue.
Make boxes.
Show leather.
Hide heel bare gasp.
Shoulder.
Oval.
Oval then.
Not a knife night.
Nut papers.
Crackers.
Bent on in.
Birds birds birds.
Place of peas.
Why do you take it.
Peas stay still.
What is an expletive.
Cow come out with a shout.
What is an expletive.
Colon. Opera glasses.
Opera glasses, thunder and simmer.
Thunder. Register.
Register pints, leaves open.
Open. Oh why should the joint sleeve of all the rash velvet
rash velvet and spacious and near sleeves and all. Is it a chance to
believe. Call the puss.
It is a name a name went. Stir.
Apples.
Apples apples apples.
Apples.
Apple.
Apple going apple.
Apple against.
Apple Apple Apple.
Wednesday.

Apple Wednesday.
Door a dog.
Door or.
Door or dog.
Door Door.
Door Door.
Flying steep steps.
Flying steps.
Saturday.
This one is longer.
This one is longer and longer.
This one is higher.
This one is longer this one is longer this one is longer.
Longer and higher.
Higher.
This one is longer longer and a different size.
This one is exactly.
Exactly longer.
This one is a rug.
A rug has a bottom.
A bottom is below.
Below.
Below below blue.
Blue is name name of red.
Blue is name of red blue is blue name blue is. Name.
Rug.
Apt to be blown.
Apt to be.
Apt to be remain.
Thirty for in a day.
Needless to say spend or tall.
Mary Bell, Mary Bell, Mary Bell, Mary Bell.
Mary Bell, bell, belly.
The redivisible filling.
Necessary to-day birthday.
Respect oil will.
Respect elastic respect elastic tuck.
Respect selection.

Study staining.
Believe checks bother noses.
Noises.
What is a prints fatigue or.
What is a lender might.
What is a wheeling breakfast.
What is a coupon.
What is a soiled butter.
What is melody.
What is chopping.
What is circle circle.
What is a service.
What is pins.
Around top and bottom.
Little least nice.
Honey meet and a velvet tie and nearly old age between,
rest or rester or restless.
Blue eye.
Marble. Marble green.
Green marble.
Lessons in behavior.
Matches.
Claims of paler clouds.
I want a long one.
If you can tell a seller.
Salt cellar.
Come.
Come.
Come Come.
Sever yet.
Serve or even.
Mat or ease.
Seven.
Mat or ease.
Seven.
You You.
Never a shape sweet.
Never a nose.

Never a nose.

Maintaining.

Cost cost cost cost cost.

Surprise.

Surprises.

Surprises regulate accentuation.

Administration show more chirps.

Chirps are bitten.

Oh key tea hall oh key tea hall oh key tea hall excellent tube hurt it since. Hyacinth.

Plants.

Plants coop.

Solemn.

Solemn ten ten.

Fount tin.

Take a soup to a mounting leave all the beets for the regular supper, show persian show persian or a shrine show it plainly so that there is protesting.

What is a box been.

A box is where in there has surely longer surely longer surely longer so to see so to see so to see so to see.

Not a nice.

Not a.

Not a nice.

Not a.

Not a period not a period to.

Not a period.

Not a period proclaim.

Enjoyable singling extreme.

Enjoyable procelain.

Enjoyable sailing extreme.

Enjoyable feathering.

Feathering.

A large size.

Paper sun burns.

Burns.

Paper burns.

Catch a can.

Can.
Too neat too sweet.
A loaded light and a berry in sight.
Two teeth.
Was in station.
This is a joy.
Supple split.
At a slant.
Slant or.
At a slant or.
At a slant or.
Noises.
Beaded lay tea.
At a slant or.
Beaded lay tea.
Climb.
Climb.
Lucy or see.
Monday Monday.
Capable by.
Extra section, section of what.
Section of reasonable peals peals of it peals of it and, it and
extra sensible ejections. Ejections mean of course.
We have not decided.
Neck.
Neck is a standard.
Standard bearer.
Stand and bearer stems.
Two years.
Two years without.
Without why.
Without when.
Nevertheless.
Spend or less.
Nevertheless.
He said he said.
Charis.
Boiledness.

Boiledness with steam.
Steam
Steam.
Steam steam.
He said.
To come.
Taking.
He said to come.
Talking.
He said to come.
It is a way to go.
It is a way to go.
It is a way to go.
It is a way to go.
Bestowing.
Bestowing.
Hems.
Hem stitched.
Sheet.
Sheets.
Hem stitched.
Towels.
Hem stitches.
Soils.
Soil towels.
Hem stitched.
Hem stitched.
Towels.
Churches.
Chairs.
Heaps.
High.
Heard.
Hand.
Elderly swim.
Climb ate.
Eight.
Color.

Copper.
Copper gate.
Steel.
Steel bite.
Shape.
Shape.
He told her.
He told or.
What is sweeping.
Swept.
Or swept.
Or swept or or swept.
Not a pole sad.
Not a sad pole.
Not a pole sad.
Shape.
Shape err.
Shape fur.
Fur boat.
Fur.
Shape.
Let us.
Let us elevate.
Let us ever ear resist.
Ever ear.
Ear.
Ear.
Not a cellar.
The shape.
The shape that catch.
Scratch.
Noticeable.
Noticeable eye.
Noticeable eye oh.
Noticeable eye oh
Noticeable eye.
O.
Noticeable O eye.

Eye.
Eye.
Eye.
Nape.
Nape.
Pillar.
Pillar or.
Not such a.
Not such a such a.
Such.
Even.
Ed.
Eddy.
Shield.
Shield why.
When.
Worry.
Worry.
To begin a seven even
Seven.
After a soon to win.
After to a soon to win.
To win.
Way.
To win a win.
To win a win.
Never ceasing sofa sea.
Why.
Wax or cool coaling.
Weed sell sell sell.
Changer.
Jet.
Jet.
Why water.
Why water.
Actually.
Be case.
Hand.

Hand hand hand hand.
Hand hit.
Hand hitter.
Hand hitter hand hitter.
Hand.
Hand hit.
Lay lamentable.
Pea simple.
An attachment.
And attachment.
Shall a.
Shall a of a son.
Shall of a son and.
Shall of a son and brother.
I agree I agree. I agree baby.
A sudden.
A sudden.
A sudden.
A sudden.
A sudden.
Exactly.
Exactly sucker.
Exactly sucker.
And a say religion.
And a say more.
Knee delays.
And a estimable.
Needles.
Needles.
Package.
No whatever.
Ever so much.
Thank you.
Suddenness.
Excellent.
Utensils.
Where with all.
Next to lime.

Crave hen.
Crave hen.
Neither to spoke.
Neither to spoke
Car lock.
Car lock.
Car lock car lock cut or cut lock lock.
Car lock.
Car lock.
End in to a seam.
Seam it.
Able it feather.
Feather.
Car lock car lock able it feather.
Able to it feather.
Car lock car lock end so or seem.
Car lock car lock end to it seam.
Car lock car lock able it seem.
Car lock car lock able to it seem.
Car lock car lock able to it feather able to it feather.
Able to it feather.
Able to it feather.
Rose.
Rose.
Rose up.
Rose.
Rose.
Rose up.
Rose.
Rose up.
Able in stand.
Able ink stand.
Rose.
Rose.
Able in ink stand.
Rose up.
Ray chest.
Ray curtain.

Ray curtain record read loss.
Ray chest.
Ray chest.
Record record less.
Peas in nut.
Peal Peal pot.
Peal not so.
Not remarkably sew.
Not remarkably.
Not remarkably so.
Shutter.
Not such a regular sudden shirring shirring with bends bends
top top or top or top that that when there is no separate sepa-
rated separated cabling no separated cable cats cats shaken.
Shaken kinds.
A fly.
Thunder.
Poles.
Ink piles.
Neither season.
Shout up.
Not so to speal needed.
Yes yes.
Yes yes.
Boil.
Technical.
Technical with a tremble.
A tremble.
Another wipes.
Another wipes.
What is pink.
When is tea.
Where is a lot or.
Why is not for.
Reckless.
Real thick less.
Told.
Old soap.

Where belly.
Belly the sail.
Best to see.
Sitting.
Sitting let us secrete sitting.
See sitting, see sitting sitting.
A chime in lady.
A chime in lady.
Not an unfold.
A chair.
What is a chair.
James.
Oil sleeping.
Oil sleeping sleeping.
If you indirect a remarkable no no no.
If you indirect a remarkable.
Not a proof.
Not a proof.
It is no use.
Urgent in urgent in.
Not a pine. Not a pine.
David.
David is a blouse.
It was spilling.
Show air sleep.
Hire head.
Hire head. Hire head.
Twelve it spoon like an elderly person.
Neglect.
Velvet spoon.
Spur ringer.
Velvet spoon.
Spur in ringer.
Real old cake or.
Real old cake for weather.
Real old cake forty.
Real old forty weather.
Old cake for.

Four twenty for.
Lend us letter us.
Cooking.
Cooking.
Sole in a reason sobbing.
His see it.
Color aloud.
It was an example swing.
Color cloud.
Go white go white.
Neat shelter chose.
Chose what.
What.
Way suit way suit why call a class why call a class. Way suit way suit why call a class why call a class, way suit way suit way suit a gold.
Color.
Seasons. Seasons sop or sop or.
Loud extra.
Allowed extra.
Nibbles nibbles nibbles elephant.
Elephant.
What is hide.
Hide in capable.
Chosen separate.
Separate.
Separate.
Round cooler.
Veins.
Measuring.
Measuring. Measuring from.
Measuring from little yellows.
Measuring from little possible sweeter. Measuring. Single.
Violences.
Call it.
Call it.
Shades of. Sample.
Not or difference.

Left wheel. Left or. Origin.
Or joints.
He is come back.
Thirty.
Shows.
In a insist.
Bender.
Not nickles.
A milk or.
Little lays.
Not let.
Not let so.
Not piles.
Not piles so.
Collar.
Collar what.
Sauces.
Sauces how.
Fire.
Up it is make shall.
A bill what a bill loss a blaze where a shut up.
Shut up. Shut up.
Nice sense.
Nice sense sense sense.
Not sell dress not sell dress dish not sell dress copious bean.
Esther.
So silence so shall.
So shall it second see.
So shall it.
Not about.
A beat.
What is a pump.
A soiled cover.
Really soiled.
Really soiled.
It does matter.
It does matter.
Not a set.

Not a set of dailies.
Not a set more.
More of a collected.
Collected person.
Sand.
Paper.
Sand paper.
In a lean.
Not noisy.
Feel rail.
Rest.
Roll.
Right.
To shown.
To shown glass.
Arouses.
Arouse arouse.
Pointed.
Not a stopper.
Not a stopper stopper.
While out.
Supper.
Supper.
Presses.
Velvet a spoon.
Not so.
Careless.
Not so careless.
Careless.
Erect.
Erect erect.
It was a rendering.
It was a rendering.
Knee sew.
An in mine.
Commending.
Not a special.
Sew or up.

This is a wise this is a wise this is a wise to seam.
Soleing.
Shut up.
Train.
Shut in.
Train.
Shut in.
Around a stool.
We never went yesterday.
Cooking is very different to what to what.
Collection.
Paragraph.
Round numbers.
Pet pet.
Lizzie.
He said he could he said he could.
Sleepy.
Mabel.
Henry.
Heard.
Heard.
It was a sleep.
Asleep.
Slants.
Slants slants.
Plough strange.
Curly goats.
Centre.
Awful.
Awful.
Vein.
Weigh vein.
Vein.
Sight.
Since.
A blame to a.
A blame to a blame to a.
A blame to a blame, to a.

A blame to a blame.
A blame to a blame.
Cooking.
Not a house.
Very well.
What I have done with those.
Not now.
Curving in curving in curving state.
Curving in curving in curving.
Curving eight.
Curving in curving in curving.
In curving.
Led bones.
Led bones but tons.
Led bones buttons.
Not necessary.
Not nestle.
Not a cream mean.
Not a cream.
Creature.
What is or.
Or is a.
Shook it.
Head.
That is a glance in plaster.
Plaster or.
Not a circumference.
Not a circumference. in.
Bellying. Bellying bellying in close. Bellying in close
A four in sound and a recollect call recollect call soup.
To be brought up away from that to be brought up in supper.
To be brought up away. Away from it. Away. Away from it.
To be brought up. Soup.
Sachet.
It was chopping.
Come a cold.
Hearing.
Hearing.

Swept.

Swept.

A whole wall.

A whole wall wet.

Just sign.

Just sign there.

Just sign outside and more moreover and extra study an extra study to show what what means a lot a lot of calling.

Calling to. Calling.

Calling enough anyway.

A chance.

A chance why.

Why.

Why not.

Why not for.

Why not for.

Not avoid.

Not avoid.

Avoid a.

Between

This is so.

This is so to mutter.

This is so.

This is not so.

This is not so.

This is not so.

This.

This.

This be tea.

This be.

A chance to buy.

Journey.

Journey to not.

Not very.

Since.

Since only

Since only by.

Example for.

Join.
Join coral cedars.
Not this.
That was a mistake.
That was a mistake.
Vein.
Vein why.
So number.
Least
Least o.
Or white.
Or white.
Or white.
Oil.
Oily.
Not oily.
Not beside.
More.
More.
Able to spin.
Able to spin.
Spin.
Nodding.
Nodding.
Will you pour.
Out.
Outside.
More outside.
More.
Outside.
More outside. More outside.
Careless pushing.
Pushing is grass.
Pushing is not in.
Pushing.
That was a sea lion.
A really pillow.
A really pillow.

Treasure.
Not an exchange.
Hardly more.
That.
Please light.
Please light almost again.
Not.
Not.
A shed. A shed.
Standard cups.
Standard cups with.
Cups.
With.
With.
With
The.
The.
It was a change from nearly missing to almost missing almost and nearly.
Nearly.
It was a change from nearly missing.
It was a change from nearly missing the half the half of that. It was a change from nearly missing half the half of the rest. It was a change from nearly missing beside it was the same almost the same. It was a change from missing it was a change from missing the half. It was the same it was a change from nearly missing missing. Neglected posts. Neglected. Neglected so. Some.
Come again.
Call water.
Where do you call.
Reason, reason for a crate.
Are to be are to be are to be.
Chamber chamber why.
When.
When in.
Iron.
Oat.
Labor.

And.
Opera.
Opera coat.
Coat.
If a.
Stamp.
So lets.
Wishing a stick.
Nice knees.
Wishing a stick.
Nice.
Colored goat.
Piles.
Piles.
Piles.
What a red.
What in or red.
What in or late mine.
Suppose a chair has a learning really learning, posts, near seat,
bold jacinth and meadows, horrors, little levers, and most most
shine.
A way at.
A way at a table a building and countenance.
Countenance.
Countenance.
Do not let me listen to you again.
Why is reading shall you.
It was a million.
A million or three.
Twenty.
Twenty two.
A little page.
Page Folder.
Folder elbow.
Rather shot.
Rather shoe shut.
Rather roast.
Roast why.

If spring.
If spring.
And winter see.
And seldom bless.
And towels.
It was not an s.
A chance to puzzle peas.
Peas four.
What is let.
Be there.
Be there.
Be there.
A change.
Be there.
Wideness.
Not a rain in water.
Closet.
Closet.
Pie.
And does it.
Does it about
Able to pay cutlets.
Whistle.
Mary had.
She had.
Angles baby.
Oh miss.
Needless to say.
It was expression.
This is not grass.
And happening.
Forward.
To believe.
To relieve.
To pillow case.
A change purple.
Lantern.
Anxious to read.

Anxious to prevaricate.
Real outer old stones.
Not with care shell.
Care shell.
What is it.
What they bring in.
What they bring in.
Do you see a class.
Do you bewilder joy.
It is a pleasant share.
Has the natural and really best really more and the playing
every one day every day practically not nearly so. What they
bring able to not nearly.
This is the change that occurred.
In a little while there was more.
Picture.
What is a picture.
What is a culmination.
What is a real wearing sober shellack.
And not nearly more cheese.
Not nearly more cheese.
Any plan.
Most nestle.
Happy.
Very.
It is a real shoulder.
It is.
More.
More.
Come.
In.
Just a position.
London bridges.
Able.
Since.
Not since.
Net us.
Net us spike.

Class call.
Class call spine.
Lead pallid lead pallid lean.
Clause.
Clause what.
Butter cups.
Wife or.
Nose upper.
Suppose this is a joint.
Suppose celebrations are lucky.
Suppose language.
Suppose sore.
Soar.
Real sore.
Supper oppose.
Nails.
Nails fish.
And fish.
A land of what over.
Pleasure.
Is.
Like.
Call.
Baby.
See.
Shell.
Plain.
Tie for.
Resolute.
Person.
Shares.
Shares shone.
Shares shone.
Why well.
I am excited.
Ceiling.
Ceiling.
Wait. Wait.

Color weight.
Weight.
Weight.
Never see.
Ceiling.
Plan.
Next to a note a corner.
Please a corner.
Please a corner.
Sumptuousness.
What is dinner.
Dinner and dinner and meddle.
Kernel, kernel a dot.
It was explained that nearly all the time and meaning little ways with sent sent in and a likely a mender mender into what, shame on in.
Mender what.
One after in other.
These were the things leave or leave or standard dish. Stand or dish. Stain dear or dish.
What is a chance too spring.
Charming edge or says.
Reason, reason close reason janitor reason to be Sunday, reason to be alright, reason reason where, reason to be.
Nancy.
Will he.
Public spirit.
Public spirit.
Resell well.
That is a blow.
This is a pine sore. Let me be.
Be when.
Be when.
Public shall she. Public shall she. Shore she spread.
Leave us.
Then a narrow neck.
Then what a stolen. Then then.
The upper.

Enticing.

Enticing meal track.

Enticing.

Recent.

Wrestle.

Wrestle but.

Lay oh lay oh lay oh lay oh leap leap oar.

Weigh edge.

Way edge.

It is much better, better, to, not to able to stay and nearly poorly.

Plan.

Plan

Hill shock.

It was a last time and to be related and sealing not an ever way shall it not this time. All again.

This.

Now.

Now to be.

We went into the early and saw that it was never dinner. This made a stretch and a stretching a stretching showed the same nearly the if it was and was and all of it but the all the change and more shake.

More shake two pause.

It did sent center.

Go on.

In.

In ear lily.

Shames so.

Another chair.

When these.

When these.

Is your father living yet.

Not yet.

Wipe.

Wipe it.

Wipe with it.

With it.

Wipe.
Wipe lay it.
Wipe loan lying.
Wipe laying.
Wipe.
Wipe with.
Wipe with stretches.
Stretches where.
Very shall he.
This is a sunny.
This is a ceremony.
This is a selection.
This is relay a coin.
A coin leave.
No. No.
Not a little sixty.
Not a shelling.
Shelling what.
Vegetables.
This made a change.
All the salt.
That was nice.
Bread and butter.
Able to fancy.
Nelly.

MEAL ONE (*1914*) *is similarly hermetic.*

V.T.

MEAL ONE

Meal one airs.
Pour leash.
Meal one.
Pour leash.

Pour leash.

Least o crater.

least o crater spores.
Least crater spores styles.
Least spores styles store is.
Least spores styles stores miss.
Least spores styles miss core brake. Least spores miss core brake stale so did usher.

PART II

Onion pear layer.
Not in oxes not in oxes glass.

Par lower but.

PART II

By we linen.
Coil and I run.
By the time span well.
Old in geranium hop elevate pierce fixtures.
No it is in joy rest vestibule.

PART III

Please power pot in the pour rim.

PART III

It was no, eat was nor.
Eight was knot for.
Heat hate was not five forty four.

Kind climb back bore box.

It was a sugar four state.
A lime lump, a lime lump weather.

PART III IV

Live louise loo.

PART IV

Neat space pin summer mourn.
Neat space pin some mere same.
Neat space pin simmer more sum.

PART IV

It was a straw such.

It was a straw such to boom.
It was a straw stretch to boom.
It was a strum straw stretch to street boom.
It was a train straw stretch to strew boom.

PART V

Excellent singing excellent singing in a hinder pay tight. Excellent singing excellent singing.

PART V

No No No No No No.
No no no, no no no.

PART VII

Was it a stem, was it a steam was it a stem to taste.

PART VIII

Was it a stem was it a stem was it a stem to taste.

PART IX

Neglect so is.
Neglect, so is a china.
Neglect so is.

PART X

It was a wade.
It was a wade too sue.
It was a wade to sue bay bays.
It was.
A wade.

PART X

Pea dear cut less.

PART X

Not a count in near sun net sense.

PART XII

Pea let sit curly lip.

PART XI

A go lasted to a pine net a pine net feel.

PART XIII

On account of noise.

PART XIV

The middle hear.

PART I

Pick her let.
Peculiar peculiar hyphen.
Not a sound in, not a low pin.

PART I

Pledging a real sodad sue seen.
Not a single pea leaf.
This is no change.
Not butts.

PART ONE

Place a sir print in box, boxing.
No piercers coal show it out stand parts of stretch, strachey.

PART II

Poise in poise in.

PART III

Next a bet.
Next set.
Next a bet.

PART IV

Not a balcony, not a be leader. Not a bell not a bell candy not
a bell candy neigh. Not a bell candy shout, not a bell candy sheet
fountain.

PART IV

Extra a cream.

PART V

Extra a cream same tear lay.

PART V

Extra a cream, Extra a cream.
So up so up so up.

PART VI

Extra a cream.

PART VII

Put in put in close.
Curl a curl a hat.
Net, here, held hair.

PART I

Lily least lily least lily make a stuff.

PART I

Supper in parted rest match.
What is a match in pleases.
Pleases are so a glass, so necessary to re-sign, to re-sign colds.
It is so to seek. Not satchel not satchel first. No glaze.

PART I

Wet a wait, wet a weight.

PART I

Extreme recross. Extreme recross nose lets. Extreme recross
nose lets eyes lets. Extreme recross nose lets.

PART I

A prayed car.

PART I

Paces are with curls not spilled. It is a plain.

PART I

Net grass.

PART I

In is an indent in.
It is a silver snatch.
It is a burn sneeze.
It is a clause ear lay.

PART II

Let us lie nice.
Let us a window.

PART III

Not a see knee.
Not a see knee no.
Not a see knee.

PART IV

Lets bake irregular.
Lets bake irregularly.

PART V

Pewter for, pewter for no.

PART VI

Lay glass lay glass.

PART VII

Season season, sack or last, sack, last.

PART VIII

Necklace necklace to necklace to waist, necklace too necklace two necklace two necklace two.

PART IX

Woe under woe under.

PART X

Soon seen, soon seen soon in seen.

PART XI

Cold in ups, cold in ups, cold in cold in ups.

PART XII

Nice is a grass nice is a grass all the gas is greening.

PART I

Pile in so in, pile in so in, pile in, so, in.

PART II

Neglect. Neglect cause. Neglect.

PART III

East and rain east and rain chin east and rain chin win. East and rain chin win suck. East and rain chin win soak suck.

PART IV

A neglected english woman.
A neglected in chest woman.

PART V

It is a tall it is a tall it is a tall to matter.

PART VI

Heavy next heavy next to throat, heavy next to throat dish.

PART VII

Loud crane loud crane makes a creek. Loud crane makes loud creek. Loud crane makes loud crane. Loud crane makes loud crane makes, loud crane loud makes loud crane.

PART VIII

Next next next to make.

PART IX

Little lily little lily lily.

PART X

Next in the settle sun to poke and night where night where in a sun, in a sun and next to bay seen sun and never exchange readily.

PART XI

Why o x why o x.

PART XII

Nose where, nose where stow sakes, nose where stow sakes.

PART XIII

Roe beast in roe and a selected thunder exact leaf tree.

PART XIV

Why poor cress.

PART XV

Read writes.
Pot or fine.
Please sacks.

PART I

Color or tour hair.
Color or four hair.
Four head.

PART I

Pin tea pin tea pin pin pin oh oh oh eye sacks.

PART II

Bird nickels.

PART III

Excellent and stays, excellent, note a grass, note a grass.

PART IV

Nervous in sue sees, nervous in sues sees. It was a chinaman,
it a was a china mean on.

PART I AND II

Excellent sizes of old pieces I remonstrate.

PART II

Stone curls.
Neglected instance.
Not a docks hundred.

PART III AND IV

I demur, I demur to a stroke and hand in hand.
I elaborate, I elaborate and pale coil pale coil of tender tunes.

PART V

We the search we the search cotton, we the hold hold hold.
We the time tell bill, we the so plain record to the marble fire
place which is not where, which is a behave tone.

PART VI

Part lessen part lessen no more. Part lessen no more in a pan.
Part lessen no more.

PART VII

So plenty in white sneezes and columns. No cool ore off.

AT, EMP LACE, FOUR, DATES, FINISHED ONE, *and* TILLIE, *all from 1914, express the same preoccupation with verbal concealment.* CRETE, *written in the spring of 1914 in England, begins with a mention of the classical scholar Jane Harrison, here referred to as Miss Clapp. It is not a portrait, however. It is a landscape or interior scene with people in it.*

V.T.

AT

> I think so.
> I think so.
> I see that.
> The rest is right.
> The leaves are mean.
> The practical case is Chinese.
> All the shoulders are there.
> Waiting houses all wind houses all wind houses besides,
> Not leaning.
> Never sold in foreseen.
> Not leaning.
> Not particularly blaming.
> Not in seen.
> Not leaning.
> Not leaning.
> Not leaning four.
> Please do please do say sore.
> That's the rest.
> I don't care to make a recent entrance I don't care to sign.
> That's it. That's the rest.
> I shall be seeming.
> I shall be seaming.
> I shall be seeming.
> I shall spool.
> Not it. That's the rest.
> I love eating.
> Spread threading.
> Go on in.

I leave ate eight eight.
Height.
And in an exceptional rejoining.
Top.
Please come across.
Please.
To please.
To please sleeping.
Please come across.
You remember what you can.
Would you mind putting the pink up to my knees.
It's touching the butcher.
For touching for touching touching a fork.
We have decided that we will get a teacher.
Touching a fork.
Please Isabel please.
Yes it would.
I can shelter fifty seven and make eight say that and celebrate forty more and believe nothing.
Calling counts.
I can finally get winter nellies and San Francisco.
Oh yes but I do.
But it is an expression if you do you do.
Thanks for an indelible pencil.
I don't mention it.
Sighing grinding.
I was just quieting myself.
I was surprised to prepare to ask and to be altered and to be reasoned with to be reasoned with.
Mentioning a position.
I don't care to take all of it.
Only if they're aired.
Very young.
I should say.
Vehicles.
I believe in the raining of undulating beams borrowed by the way from all of us.
I need not stretch.

Not in a night for that night.

Let us change not glasses let us change pages. Purses are receptacles for gold.

I do hear I do hear a name.

What is the matter with all paper.

There were noises in in solos.

What and whatever.

I mean to be rich.

Why should I seam it because it is necessary.

Oh my silver.

I believe in hurrying.

They are worrying her.

It does make it rather strange.

Not being used to eating it with a knife and fork it tastes like a pineapple.

I don't want to listen to well yes.

A spending sending.

No I don't mean that.

Thanks so much.

EMP LACE

Emp lace.
Miserable.

Next n time

Seat.

What is a say mow grass.

Night a steam pen.
Night a steam pen penny.
Night a steam pen penny pennier.
Night a steam pen pennier penny.

This is puss.
Polar share.
Pole pair.
Polar.

Knee nick.
Nickle.
Knee nickle Knee nick.
Knee nickle Knee nickle.

Picture and steam boat extra sail boat.
Not a no not a long suit pale mail.

Why is a sole a dumpling.
A sole is a dumpling because there is swimming.

Little lights of kindness news in all the branch where all is the weeding when the perfect set of tracing is poodle. Poodle when.

Pole in ore. Pole in ore up till. Pole in ore up till soon lay. Soon lay spook. Spook tie. Spook tie told top.

Oh my way sit.
Oh my way sit how glass.
Oh my way sit any an now.
Oh my way sit any earn now.
Oh my way sit any now.
Oh my way sit any an now.

Net and some silk.
Suppose it was in glass. Suppose an investigation and a relay a relay of large size. Suppose it is a burst, suppose it is egg glass. Not in sent.

Not a sill in bellows.
Noise is claim climb.

Are perches in cream.
Not or nest or.

Little thunder brick ates.
Let or mine shine.

There is no use in a pilaster there is no use in a peel laster, there is no use in a pilaster.

Color it cup, color it cup why is why is hair is.

Climbing in tights climbing in tights climbing bits of button.
Tiny nuts tiny nuts make week, tiny nuts make week straw.
Legs look like less. Leg look like less.

Tiny week tiny week hum moan day, tiny week hung moon,
day, tiny week hung moon day secure.

Neck lace in laces, laces and keeps back, necklaces and keeps
back.

Not a peal not a peal sounder, not a peal sounder eggs use.
Eggs use twos, eggs use twos two specks. Eggs use two specks.
Two specks sounder. Two specks sound in admit safe. Two
specks are or in is it, are or is in it in, is it in or is it, is it in or, or is
it in.

Next a place next a place hawk next a place hawk cough.

Angel of weeding cake, angel of weeding cake, angel of
weeding cake ate, on a step by a stem, all a pack sew a glass necessary necessary by wear eight.

Tender piece of a section of is to there. Most so.

Lack of roaring mutton. Sold pigs sold pigs wretch wretch
eating wretch.

Knock about gate knock about gate must it must it must it.

In the agreeable, in the agree silk great or in the action not a
shape or paid a sacrament to be a real coal leaf or pass. A curtain,
next sugar rest, rent sugar rent not a smell not a smell salt.
It was funny it was peculiarly reacted by a necessary white
knit way boat, way boat when call the looks for it. What in lace,
what in lace to, bowl of nor or so let or.
Nest let nest let be. Accent and be have accent and be have no
no sigh wake no sigh wake peace or.
It does get funnier it does get funnier, it is does funnier, it
does is funnier, it does is dunnier. I have no inclination to be
scolded.
Come to pearl ton leave stretch, most or climb step, climb step
tight.
Pail of clover. She was a spectacle to win to win a dressing

table. She was a spectacle to win a dressing table. The nice nine, the nice nine pours.

Earn east in gay, earn east in gayly, earn in east in gayly good, earn in gayly.

When should the ill boat show excellent pail, when should it cause a fly beam.

Nest to extraordinary and curtain and little special, real trimming, not a shade, not a horizontal piece of coat, not nearly finish.

Please sudden please sudden dough, please sudden dough nuts, please so rendered so rendered so rendered.

Later exchange no pet is stolen oh the lovely cool satisfactory on when on when.

Plunder in collars plenty in collars plenty in plenty in collars. It does change nuts. It does reduce burns. It is sell out in.

Earnest. Earnest is a chamber.
Earnest. Earnest.

Representative essence. Essence.

Following feet, following feet for, following feet furnish.

A longer curious a longer cup and stand.

Pledges pledges nearly.

Please fasten white please fasten white, please fasten white white please fasten white.

White eye-glasses, white eye glasses and a ribbon a real ribbon a glow a glow a gone gather a little seed spell and a natural gas. Piles of strange piles of strange in a special reason. If it is warm it is an hour glass, if it is cold it is a saddler glass if it is rain if it is rain, if it is rain it is a celebrated glass, if it is rain if it is rain if it is rain it is a safe in last old solid, last old solid grain last old solid grain of trained lips.

Clouds of willing seen in the bird day.

Able to exact bicycles.

A personal survey of frost.

In general.

Perhaps he has perhaps he has.

A wood below a wood below jerk, a wood below a wood below aid or excellent.

It was a transitive a transitive leave height.

Allowing allowing allowing allowing.

Put a pull put a pull all leather.

This time not so well on limb.

On none part let par on eat touch par.
Going to stop singing stop it stop it stop it stop singing.
Perfect pleasant place wire lily.
Put see put see put see put see.
Leave a glass mass leave a glass mass curling is a pressed sense.
Words cousin by words and cousin by, words and cousin and by words and cousin and by words and cousin by.
Left grapes or shade of real colds or pieces steak or little way shoulder steps.
It comes to the present interdicted and really poised really poison really pointed necessity to be collided agreeable and a commoner a comprehensive rendered so present and nearly persuadable nearly power.
It is a credit to be it is a credit to be.
Nearer a glance to thee.
A little reasonable parcel a little reasonable parcel.
Shatter a pan cold more a ground lease with mite and less line and check go lights with peaked peaked pats widow grown not a spell soup not a spell soap actually actually in in.
Morning gate. Pepper calls. No use.
Read oceans right burn rubber hose nerves color in a ten agreeable and a lest woes.
Knocks eggs know better. Knocks eggs nor better. Knocks eggs nor eggs nor eggs nor better.
Lay colonel lay colonel.
Paper chews.
Hinting and boldness, hinting and boldness, way waiting, way waiting.

Mention leader.

Little stands make meadows and beneath all and beneath more and beneath pants.

Have it at hand, have it at hand have a pear to smear why it.

Able stamp planter able stamp curtain, able stamp bowl dear slow.

Pearls, pearls pages, extra summer one, minor chin laugh, pearls pearls pages, extra some more one, leave minor changes, let powder let powder let powder.

Extraordinary purses, extraordinary purses.

A pleas rather fine a pleas rather fine.

It was a pew it was a pew it was a pew in places.

Widen pour lets.

Papers of cranberries.

Laps in covers.

Age in beefsteaks age in pear shapes age in round and puzzle.

Witness a pair of glasses. Extra win eager extra win eager.

Piles piles of splinters piles piles of splinters.

English or please english or please or please or please or please or please.

Weighed in skirt weighed in weighed in skirt.

Anguish anguish anguish.

Puzzle a tower.

Real button.

Real butter or nuts.

Real button nuts.

A measure of muss, a measure of a muss meant.

Little eyes of peal ax resting by the clothes makes a pillow show a grain and makes a left hand restless back wards.

After noon. Extra toweling.

Persons.

Persons nearly bower.

Plain tags to a dozen. Yellow sponges to a piece.

If it was necessary if it was ameliorating, if it was ameliorating.

Loud center wheel loud center wheel.

Paper satchels.

Little sequestered lot shown countenances.

Angles agreed.

When stares.
When stares.
When stares.
Flute flute how are you.
Way of web stairs way of web stairs.
Why or lean.
Door hum door hum sew.
This is a change.
Wheel or wheats.
Lettuce excuse.
Heap heap heap.
Or a plain.
Personal bestow personal bestow buck eat wheat. Personal bestow buckwheat eat personal bestow buck eat wheat.
An irregular an irregular and irregular an irregular.
Please lean wheat.
Away in pay real suspect away in pay real suspect can, in away away in pay real suspect can argue ties, away in pay suspect ties away in argue suspect ties ties.
Mounting slate.
Extra fort.
Whine cold straps, whine cold straps angle trace.
Not in corner pigeon, not a regular rice not a chin reading not worry goal.
These are oiler or glee.
Wade in cake.
Come in.
One one.
Come Come Come Come.
Two queen.
Come into so.
Of two or two.
It was necessary it was necessary to purchase twine it was necessary string it was necessary so on it was necessary reasonable sweet, it was no pole it it was an example.
Let it agree.
Lovely eye lamb.
Red in red in parlor notes red in red in parlor notes.

Red in eye lamb, red in red in parlor notes.

Red in eye lamb red in parlor notes red in eye lamb red in parlor notes precious precious precious precious.

Red in parlor notes precious precious precious.

Red in parlor notes red in parlor notes red in precious precious.

Lovely eye lamb red in red in precious

Lovely eye lamb red in parlor notes.

Precious Precious Precious.

Smiles and miles.

Colored board.

A collection a collection poor at a collection poor at pencils, a collection poor at pencils patients, a collection poor at pencils patients.

Please over debt please over thumb.

Lender tender.

It was putting.

Scissors or cheese scissors or chase scissors or james.

Lamp lighting.

Pen a sable.

Peacocks. coil balloons.

Tea knows.

Lick in plains.

Cannery. Cannery catastrophy.

Length.

Weed spare those.

Able able to take sugar.

Less in bright.

Not a louis in filip.

Hug or. Hug or hug or.

Lump in a wheel lump in a whole lump in cousin sand.

Narrow bend.

Twisted twisted lake.

Vestibule paul.

Near jenny.

A whole season a rode a rode a rode.

A whole season a road.

Pleasant stem.

Next to shake.

We say.
Examples and earn say burn.
Acres again acres again.
Spot or less.
Need berries hot.
Wave who mean.
Leave be leave be.
It was a positive corner.
A white extra syllable.
Neither pressure.
Can you see sit.
Cinder judge land hear.
Susan spoke what.
Susan spoke sweetly.
Read birds.
Susan spoke what.
Weighed.
Leg light.
Ancient washing tone.
Red tea let.
The power of his violin line. He transformed it into hair.
Loads loads and loads loads.
Paper cut in water water chair.
Neat niece or egg.
West in stoves.
Natural lace furniture.
Old cheap gray. Mustard.
Why should pepper mutter.
All all all all.
Ready sign tax ready sign tax.
Naturally cunning. Weather scope.
Ee's last.
Ready little a.
Color two pieces.
Wait a garment.
Not a flake hater.
Needs pearls tiles.
Oh pay oh pray open.

Oh pray oh pay open.
Not a regular bay day.
Weeding butter.
A left over into a left into or a left or into a left into over.
Nuts in nights nuts or nights.
A clamor.
Pay special stains.
Coil or puss.
Whiter ship.
Eight o'clock.
Rubbish.
Eight o'clock pussish.
Eight o'clock radish.
Eight o'clock and a lump.
Eight o'clock more.
Sew soon.
Eight o'clock equal.
Pun in baby.
A clock feather.
Eighty day.
Cunning.
Feeble foliage.
Rain air neck.
Pay stairs.
Pair recapitulations and tender tender tender titles tender
tender tender titles.
Able to seize able to seize separate separate separate.
What is a dictionary, a dictionary is thanks.
Nerves curves nerves curve less nerves curves curves curve
less nerves nerves less nerves nerves less nerves nerves less.
Waiters double cherry waiters double cherry.
In the course of conversation. In the course of conversation.
Needs a pin.
Needs as a pin.
Come out.
Come come out.
Out.

Mercifully mercifully mercy fully mercifully.
Which is a lit.
Lighter.
Wedding chest.
Wedding chest pansies.
Hat is across.
Across far.

Next to next to near soled tip, next to next to near to next to near to near to next to. Next to next to next to near to next to near to.

Cow come out cow come out cow come out come out cow cow come out come out cow cow come out cow come out cow come out come out cow cow come out come out cow cow come out cow come out cow come out cow come out cow cow come out cow come out.

Honey is wet.

Paint on paint in paint in paint in paint in paint in paint in.

Left order neither.

Yes I have been to come. Cow come out cow come out cow come out come out cow cow come out come out cow.

Become become. Polish.

Dress well dress well dress well.

Funny little bore or link

Next next.

It was a way to say say say say.

Inch and inch met or met scale or stamp, stone or paper drawer, rent or rent needs address excel wood and wood and only stick out either, by a place but not more sudden when and all July.

FOUR

Fine

Neither your fathers nor your mothers nor your brothers.
Finally see sees.
Neither your mothers.
Finally see see.

Neither your mothers.
Finally see see.

Of

Nest.
Nest of course is.
Nest.
Nest.
Nest of course is.
Nest.
Nest of course is.
Nest.
Nest of course is.
Nest.
Nest of course is.

Brother

Lay up.
Other see sees.
Pray shoes.
Pray shoes.
Other see sees.
Brother.

Firm

Twenty.
Nine teen.
Finally see see.
Finally see see.

DATES

I

Fish.
Bequeath fish.
Able to state papers.
Fish.
Bequeath fish.

II

Worry.

Wordly
Pies and pies.
Piles.
Weapons.
Weapons and weapons.
World renown.
World renown world renown.

III

Nitches.
Nitches pencil.
Nitches pencil plate.
Nitches vulgar.
Nitches vulgar pencils.
Nitches plate.

IV

Hopping.
Hopping a thunder.
Credit.
Creditable.

V

Spaniard.
Soiled pin.
Soda soda.
Soda soda.

VI

Wednesday.
Not a particle wader.
Aider.
Add send dishes.

VII

Poison oak poison oak.
Stumble.
Poison steer.
Poison steer humble.
Prayer.

Irene.
Between.
Conundrum.
Come.

VIII

Wet yes wet yes wet yes sprinkle. Wet yes wet yes wet yes
sprinkle.

IX

Thicker than some.

X

College extension.

XI

Pass over.
Pass over.
Pass.
Pass.
Pass.
Pass.
Pass pass.

XII

Not a night sight.
Pay sombrely.
Are and n and no and pail. Are and n and no and pail. Are and
n and no and pail.

FINISHED ONE

Finished I finished.
Purses.
Continue.
Not in sentence.
A.
A plan terrier.
Police cat police cat.
Sunday.

Seldom.

Sunny seldom.

Change when a change when it is double when it is a plan to control a patience. Suppose to-morrow.

Suppose to-morrow.

Weeding day.

Weeding day provoking.

Discharged you are discharged.

Not a sound.

Not so sense. Silence.

Little silence.

So painful, so ill visible, so necessary.

That is a tender that is a tender circumstance.

Suppose he had a friend.

What is too listen.

Begin a blessing.

Just begin it.

Sample.

Furniture.

The reason there are pieces is because of duty.

Lend a catalogue, lend it.

Really nearly all of it is able to surmount.

Sir.

Sir.

Photograph.

Rent it.

Rent it easily.

Noisily.

Noisy vellum.

There is no use there is no use in using any example which is plainer. It is plain. It is plain enough. It is plain enough.

It is plain enough.

I can go on.

All the time.

I am tired of that.

High since.

There is an excuse.

Extreme.

Rumpelmayer ice cream.
Finished.
I finished what.
Handsome.
Pills.
Pills.
Curb it.
This is a particular selection.
The reason for it.
By it.
Another bee.
Be mine.

CRETE

Is Miss Clapp at Newnham now. She has been about ten days
in bed. Oh I am so sorry. I relieve that mention of a yes, I relieve
that mention of a yes. Oh I am not so sorry. Not so sorry. Official
time table. Official time table art dyers. French dry cleaning.
Official time to table. I wonder if they mean to be begged. I
wonder if they mean to be begged. Oh I am so sorry. It might
yes. It might be possible that something delayed the train especially as the wind went Westward. Shall it be an appeal. Yes.
What a pity. What a pity. Every dog here is called Bryce. This
is because every house here is called all the delicate attentions.
Three black dogs which are practically very like each other and
they have a family name too. She said something and I did not put
it down. I put down Donald. It's funny that I never thought of it.
How can we be a curly shattered betrothed spotted if he invari-
ably has a spot of skin. He has a spot of hair. Didn't you know
that. He is a sickly one and went and died of it. It was not quite
merry. He wondered about it. It was so unladylike. About two
days after they picked out one. Any one would not have done.
I can't get a house to suit me so that she put a finger on the map.
She once stayed in a house before breakfast, a little box of them.
What was it that was around the dining room. They used to select
the best of them and send him to be educated. Blanche the eldest
sister was two years in these girls. Their names were I've for-

gotten what their names were. After a little while she had an ambition to have another name beside and she called herself Miss Josephine Bee. It ends up with an i. It's folded. Do you remember my father I didn't darling.

TILLIE *(the title suggests) may be a portrait.*

V.T.

TILLIE

Tillie labor Tillie labor eye sheds or sheds, Tillie labor Tillie labor late in shells ear shells oil shells, Tillie labor Tillie labor shave in sew up ups ups, Tillie Tillie like what white like white where, like, Tillie labor like where open so or Tillie labor. Tillie lay Tillie laying Tillie laying, Tillie lime, Tillie Tillie, next to a sour bridge next to a pan wiper next to ascent assent, next to, assent, assent.

SERIES *was written in 1914 before the trip to England. My informant remembers that Dr. Claribel Cone used to enjoy reading it aloud in Paris during the winter of 1913–14 or in the spring. It is a picture-like abstraction in which visual nouns predominate.*

V.T.

SERIES

I

Egg last.

II

Peace in a mine
purses and strawberrie.

III

A seat each.
Leak or moister.
Peas miss peas miss miss miss.

IV

Oak in a bone.

V

Leap a please.

VI

What is a near roll.
What is a near roll.

VII

Standard coal glass.

VIII

Lamentable table back.

IX

In a complete boot by, a reset passenger rolled tied for real
in pay see, what is wheat eat.

X

Not a sister.

XI

Oil in join, oil in join show, oil in join shoulder shoulder
shoulder show.

XII

Next is cutter next is ease cutter next is geese.

XIII

Sublime sublime real in real pin pin in in real in pin in real in.

XIV

Banner makes a cheese.

XV

Why does banner make a cheese.

XVI

I feel no impulse to be scolded.

XVII

An estimable wheeler, Note so soon. A track a track chart, a
leaver in a below. Why is a pear. Why is a pear lay cross. Consider that the sun is tired and leaves and leaves and leaves and.

XVIII

Cause a galop, sudden spool, a pealing water melon.

XIX

Needless to say.
A goat makes color.
Webster and webster and webster.

XX

Lemons slice.
Letter paper.

XXI

Ever or bequest.
So lay done ring.

XXII

A little gray so meat to style.
Knee but knee but to sealed.
Able lamb bird.
Or knee so or knee so red pale, or near so red pale pallor pet.
Or knee so relay age or knee so relay.
Or knee so relay age or knee so. Or knee so relay age.

XXIII

Please pitch a line chest.
I might in the wet.

XXIV

Ways in the spoon ways weighs.

XXV

A whole collection of silver, please pitch a collection arrangement to the for or half. A whole collection of silver.

XXVI

Next to neat. Next to neat.

XXVII

Vent or rind or.
Become a whistle.

XXVIII

Lean not neglected throw bed.

XXIX

Nervous or nervous or exchange nervous or boats.

XXX

Left a place in care of left a ring or level, left a change between, no glance up.

XXXI

Place between care, place between care place between care where.

XXXII

Leaves of oil skin lower shoulders as they below not a section no silence no real rubber strange.

XXXIII

Cannot fish cannot fish in corn or new cannot fish in.

XXXIV

Neglectful peas, neglectful of colors and real papers and almost all the shutters really neglectful of underneath recent calamities almost neglectful of resemblances and butter creams.

XXXV

Able to see able to see able to see to see, able to see able to see able to see able to see.

XXXVI

Why is wet why is wet example of finisher, example to finish is capable of relight example to finish is capable.

XXXVII

Woods. Misses Woods.

XXXVIII

Credit to all ice, credit is sane it is peculiar it is really a little critical it is really a wholesome never seat. It is nearly always perfect.

XXXIX

Borrow him.

XL

Leaves color goat, leaves color black, leaves color color color leaves color girl.

IN ONE (*1914*) *seems to be the abstraction of an explanation. Its words are reasoning words though its shape is musical.*

V.T.

IN ONE

I suggest that that is not what I ordered. I relieve more feathers that way than any other. I hesitate to establish necessary we know of no better and I do mean to oblige. I do mean to offer paper and I do thoroughly reasonably chuck out what has hitherto hindered office of origin. Office of origin has become to me so presently agreeable that between needing it and not needing it, between needing it and not needing it between needing, it, between needing it, shall it be a village. Offices of origin.

LOCKERIDGE, *written in 1914 either in England or immediately after Miss Stein's return from there to Paris, is the name of the village where Miss Stein's visit to the philosopher Alfred N. Whitehead and his family was prolonged for several weeks by the outbreak of World War I. It is a portrait of certain people in the house party and of other guests, delineated through their conversation. The people do not speak to one another. One merely overhears them making characteristic remarks. Extended conversations of this kind are to be found throughout the author's portraits and plays. She tended always, in fact, to view conversation as an expression of character rather than as an exposition of ideas or as a medium for dispute.*

V.T.

LOCKERIDGE

I like grain and chapters and whole bridges. It doesn't make the difference. The same white ball is smelling. It does hinder more sound. It does let us stay.

That's what he said.

Another rubber.

I cannot stir without shapes. I simply cannot please more than size. I cannot I can not.

Eric.

Why is the under step steep, why are old, no I don't like mirrors.

Eric.

I shall say hurry.
What a wind calling.
Out banking.
Showers.
Hold if.
Hold if.
Pump. Letters.

I don't know.

It won't be quite the same.

GENTLE JULIA (*1914*) *was probably written in England a few days before the outbreak of war, because the person it describes was a guest of the Whiteheads just at that time.*

V.T.

GENTLE JULIA

I'll make literature about the old lady to-morrow perhaps. Very well I'll go alone. Have you. Have you. I intended waters. I'll make literature about the old lady shelter perhaps. Jessie. Vera. Eric Sidebotham. Do I spell the name. Do. Do. Distinguished heat. Plan planets. Not likely. Not likely to go not is it not gently whether. I cannot believe about Julia. Why mention names why not mention names presently. Do let me see. I remember that the best plan was the one that was made before there was a place to suggest, I remember more completely.

Will you let me know when you're ready.

BIRD JET, TUBENE, *and* ONE OR TWO. I'VE FIN-ISHED (*all from 1914*) *are abstractions again, hermetic works to which I have no key. Miss Stein was particularly fond of the last of these, quoted it to me approvingly in the late 1920's, though I do not remember in what connection. Perhaps it was a case of "demonstration." There is certainly a conclusive gesture about it, just as "Halve rivers and harbors" is the no less formal beginning of a similarly theorem-like demonstration.*

V.T.

BIRD JET

Colored Kindling
Eight cakes acting. below a cyst, bundles clean an asparagus.
Cut your heat off below the fan. coop end of flannel.
Eight eggs. acting.

TUBENE

Not bend be low not bend below, not bend bed low, not bend bedlow.

Not bend bid low, color hair, hair head, hair head by lead, hair head lead by by pieces of wood next to air shatter shatter a spine held by a gone soon, gone soon begone be soon. Begone be soon be soon show that it by then.

ONE OR TWO. I'VE FINISHED

There
Why
There
Why
There

Able
Idle.

WHAT IS THE NAME OF A RING *begins with mention of a cigarette holder. This was not made of aluminum, as the text suggests, or of platinum. It was of jet set with chip diamonds. It still exists. It was bought late in 1914. "Swimming" is a reference to Dr. Rosika Schwimmer, who accompanied Henry Ford's unofficial peace mission (on the famous "Peace Ship") to Sweden in the spring of 1915. The "automobile" referred to is not Miss Stein's Ford truck, which she acquired only in 1916, but an ambulance bought for service in Serbia in 1915 by a rich American lady whom Miss Stein was seeing. The year 1915, therefore, seems to be the best dating for this poem.*

V.T.

WHAT IS THE NAME OF A RING

A holder.
A cigarette holder.
Aluminium.
Also platinum.
Thank you so much.
Have we been praised.
We have been praised again.
I do not dare to despair.
Oh no you are very happy.
How well you read me.
And the automobile.
Indeed you do me justice.
I am very happy in winter.
And in summer too.
We go soon.
And enjoy it.
And we are eager.
And resolute.
Then we will have success.

There you are right.
Can you see me swimming.
No but being in a pleasant country.
In an automobile.
That is what I feel.
In this way you can say.
We enjoy the day.

STUDY NATURE (*from 1915*) *is an abstraction and deals with
the isolation of words.*

V.T.

STUDY NATURE

I do.
Victim.
Sales
Met
Wipe
Her
Less.
Was a disappointment
We say it.

Study nature.

Or
Who
Towering.
Mispronounced
Spelling.
She
Was
Astonishing
To
No
One
For
Fun

                              Study from nature.

I
Am
Pleased
Thoroughly
I
Am
Thoroughly
Pleased.
By.
It.
It is very likely.

                              They said so.

Oh.
I want.
To do.
What
Is
Later
To.
Be.
Refined.
By
Turning.
Of turning around.

                              I will wait.

DO YOU LIKE YOUR SUIT *and the next four poems may
well be all one poem. If so, they are probably from 1916, when
"Aunt Pauline," the Ford truck, was new and a source of great
satisfaction. In 1917 and 1918 it was "an old habit" and less likely
to appear in Miss Stein's poetry. "Sheep put in bouquets" sounds
like a picture of sheep standing in a round clump with their heads
all pointed toward the center, a view not at all uncommon in the
southwestern part of France.*

                                                    V.T.

DO YOU LIKE YOUR SUIT

Very much.
I can say some more.
Indeed you are becoming.
To it and the hour.
Can we be bold.
We are
And we go.
Please me to see.
The tan.
I can not need to say it. It will have its effect.
Then we can tease.
Not in the summer.
We never do in the summer.
We will go in that way.

THE FORD

It is earnest.
Aunt Pauline is earnest.
We are earnest.
We are united.
Then we see.

CALL IT A TABLE

Do not dispute me.
Oh no.
Do you call it a table.

THIRD DAY NOT THIRSTY

Clamor in coal.
Coal white.
And wood.
Wood sore.
And lambs.

Put in bouquets.
You think I am fooling. Not at all. Sheep put in bouquets.
This is that door.
They are perfectly capable of eating their mutton.

CAN CALL US

He can call us by name.
Do not be greedy.
We are not.
We are boastful.
Do not be hoarse
We are not
We are loving.
Do not be orthodox.
We are not
We have a Ford.

OUR AID *was written in Nîmes in 1917 as a requested contribu-
tion to the bulletin published by the American Fund for French
Wounded. Needless to say, it was not printed, though today it
reads fairly easily.*

                                                            V.T.

OUR AID

In the middle.
All around
And the wedding.
It is bound
To release the middle man.
And we can be left to fan.
What.
The nearest of kin
We have met many of them. Some look like Leon Bonaparte
others look like brothers and some just like children.
And all of them.

All of them are worthy of a caress.

The little English that we know says, We cannot miss them. Kiss them.

We meet a great many without suits.

We help them into them.

They need them to read them to feed them to lead them.

And in their ignorance.

No one is ignorant.

And in their ignorance.

We please them.

DECORATIONS *describes a Fourteenth of July parade held at Nîmes in 1917 in which American troops participated.*

V.T.

DECORATIONS

All decorations are Degallay.

It makes a great deal of difference who sews it on. Everybody sews it on themselves.

This is the same as Leon.

Leon is a lion and Henry is a king.

All of the date is the general. If the general goes first they all follow him. If the captain goes first those follow him. If the officer goes first they go behind him. If the iron wire is torn they go if not even though they be the children of everything they do not need to go.

This was said to me.

To us.

The best way to go is to believe in reading. Candles are very good. They burn to-day.

What was the life of the bee.

I forgot to mention trumpets. Whistles are known.

Sit in the chair with the pleasure of seeing the old women mutter why do they mutter and say have you got a window for to-day.

I need to sleep.

I saw a great many to-day.

Bigger.

I am very sorry not to have been able to see you again.

Sing to me.

Irene sings to me.

We will rise up and say how do you do things have changed
I have a beautiful cane. You are making fun of me. Not at all.
I am literal. I say they do not drink coffee there.

I do not wish to write down what I hear.

Do you remember what you read about.

Collect Willy.

Willy is his name sir.

Decoration bee.

We will sing together and one will be won together. This
is what we think.

What did I do in the garden.

I played with soldiers.

You mean the soldiers prayed. I mean the soldiers played.

Ask me to mention it.

Treasure little treasure I adore but thee.

Did I make a mistake about decoration.

Embroidery.

The class of 97.

They can make systems.

This is not what he said. He said nothing.

Listen to the king.

Listen to that.

Listen to the country.

My dear Ezeroum my dear Trebizonde my dear Erzingan.

To go with you

With us.

There little Edstrom.

What is the meaning of decorations.

I know the meaning of decoration.

This indeed is a decoration.

Days of grass.

Dazed.

I can answer any question.

So can Mr. Gilbert.
I believe what I hear.
Mr. Louis.
Yes Mr. Louis.
Poor Mr. Louis.
He has soldiers.
And pupils.
No not to-night.
Placing William to-day.
Little clinging necessary.
A great many have sisters.
Oh dear yes.
Can you see.
What I say.
When I go.
I say yes.
And then
I see kings.
And then
Not this again.
Knot this again.

w o n *is about winning the war. It must have been written in
Nîmes in 1917, since it describes the arrival of the first American
troops—"thousands of trucks and hundreds of marines." "Aunt
Pauline," already a year old, is "losing oil" but "will justify herself."*

V.T.

WON

Thousands of trucks.
And hundreds of marines.
And in between then.
Aunt Pauline losing oil.
We will see.
Can you think about a dish.

We will have a dish.
Radish.
That is good as food.
Aunt Pauline will justify herself.

WHY CAN KIPLING SPEAK (*1917, Paris*) *is about the war.*
The Kipling named is not the British author but an American
Army (*or possibly Red Cross*) *officer of that name.*

V.T.

WHY CAN KIPLING SPEAK

In asking this we ask no more than we need.
Indeed we say indeed why can that come about. In place of
that we have heard. What have we heard. Nothing that is to
disappoint us. Can we be careful enough. We can not be selfish.
Indeed we have a great deal to arrange. We have system. And
then praise. We have no remembrance. This is after all the need.
And then we like the grey color and the yellow color. Which
is the best. The last mixture.
We are never disappointed.
They are never disappointed.
In asking him to cluster.
Allow me my belief.
Can you speak to me.
Call it a wind sir.
I call it a mind sir
So do a great many wishing to steer.
And then they mean mischief. We never think in gold.
All men are elfish.
In that way birds have credit.
And horses.
Can you think of me.
A great many pledges are wonderful.
And then there is the pleasantness of wondering why there
is gravity.
I do not like to close.
But you must.

T H E W O R K *was written at Nîmes in 1917 for the* A.F.F.W.
Bulletin. *It is about the war work with which Miss Stein was as-
sociated, and was printed in the* Bulletin.

V.T.

THE WORK

Not fierce and tender but sweet.
This is our impression of the soldiers.
We call our machine Aunt Pauline.
Fasten it fat, that is us, we say Aunt Pauline.
When we left Paris we had rain.
Not snow now nor that in between.
We did have snow then.
Now we are bold.
We are accustomed to it.
All the weights are measures.
By this we mean we know how much oil we use for the
machine.
Splendid.
We say are they plateful.
Girls are.
By this we mean that it is reasonable to be well fed and they
are in France. It is astonishing how well everything works.
Women.
Treasures in song.
I mean that we feel that way.
Really we do not sing and as yet we have no phonograph.
The soldiers would like it.
I see a mountain wheeler.
This was when we were frightened and there was no reason
as the wheels were good.
I see a capstan.
This meant that we knew the direction.
I see a straight, I see a rattle, all things are breathing.
This means that I had learnt to go down hill.
Then we came to warmer climbs.
Can you say see me.

Hurrah for America.

Here we met a Captain and take him part way.

A day's sun.

Is this Miss.

Yes indeed our mat.

We meant by this that we were always meeting people and that it was pleasant.

We can thank you.

We thank you.

Soldiers of course spoke to us.

Come together.

Come to me there now.

They read on our van American Committee in aid of French wounded.

All of it is bit.

Bitter.

This is the way they say we do help.

In the meaning of bright.

Bright not light.

This comforts them when they speak to me. I often discuss America with them and what we hope to do. They listen well and say we hope so too. We all do.

Light to me.

Then say the essence.

Here I must confess I am introducing my own troubles. There is always a certain amount of trouble in getting essence but everybody is so kind.

Not a nightingale.

We hope to hear one soon.

Wild animals are not fierce neither are sponges.

This means that the french fight well and make no suggestions. They like to talk about life. They say it is for you to decide what you will bring them. They can criticise but you know how to ask them to tell you what they meant. They are so reasonable.

Can you see her dressed or him.

In this way we cough.

This makes me sad. I hate to hear of them that they are not going to be well. We need them. Not to fight only but to live. You can imagine how I feel.

What can a mayor do.

All the mayors have been most kind.

In this new school in this new school they are ladies and now you mention gifts and lists.

This refers to long conversations and after all they are devoted and all devotion begins with one another. They feel they must answer for all. In this way we know whom to ask. We cannot say we can be pleased but we are very careful in our distribution. That is as it should be.

Can you believe.

Then then.

All the leaves.

This means that as we went South there were leaves.

All the hotels.

Of course there were hotels and many of them were most sympathetic. I remember one where the landlady told us of her son. She had another one. He was then the one the one the only one and he would not be the one to do what was offered him. To remain. Not that he would do more than he did. No indeed. And a boy was an officer. Not one of her children. Were they fighting. They would never remain different in living. Let us hope they are not dying. I cannot tell you what it means to be fighting.

Cooks cook.

We are so happy.

In the land.

You mean a lady.

Nobody speaks of that work.

They do love rabbits.

Can we have imagination.

They ask have we a stocking.

This is apropos of the colonials. We see a great many. They fight so bravely and as they have many of them no people they are so grateful we like them so much. And they have such pleasant ways of speaking to each other. We get to talk to them.

We have to.

It is not a joke.

A war is not a joke.

Did he die there because he was mortal and we leave Rive-saltes. Be nice to me.

This is apropos of the birthplace of Marechal Joffre. We visited it and we have sent postal cards of it. The committee will be pleased.

It is not a bother to be a soldier.

I think kindly of that bother.

Can you say lapse.

Then think about it.

Indeed it is yet.

We are so pleased.

With the flag.

With the flag of sets.

Sets of color.

Do you like flags.

Blue flags smell sweetly.

Blue flags in a whirl.

We did this we had ribbon of the American flag and we cut it up and we gave each soldier one with a pin and they pinned it on and we were pleased and we received a charming letter from a telephonist at the front who heard from a friend in Perpignan that we were giving this bit of ribbon and he asked for some and we sent them and we hope that they are all living.

The wind blows.

And the automobile goes.

Can you guess boards.

Wood.

Naturally we think about wind because this country of Rousillon is the windiest corner in France. Also it is a great wine country.

Can you guess hoop.

Barrels.

Can you guess girls.

Servants.

The women of the country still wear the caps of the country.

Can you guess messages.

Indeed.

Then there are meats to buy.

This is apropos of the small Benevol hospitals who try to supply the best food.

We like asparagus so.

This is an interview.

Soldiers like a fuss.

Give them their way.

This is meant to be read they like a fuss made over them, and they do.

Yes indeed we will.

We are not mighty.

Nor merry.

We are happy.

Very.

In the morning.

We believe in the morning.

Do we.

This means that I have always had the habit of late rising but for hospital visiting I have to rise early.

Please be an interview.

This is when we do not think we would know what to say.

Please be an interview with dogs.

Please comfort me.

Please plan a game.

Please then and places.

This is apropos of the fact that I always ask where they come from and then I am ashamed to say I don't know all the Departments but I am learning them.

In the meantime.

In the meantime we are useful.

That is what I mean to say.

In the meantime can you have beds. This means that knowing the number of beds you begin to know the hospital.

Kindly call a brother.

What is a cure.

I speak french.

What one means.

I can call it in time.

By the way where are fish.

They all love fishing.

In that case are there any wonders.

Many wonders are women.

I could almost say that that was apropos of my cranking my machine.

And men too.

We smile.

In the way sentences.

He does not feel as we do.

But he did have the coat.

He blushed a little.

This is sometimes when they can't quite help themselves and they want to help us.

We do not understand the weather. That astonishes me.

Camellias in Perpignan.

Camellias finish when roses begin.

Thank you in smiles.

In this way we go on. So far we have had no troubles yet and yet we do need material.

It is astonishing that those who have fought so hard and so well should pick yellow irises and fish in a stream.

And then a pansy.

I did not ask for it.

It smells.

A sweet smell.

With acacia.

Call it locusts.

Call it me.

I finish by saying that the french soldier is the person we should all help.

A POETICAL PLEA (Nîmes, 1917 or 1918) is about an American officer, a Captain Dyar, who "at everything his eyes lit on" always said "I would like a photograph of that."

V.T.

A POETICAL PLEA

I would like a photograph of that said Captain Dyar.
Of what.
Of villages.
Of villages of course.
I need the money to give away.
To the mutilés and the reformés.
The reformés of the war.
Let us do arithmetic.
Let us do the arithmetic.
Can you see how many days in the year.
Answer. Three hundred and sixty five.
There are double that number alive.
This is the way we sing.
If the government gives separation allowance they can live.
If the husband comes home and they have a pension they can't
live.
Do you see.
Why not.
Because the man is sick and he makes it less.
But you must not be stupid.
We need the money to give away.
To the mutilés and the reformés.
The reformés of the war.
In this way we must.
Excuse me.
In this way they must
You excuse me.

The SELECTED POEMS *were written mostly in Nîmes, in 1918.*

V.T.

SELECTED POEMS

A M A R Y L L I S *was Miss Stein's nickname for Dr. Claribel Cone, though the poem is "not about her."*

V.T.

AMARYLLIS OR THE PRETTIEST OF LEGS

Thank you so much.
What can you say to shoes.
I don't like the leather.
What do you feel about the cut.
The sole looks pretty.
The sole looks pretty.

A N I N C I D E N T *recounts a misunderstanding between a French nurse of good family and breeding and a soldier of the Foreign Legion. Class tensions of this kind were common at the hospital in Nîmes.*

V.T.

AN INCIDENT

Don't be harsh to me Misses.
I am full of kisses.
As the soldier said it in English the nurse did not understand.

W H A T I S T H I S *takes place in Perpignan. Crystal and Cross are two ladies.*

V.T.

WHAT IS THIS

You can't say it's war.
I love conversation.

Do you like it printed.
I like it descriptive.
Not very descriptive.
Not very descriptive.
I like it to come easily
Naturally
And then.
Crystal and Cross.
Does not lie on moss.
The three ships.
You mean washing the ships.
One was a lady.
A nun.
She begged meat
Two were husband and wife.
They had a rich father-in-law to the husband.
He did dry cleaning.
And the third one.
A woman.
She washed.
Clothes.
Then this is the way we were helped.
Not interested
We are very much interested.

A LESSON FOR BABY

What is milk. Milk is a mouth. What is a mouth.
Sweet. What is sweet. Baby.
A lesson for baby.
What is a mixture. Good all the time
Who is good all the time. I wonder.
A lesson for baby.
What is a melon. A little round.
Who is a little round. Baby.

A RADICAL EXPERT

Can you please by asking what is expert. And then we met one another. I do not think it right. Marksman. Expert. Loaf. Potato bread. Sugar Card. Leaf. And mortar. What is the meaning of white wash. The upper walls.

That sounds well.

And then we sinned.

A great many jews say so.

A M E R I C A *is about war work.*

V.T.

AMERICA

Once in English they said America. Was it english to them. Once they said. Belgian.

We like a fog.

Do you for weather.

Are we brave.

Are we true.

Have we the national color.

Can we stand ditches.

Can we mean well.

Do we talk together.

Have we red cross.

A great many people speak of feet.

And socks.

Y O U R O W N *is "just war."*

V.T.

YOUR OWN

Complain to me.

I like it better just that much better.

You are sure of that.

I think it's too wet.

Now how do you feel about summer.

Sunny isn't hot.
I prefer painted wood.
I am right about wood.
I prefer knitting to crochet.
Because it is pleasant and because it is a third part of an art.
What do you feel about windows.
I prefer windows french and long and open.
And what is your idea of resistance.
And fruit.
And sweet.
And what do you think about leaks.
Leeks are the asparagus of the poor.

LET US TALK ABOUT WAXING *is about household matters and may have been written in Paris.*

V.T.

LET US TALK ABOUT WAXING

Will I do any work to-morrow.
Whom did I think did the marketing.
Veal I think would be best.
They take them as a parcel.
Some have a work bag.
We smile sadly at each other at their pretentiousness.
No no no no no.
A farmer's life is a hard hard life.
Lawyer's daughters who are hard up.
Well that is wicked of them.
Oh dear oh dear.
Without working.
He didn't try to tell the American equivalents.

IN THIS WAY, KISSING *is a love lyric.*

V.T.

IN THIS WAY, KISSING

Next to me in me sweetly sweetly

Sweetly Sweetly sweetly sweetly.
In me baby baby baby
Smiling for me tenderly tenderly.
Tenderly sweetly baby baby.
Tenderly tenderly tenderly tenderly.

CAN YOU IMITATE DISASTER *refers to the second battle
of Verdun, by which Miss Stein and her friends "were not so
frightened" as they had been the first time.*

V.T.

CAN YOU IMITATE DISASTER

In Verdun when there was weather we used to say we like
the sun. Now what does heating mean.
It means that it makes us very thoughtful.
But it was not a surprise
It was a surprise to them.
Then they cannot think about it.

IN THE SAME POEM *is a hospital scene.*

V.T.

IN THE SAME POEM

In the same way he and whom do we mean by her. We cannot
choose them. They ask for socks and are they William Tell. I ask
them are they William Tell.

All bothers are as washing and mending is. Not done. They
are often done. Then listen to that siren. We do not speak the
words! When we speak the words we know it is not true.

I bless you too.

AN ELEGANT ESCAPE *mentions Anne Veronica, a character out of H. G. Wells.*

V.T.

AN ELEGANT ESCAPE

In the midst of the wind there is a milk bottle.
Not now.
And in the midst of the water there is a flower.
So there is.
There is a difference between Anna Karenina and Anne
Veronica.

CAN YOU CLIMB IN LITTLE THINGS *is about nuns.*

V.T.

CAN YOU CLIMB IN LITTLE THINGS

In the midst of brushes there is war.
Can sisters replace each other.
Can a sister be a mother.
I Wonder about Therese.
No you wonder about Claribel. I do not wonder about Mrs.
Nightingale.

WE CANNOT

We cannot have prunes.
You mean it does not agree with our pursuits.
I mean I like the right side.
Then thank me.

WHY CANNOT YOU SPEAK IN PIECES

Why cannot you speak in pieces and say no matter.
Because boards vary.
So do crosses.
So do porcelains and so does pewter.

MAKING SENSE, *probably begun at Béziers in 1917, describes
a fountain. Later it speaks of Beffa, Miss Stein's concierge in Paris,*

where the poem was probably finished. After the quarrel with Beffa, it goes on to current events and domestic incidents.

V.T.

MAKING SENSE

Now I do mean this to be reasonable.
In the middle of Béziers there is what. A fountain.
And what does it do.
It sounds like rain.
We have never heard rain here because when it hailed in Perpignan
We were not there
Now about Narbonne.
We do not like Narbonne exactly.
What do you mean by that indeed. It means that there is a type of hotel called Grand. You mean you don't like the Grand Hotel. I mean I do not care for Negro minstels. You don't remember those. Really. In this way there are a great many visitors.
In reason.
In case of wine.
What do you mean by cooking berries.
A drink.
Cherries.
Not a drink.
Byrrh.
A bottle.
Words.
Maria Eustasia.
I do not believe in stars.
Can you think.
Clearly.
In this way I came back to this walk.
Indeed indeed indeed.

In this way we stink.
Was I angry at Beffa. I was very because he disappointed me. He made a botch of the room. He did not finish the work when he said he would and last year he made trouble with the servant.

I do not appreciate his nature. Beside that I feel that he is married. This is not because his wife desires that he works. That is natural as it is difficult to please but he he says a soldier is not brave. That is easily said as his nephew was a soldier. And did he disgrace himself. Not at all he looked like William Tell at least his friend did. In this way he has no value and indeed if it were possible to have any one else do what he does we would but it is useless urging him to be there. He refuses to go to see the man at the back and we we are afraid of rain and it is not foolish we have reason to be on our regard. He refugee. She is not a mother of a million but three. Three and a head. Ahead of the game because Paris is so kind. I do not mean to speak of Beffa. Why is Beffa not content. We are not content because of him and we are not difficult to please. We are very difficult to annoy. We are not amiable nor good natured. There is a french word for that. When this you see remember me. Occasionally in talking I feel like Elizabeth Stuart and American lady.

Let me leave me. This is not what the island will say.

And then why are we careful.

We are very careful in joining the army.

What does the island feel. The island feels that it is french.

And in that way does it suffer. It does not know very well that there is present the one that is entitled William Tell. Can you make a joke. Can we make it. Can we be learned. About the two names in a village. Yes Beffa and Beffa. But that is only one name. It is only one name but there are two families William Tell.

Can you be sorry in an island.

In a photograph.

And will the photograph be shown.

To a sister.

And why shouldn't he be a general.

No one is a general who eats.

And drinks.

He is said not to do so. In this way he deceives no one.

Kindly be strong.

In feeling well we managed together.

Remember that the island says dinner.

And we give dinner

We give a dinner.

When the cap has been chosen and fits and hats are not worn because of the air, you mean flying yes I mean flying, do you see why they take me.

Of course we do you have had so much experience.

And I talk french.

Yes a workman's french. That's it.

CAN YOU SEE THE NAME *was written in Nîmes in 1918. At this time Miss Stein was reading Queen Victoria's letters aloud at night. Hence the reference to Lord Melbourne.*

V.T.

CAN YOU SEE THE NAME

The name that I see is Howard.
Yes.
And the water that I see is the sea.
Yes.
And the land is the island.
Yes.
And the weather.
And the weather.
Cold
Indeed.
And the cause.
The cause of what.
The cause of lust.
Lust is not a name.
Indeed not.
And bushes.
Can you fear bushes.
Not I.
You mean you are braver.
Braver and braver.
What is the meaning of current.
Current topics.
Yes and then.

And then colors.
Green colors.
Lord Melbourne says blue is unlucky.
This is fear.
When can you see us.
Whenever I look.
And when are you careful.
I am very careful to smile.
Then we have our way.
Indeed you do and we wish it.
We are glad of your wishes.
It is not difficult to drive.
Curtain let us.
We do
We will.
Thank you so much.
You learnt that before.
I learn it again.
Do you know the difference in authors.

WHY WIN WINGS. ON A HAT (*1918*) *is apparently about
some incident of the day.*

V.T.

WHY WIN WINGS. ON A HAT

We had it to-day.
And we were pleased.
We can not be nervous.
All the drink saw it.
We did not say the taste.
We are satisfied.
We cannot conceal.
Then you say.
Necessity.
Can we be careful together.
Can you mention a dog.
She will not let me finish.

IN THE MIDDLE OF THE DAY, IN THEIR PLAY, CAN YOU BEHAVE BETTER, *and* MIRROR, *all from 1918, seem to be occasional pieces. "In Their Play" has also a touch of the literary exercise about it, of a writing problem approached abstractly.*

V.T.

IN THE MIDDLE OF THE DAY

Can you be present.
I can be present earlier.
Before the middle of the day.
We will have wishes.
I wish to say the time of day.
Then we cannot repeat this idea.

Part II

Can we say that. Can we say that.
Do not mean presently.
Then when can we mean.
You can mean soon.
We do.
We will.

Part III

You can you can make it go funnily.
Indeed we know that.

IN THEIR PLAY

Play in the men.
Play in the changes.
Play in wishes.
Play in orthograph.
Can you hear pillows.
Can you imagine mistakes.
Can you understand why he left.
Can you see that he did not.
Indeed he did not.

He told us of wishes.
I do not understand defence.
Can self defence be strong.
I doubt.
It is this that we are able to say.
Can we say to-day.
Can we again say to-day.
Can we mean to be elfish.
Is this their assistance.

CAN YOU BEHAVE BETTER

Can you behave better than what.
Can you indeed.
We do not like the voices when they have been changed in
there.
You mean out there.
Yes indeed.
In a minute.
It was very funny.
In that way.
Can you consider it to mean the window.
In there.
Can you see
Can you see
Can you see further.

MIRROR

This is not the same.
Mrs. Gassette.
This is not the same
The rain.

EXCEPTIONAL CONDUCT

We are exceptional.
Really exceptional conduct.

Can you please
If you please.
In the likelihood that there is.

LIGHT BUTTER

You mean as fuel.
Taught.
Taught to close.
A great many vessels are paper. You mean to keep warm. Of course calico is cloth.

In the meanwhile why listen to me. Not to blame another and scald the weather. How can winter be not. It is in Australia. Say it around. It was a disappointing thing.

JAMES IS NERVOUS

James is another.
He is not in smiling.
No indeed he smiles.
Can you be a gate.
A gate for whom.
For Ruth Casparis.
And then smiles.
Oh so many do not sing.
So many do not sing.
I will not say that again.
James is not nervous.
Any more.
Indeed he is general.
Goodbye to coffee.
Goodbye to coffee where.

IN THIS SHAPE WOOD

Indeed I do love wood.
And coal.
And speak of horses.

We do not mind coughs.
You mean of a machine.

CAN YOU SPEAK

Can you speak
Teaches.
When can you please me.
Corn bread.
Corn or bread.
In the midst of plenty.
In their plenty.
We do see watches.
And mistakes.
Can you sit.
And stand.
Walking has a name.

CAN YOU SIT IN A TREE

Can you sit in a tree comfortably.
And mean to be alright.
And then pleasantly say.
Whose is the car.
Do not mistake a white for a red.
Or a woman for a man.
Do not be in error.
In this way many exchanges are
made, we get an oiled coat and we prefer it. Such pretty color.
Do you always believe in that. I believe in the woman of my
choice.

WHITE WINGS *must have been written before or just after
November 11, 1918, since it contains references to a number of
American soldiers known at Nîmes and since Gertrude Stein left
Nîmes for Alsace almost immediately after Armistice Day.*

V.T.

WHITE WINGS

> White Wings they relieve Jan.
> Baby stars they whistle to Duncan.
> Glittering pets they wake up Childs.
> Tall boys they don't need Humphrey.
> All movies they need Americans.
> See D.

I EXPRESSED MY OPINION

> In Iowa
> In Idaho
> In Illinois
> In Tennessee
> Indeed
> In there.
> And what did they say.
> They said they don't like puzzles.
> We give them jam.

ANIMATED

> By animated we mean listen to them.
> By that we mean that we move in one way.
> We move in one way and then we say
> Fifty five alive.
> Fifty five alive.
> Don't be foolish.
> Don't be foolish.
> Do we say don't be foolish.

LEFT POEM *must also be from Nîmes and 1918, since it tells of Lucky Strike cigarettes, first seen by the author when the Y.M.C.A. appeared, selling them, that spring.*

V.T.

LEFT POEM

Why do you walk and ride.
Do you mean me.
There it is.
What.
A Lucky Strike.
They just grew.
That's what they do.
And everybody is so satisfied.
We like he.
We like he.
Love all three.
Who work for me.
That's what they could sing if they were not so busy singing.
We like me.
We throw easily.
What.
What we threw, that which we throw.

PRIM ROSES (*1918*) *is about winning the war.*

V.T.

PRIM ROSES

This is not the name.
          Roosians.
It's a shame.
          Success.
We sing.
          Will we then win.
We will then win.
          Dogs.
They sing and bark.
          Where.
In the square.
And then what is it.
I cannot see why we need to deny it.

Patience and wishes.
Wishes with fishes.
They knew the day.
We will sway and pay.
We will pay them the villains.
Keep sober and all.
We will be tall.
We are tall and strong.
We will take long.
Thank you as we win.

THE PRESENT

THE PRESENT

Tiny dish of delicious which
Is my wife and all.
And a perfect ball.

ITALY

And then can you see.
There can you see.
With which can it.
And then it was victory.
To the country.
In this country there is notice.

THE LIBERTY LOAN

Eradicate money.
The blind can see.
Eradicate mine.
We are rich.
We have come.
All birds.

SACRED FOUNTAIN OF BELLOWS

Can you believe the wind.
The moon does
And what do we do.
What do we do.

SAY IT AGAIN

I say again that Italy will be victorious. You have the feeling
I have the feeling.

POSTAL CARDS

Were you it.
Were you a postal card.
Were you on a postal card.
I do not care about imitating narratives.

OLD DOGS *and* KICKING (*1919*) *are straightforward lyrical poetry, expressions of mood.*

V.T.

OLD DOGS

Old dogs.
Old dogs are we.
Old dogs
Old dogs merrily
We see.
Hurrah.
Sunday.

KICKING

Kicking is relegated to the Midi.
I understand.
Disturbances are confined to the North.

So I hear.
Money comes from there.
We adjourn.
Longing comes from home.
We bemoan.

THEN STEAL *is from 1919. I do not know what it is about.*
I consider it, however, merely obscure, not hermetic.

V.T.

THEN STEAL

Can you buy a door.
Can you buy a bedding.
Can you buy oats
Can you buy measles.
Can you buy complaints.
Need you care about draughts.
Not then.
Can you learn lessons.
Can you learn medicine.
Can you learn Paul.
Can you learn bicycles.
Not to believe.
Can you witness distraction.
Can you be no better.
Can you wrestle.
Do you know your verses.
Do you know pleasure in rapture.
Believe me she is a teacher.
Is she paid to do charity.
Red white and blue.

A HYMN *(1919) is about conversations held with an English*
lady who visited Paris that year. The opening line "South Africa
and me" is quoted from a speech by General Smuts.

V.T.

A HYMN

South Africa and me
We think we are so free
But then again we can
Obliterate a man.
Who is Coutts.
And then in millionaires
We never know who cares.
For a British king or queen so mean.

Indeed an account knows
Which way they rub their woes
And in the middle Christmas
There is butter.
But in the water there
Not every one can care,
What does the rectification matter.
Indeed my money is
And so is any kiss
And least of all can we remain for Smuts.
Let us not anyway
Betray what they will say
For we do with the angels in their head.

Amen.

POLISH (*also 1919*) *is about Poland and current events.*

V.T.

POLISH

Poling poling the sea into weather along.
Poling poling dogs are pretty who have such a song.
Girls and boys tease the seas.
We are capable of this ease.
Not so the Poles and their brothers the foals.
They are the ones that made the Huns, do what.
Be sick at their guns.

Not these Huns
They were the Huns, strong in their aged sashes.
How can a man wear a sash.
That may surprise you but they do.
Some over their overcoats, some over their head.
We can see why Poles are led.
They are led by their waists their hearts and their ears.
They are led.
They are lead.
Not to sink in a bed.
They elect.
They have elected.
They can elect.
They will elect.
They were elected.
Recently they were elected
Can you believe a long distance.

w o o d *(1919) means Woodrow Wilson and refers to a moment
when "the stork flew over the White House." Mrs. Wilson,
thought to be pregnant, received as gifts from the public lots of
baby clothes, later sent them to France for distribution, where
they were most welcome.*

V.T.

WOOD

Would Wood Wooed.
And the reason.
I love the real profiteer.
Who profits here.
Can horses be peace
And birds have steps.
And likenesses and countenances
And order and trunks and cases.
The goods are not lost.
They are stolen. They steal to us here in the day time with a
knock at the door.

They come in and we have every thing.
Even the baby.
Baby clothes.
Baby clothes what.
Baby clothes the express.
Train.

NAMES OF FLOWERS

Gertrude
The peace of Europe.
The Princess of Monaco.
Victory.
Tulips.
I murmur to my servant. Don't ring the bell. I also say. Don't
attack me.
By being unkind I please brothers.
Brother brother go away and stay.

DEVELOP SPANISH

Develop Spanish.
Thoughts.
Thoughts.
Thoughts.
Thoughts.

SCENERY (*1920*) *and* CAPTURE SPLINTERS (*1921*)
are apparently abstractions of writing problems.

V.T.

SCENERY

Call a man a mountain Shasta.
Answer.
Mount Shasta or Mount Blanc or a mountain in the South.
I can make geographical tastes.

We have decided upon so long.
We used to make a joke.

SEEN III

Do be again to-day.
Three mountains.
A cow, a wife and a collar.
A hat, a ring and an umbrella.
A bird, a tooth and a mother.
Dear thing. You are a mother.
Dear thing. There is a cow.
Dear wife. There is no circus.
Dear Marquis of Wellington.
Let me see blue.
I would like a whole collection.

How can you mean to break a stem. Candle sticks have no
stem. How can you mean to wear roses. A crimson rambler has
no thorns.

In a way Joselito, in a way Joselita in a way we are not sorry.
To be.
Do not scratch suddenly.
I beg you to cease raillery.
I do not like the American library. Oh yes I do.
Henry James Winner.
Howells hold all.
A glass mandoline.

CAPTURE SPLINTERS

First poise. Poison is nearly here.
Read this.
What have you taken.
A rabbit.
How do you eat hair.
Spell correctly.
A sound of a word.
Heynse. Irish.

Heinz. German.
Heins. Swiss.
Heines Austrian and
Haines Australian.
Mean for the best.
I mean it all for the best.

A SECOND PLAY

When you stagger you feel that threatening does no good.
Where is the man that sings. He sings like a mill.
Were the mills burned.
How can you see potatoes.
Potatoes do not peel they split.
In the midst of the summer.

PLAY THREE

Coughing Occasional coughing helps a court. A court is be-
tween houses.
Coughing is displeasing.
Can you be cold in some weather.
In some climates.
I say in some climates.
I realise that there are drawbacks.
Dear me do I draw back.
Indeed you do not.
And do I mean to invite them.
I hope you do.
I will really and truly do it.
I meant to believe in Noah.
I really meant to believe in Noah.

SONNETS THAT PLEASE (*1921*) *are exactly what the title
says. They read like sonnets, feel like sonnets, sum up the sonnet
by avoidance of all its conventions save that of being expressions
in the first person.*

                                                        V.T.

SONNETS THAT PLEASE

I see the luck
And the luck sees me I see the lucky one be lucky.
I see the love
And the love sees me
I see the lovely love be lovely.
I see the bystander stand by me. I see the bystander stand
by inside me.
I see.

ANOTHER SONNET THAT PLEASES

Please be pleased with me.
Please be.
Please be all to me please please be.
Please be pleased with me. Please please me. Please please
please with me please please be.

SONNETS THAT PLEASE

How pleased are the sonnets that please.
How very pleased to please.
They please.

SONNETS THAT PLEASE

I please the ribbon the leather and all. I please the Christian
world. I please the window the door and the bird. I please the
Hindoos a third. And Elsie Janis.
I follow the sonnets that please with ease.
If we must part let us go together.
I miss a trick. I sit up quick, quickly.
Eddying
How often do I mention that I am not interested. She is so
loyal so easily moved so quickly roman catholic so entrancing.
And how plainly we speak. How caressingly, all nature eats every
day.

I am persuaded still.
He was deceived by the color.
And now for Sunday.
A Sunday is measured by sawing.
Upright stands and swinging. We never sing.
Why not.
Because voices are so useful to me.
The sound of them. No the color of vegetables. Vegetables
are flat and have no color.
Flowers are irregular and have a variety of color.
And rubbish. Rubbish lies in heaps when it is not a birthday.
How sweetly birthdays bear their fruit. And trees, trees the
leaves of trees are transparent, because they have been eaten.
I can make a description.
I am excessively sleepy.
Every day will be Sunday by and by.
And now we dream of ribbons and skies.
We will win prizes.
We will announce pleasures.
We will resume dresses.
How pleasantly we stutter.

SEPARATED *and* ATTACKS (*1921*) *seem to be comments
on people or on incidents.*

                                                    V.T.

SEPARATED

She is meant to fear.
Fear nor that.
Opium den opium then opium when.
Have they hair.

ATTACKS

She is.
She is the best way.
She is the best way from here to there.

I cannot regret pouches.
Instead of pockets.
Question nicely.
Question me nicely.
If they read it.
If they read it.
Can they read it.

JOKES FOR JESSIE *was written for a friend who visited Paris in 1919–20.*

V.T.

JOKES FOR JESSIE

Parlor habits.
In England they call them drawing rooms.
The English cannot draw, they are under sleeping America.
America sleeps when it can.
One sleeps when one can.

COUNTING *and* KITES *are from the same year, 1921.*

V.T.

COUNTING

I once said something about counting dresses.
Counting dresses is not nearly so difficult as counting distances.
Would you believe that 25 miles is farther than going around.
We go around every day.

KITES

All attention is directed to traffic.
James have you a short name.
Shorter than yours.
Shorter than Jennie's and William's.

No we name ours Francis.
A little baby sleeps.

MARY *and* NOT A HOLE *(1921) seem to be meditations or comments.*

V.T.

MARY

Mary Minter and Mary P.
Mary Mixer and Esther May.
Henriette Gurney and Mrs Green can you see what I mean.

HERBERT

In a little while I smile, and then in between there is relish. I greatly relish reading what do you expect.
Mingle more names.
To-morrow I will work.
I have seen Jones.
And Mary.
Jones is Welsh.
And Mary.
Can you believe more of Jones than of Mary.
Mary Jones. James Jones.
Cadwaller Jones. Henry Jones.
Have you a very little cough.
Dear me.
I say will you sit down.

NOT A HOLE

Out from the holes Rosenberg,
Out from the whole Rosenberg.
A mountain in roses. A mountain for roses. Roads of roses.
Read rapid rows of roses. Relieve me oh relieve me.
A very little man can never deceive me.

CURTAINS DREAM (*1921*) *is about Miss Stein's new Ford car, "Godiva." "Aunt Pauline," the wartime Ford truck, has now become in memory plain "Liz."*

V.T.

CURTAINS DREAM

Measure a treasure.
We treasure a measure.
We measure and we measure and we tread that is Godiva does the distance that was the distance that is and it was Liz and it was Lizzy she would have been dizzy but Godiva is strong and for long and the song the song of the godmother prolong.
Think. Is she.
She is.

AS EIGHTY (*1923*) *reflects Miss Stein's developing preoccupation with grammar and "how to write." Its subtitle suggests an exercise in argument. But the argument, if there is one, takes place through the isolation of words, not through their composition into sentences.*

V.T.

AS EIGHTY

OR

NUMBERED FROM ONE TO EIGHTY-ONE

A DISPUTATION

As eighty-nine.
Regulation.
Regulate.
Why is it easier to have it.
Why is it easily and to have it easily and why easily.
As eighty-one.
As it easier to have it.
And now announce.
Crowding.
Finished it as quickly.

And attracts.
This is and introductions.
Eighty-one.
Commence now.
Follow tube-roses tenderly and account for it.
Eighty-one eighty and eighty-one.
One.
And one
And eighty
And eighty one.
Just to fancy
Justly just as just to and to adjust and instead. To blame. And shine and retain and absently be be presently. A pleasure in as recently.

All this introduces a man and his mother. This is the second book for my mother.

Begin now attractively.
Eighty and one as it interests me.
Eight.
And one.
And one.
Eighty and one as it interests me.
A climax.
Subdivision.
Gardening.
Caesars and arrangements.
Ordinary environment.
Religion separately.
One follows another.
Originally
Originally one follows from another.
And originally religion separately.
And also as originally Caesars and arrangements.
And originally subdivision.

PART OF ONE

Were they deceiving her.
Part of eighty-one.

Plenty of it and hand-fulls of it, plenty of it and plenty of hand-fulls of it. Do not be afraid of the transition.

Nature.

American.

Not at all.

It makes no difference.

If you care for it.

And find it to be splendid.

There is no authority for misstatement.

PART 3

Partly three.

Prettier than ever.

As pretty.

PART 4

Before very much before and have it to do.

We know.

PART 5

Back again to part five.

PREPARATION

In preparation for it.

As an instance.

For instance.

A description of every waiter as in place.

Always know when.

To always know when.

When.

When smiling.

Carefully beam.

Carefully order.

Carefully.

Very carefully.

Presented anyhow.

A long sentence.

A long sentence begins with the attention that is given not to one another but in addition, additionally it begins with a distribution and not as to places nor as arranged but not necessary as standing and in standing, no one can exhaust staring and turning and in candidly refraining, an arrangement precludes that and firstly and as understanding we signal, no more satisfactory effort has been rectified and in this easily. So then.

In ministration.

All of it as to memory.

Memory not mentioned.

Diminish not mentioned.

In aptitude not mentioned.

In refreshing not mentioned.

Nourished not mentioned.

Quadrilateral not mentioned.

In collection not mentioned.

Three not mentioned.

Their and three not mentioned.

As afterwards and they were there as afterwards as afterwards they were there.

Beginning of a ceiling.

I didn't count them in you didn't count them I didn't count them in I didn't count them.

Presenting it to them. As presents to them.

A short sentence.

Very short.

As a sentence.

As they do differ.

Deference differ.

Very much so.

In respect to horses. No horses.

In respect to horses. No horses.

In respect to horses. No horses.

Planting as planted.

Immediately as roses.

Immediately as roses.

Immediately as roses.

Having had it.

Having had it preliminarily as having had it.

Not nearly.

Another sentence as long as the other sentence.

And make more of it further and further make more of it if
in places where if the reasons remain the flood would be true
because as we were saying if in a little while all of it as it and
as it all of it then in a little no counting can destroy twenty and
twenty, no counting can destroy forty as it means to do and
nearly as more is known it might be sixty even then evenly as
even and not high enough to remember at all and remember at
all. This is the decision about it as a flood, a flood as a flood a
decision about it.

Not as in very nearly. Meaning makes mines. Nines. Such a
comfort.

As such a comfort.

I plan to.

As such a comfort.

Not so very many not so very many as there are not so very
many for instance as there are not so very many.

As she says.

Beautifully silky as she says.

As she says.

So sweet as he says: As he says as she says as beautifully silky
as she says as sweet as he says as he says.

Ninety-nine counting. Counting ninety-nine. Ninety-nine
counting ninety-nine. So pleased with you.

Don't you see this is the way this is in the way. Now press it,
what, as rested, now rest what, as the rest of it.

Pleased with me, When this you see you are pleased with with
me. Easily pray prettily. All of it as a reduction. In size. I cannot
see why collections vary. In this way a long visit is proposed.

So many fairly nearly to places here and there.

As to that.

You will all you will all as to that.

Irritated.

And now the middle is higher. The middle of what. Compare
to this end and to that end. Compare it. Compare with it. Carefully.

It is always a mistake to be plain-spoken.

Forty-five and forty-five make ninety.

In NEW (*1924*) *she is still confined to "words." The "sentence" has not yet engaged her attention as a problem.*

V.T.

NEW

We knew.
Anne to come.
Anne to come.
Be new.
Be new too.
Anne to come
Anne to come
Be new
Be new too.
And anew.
Anne to come.
Anne anew.
Anne do come.
Anne do come too, to come and to come not to come and as to
and new, and new too.
Anne do come.
Anne knew.
Anne to come.
Anne anew.
Anne to come.
And as new.
Anne to come to come too.
Half of it.
Was she
Windows
Was she
Or mine
Was she
Or as she
For she or she or sure.
Enable her to say.
And enable her to say.

Or half way.
Sitting down.
Half sitting down.
And another way.
Their ships
And please.
As the other side.
And another side
Incoming
Favorable and be fought.
Adds to it.
In half.
Take the place of take the place of take the place of taking place.
Take the place of in places.
Take the place of taken in place of places.
Take the place of it, she takes it in the place of it. In the way of arches architecture.
Who has seen shown
You do.
Hoodoo.
If can in countenance to countenance a countenance as in as seen.
Change it.
Not nearly so much.
He had.
She had.
Had she.
He had nearly very nearly as much.
She had very nearly as much as had had.
Had she.
She had.
Loose loosen, Loose losten to losten, to lose.
Many.
If a little if as little if as little as that.
If as little as that, if it is as little as that that is if it is very nearly all of it, her dear her dear does not mention a ball at all.
Actually.

As to this.
Actually as to this.
High or do you do it.
Actually as to this high or do you do it.
Not how do you do it.
Actually as to this.
Not having been or not having been nor having been or not
having been.
Interrupted.
All of this makes it unanxiously.
Feel so.
Add to it.
As add to it.
He.
He.
As add to it.
As add to it.
As he
As he as add to it.
He.
As he
Add to it.
Not so far.
Constantly as seen.
Not as far as to mean.
I mean I mean.
Constantly.
As far.
So far.
Forbore.
He forbore.
To forbear.
Their forbears.
Plainly.
In so far.
Instance.
For instance.
In so far.

A double as in half.
Follow me slowly
Fairly has.
It fairly has.
In half.
Not at sea.
To be, not at sea concerning if at that.
Not to be at sea concerning it.
Not to resist reasonably not to persist.
Fully.
Sing Song.
As at.
Attitude.
Attitude toward it.
An attitude toward it.
An
A second apart.
Bay too.
It pays too.
To pay too.
Or to.
To draw.
In a sense.
In the sense.
Attract.
Alter attract.
The same.
Here.
Anne Anne.
And to hand.
As a while.
For a while.
And to come.
In half or dark.
In half and dark.
In half a dark.
As to it.
In a line.

As fine a line.
Bestow.
Anne Anne
And to hand
As a while
For a while
Anne
And
And to hand
As a while
For a while.
So new.
So new.
So new.
Sew
So new.
As a while.
See it.
Say it.
Say it.
Say it with sailors.
Every once in a while.
There is no use. Vienna does not really produce real sailors
nor does it very, as very nearly, as so very nearly.
All of it makes it as if it is as if it will have so many times so.
As to know.
Is to show
Are to go.
Can say so.
Letters and press.
Letter press.
Luck and cress, grass and now.
And now.
And new.
And new.
And too
And too.

A COMEDY LIKE THAT (*1924*) *is "not landscape but affected by the landscape." It is about the city of Saint-Rémy in Provence and its circumjacent countryside. It has "the Saint-Rémy rhythm"; it is suffused with rigamarole and metrics. There is music in its air and in that of the two better known pieces about Provence of which this is the prototype, "Capital, Capitals" and "The Four Religions." Gertrude Stein said later that "the music in them was incidental, not the intention," that they were "objective" writing. All the same, they do sing. Perhaps this quality comes from their having been almost literally written to the sound of running water, because Miss Stein used to love at this time to sit all morning in the fields beside the irrigation ditches, sometimes talking to an old woman and sometimes just sitting. She seems to have been "much affected by the running water." The same had been true earlier in Granada.*

V.T.

A COMEDY LIKE THAT

I am going to try a comedy like that.

I am going to like a comedy like that.

Like that is like that it is like that I am going to like that. I am going to like it like that.

Which first.

Which on what on what does it depend which first.

Which first on which does it depend which first.

Which first what first on which does it depend what first.

On what does it depend which first.

On which does it depend on what does it depend on what does it depend what first on which does it depend what first on what does it depend which first, on which does it depend on which does it depend on what does it depend on what first.

On what first.

On which first.

Next evenly, next even even next evenly next evenly next even. Even next evenly next on what evenly next on which even next on which even next on which on what evenly next on evenly next which depends on what first, what depends evenly next

which depends evenly next which depends on what first even
next evenly next which depends on what first.

What depends on which first.

Evenly next.

INTRODUCTION

Just the same as another.

As always interested to know as always in the way to on the
way and before by the way when there is a part, all the way as it
is used, used and added for and so much. She has no habits here.
But she will form them. She has no habits here. But she will hear
them as more. Hear in the sense of heard, hear in the sense of
right, hear in the sense of settling.

Not only over again.

Habitually corner and corner and habitually and harps and
habitually and corner and habitually and harps and corner and
habitually.

The next time as ever.

It is and not and so and to it is and so and not it is and to and
so and is and it is and it is so and it is not and it and so and is, and is.

Further than this makes it best.

Best test.

OPENING SCENE

Seen and seen and seen as to a man which if corresponded.

Answering that.

Seen and seen and seen as to and corresponded answering
that.

Seen and seen and seen and as to corresponded answering
that.

Seen and seen as to corresponded.

In the next again and has not as yet felt it to be easier.

Not remembered as a fact.

Before scenery before scenery or more. This and waiting.
Waiting on what, can be used so as if it were as if it were a as if it
were a rest and all. To them.

Actually counted and counted it all out. And counted it all
out.

If yes, yes yes, and an addition and in addition, if and in addition, if and an addition, if yes, if in addition, yes and if and an addition, larger and better.

In answer.

And and might, as well, as it is, and it is done.

Done and done so, in place of after it and between. This then in objection. Weigh, weight, and attacked, attract, attached and after it, afterwards, beginning, and satisfactory preparation.

Here as in certain for and a threat, is a threat or a threat or a half or a part or a pressure or complete or as much as in that as a case of it.

Replied and surface if the surface has been so much sooner, soon, and accounted as finished for it, it is finished as an afternoon to-day.

If mine and mine if mine if it is touched if it is mine if mine is touched. If it is touched.

Sooner have and have it in sooner. As heard away, away from the receipt. To receive when if had it even when not as or because if in in inclined and arranged to prepare. Suited to it.

The next arrangement is made as it was. As it was and second and in arrival, as late as that. The next time. By nearly all of it.

It is more as the chance of that. Found lately.

Different to be differently adhered to there. The next in and whether to have as and forgotten.

Did she say what she said she would.

All she can remember is what happened. All she can remember is that she can remember all that happened.

The next time suitable would it be well to turn around so that if the coat which if brown and the hat which is black would continue to be as satisfactory as if when a new decision was to be made it would certainly not be influenced by that arrangement. No answer as yet.

This is on this account.

Having told and having told having told and having told having told and having told evenings and more and unaccountably.

Having told it was a pleasure it was merely an apparent day. Apparently a day and day-time.

Extra and union.

Extra and union and in union.

Extra and in union and union and union and in union.

Extra and in union.

Not and seen nearly.

Not nearly not as near not nearly not and seen not and seen not and seen and nearly.

This is the end of that.

And very nearly as it is.

To-morrow again and in and a place. A place for everything and everything in its place.

Fortunately, fortunately it was a fortunately as it was and fortunately beside.

This is not heard and seen.

This evening see this evening see, this evening see to as much so.

And as noon.

And as noon and as there was amorning and as there was morning and more than so soon and as soon.

Nearly have to say and nearly have to say it.

Coming to a station in coming to a station does a do the trains stop.

If they do does she when they do does she do so when they do do so.

After that asking to have it clearly understood as to hearing.

Is hearing and staying equal and individual. Is it a reason or is it as a season. Can there be an ounce and ounces and may there be as often as that always all of it in preference.

She knows.

When is and when is there not all of or either all if it or all of it or either or all of it. When is there after it has been as it was assured as it is to be assured that there is no doubt. It is assuredly once and more than once and once or twice and often. Often and as often and always and more so.

She was told she had bought.

Having added having added could she have and have and add, could she add and have and have and add. Could she having could she have added could she adding could she having could she be having and adding.

Cut glass cut glass cut glass and an old and sent.

If this in the morning and if she and were she, was she and in this and in the habit of it.

Satisfied to say.

Almost all and almost all and to do and to do almost all almost all of it to do.

Though she was though if she was though if she was though would there would there be any necessity for sight and hearing. In their place there is ease.

One and two, requested to use two.

Two and one one as to have it.

Repeated.

It is easier to repeat a sentence than shorter. It is easier to repeat a sentence and longer, it is easier to repeat a sentence and longer it is easier to sing.

Left after this.

Right after this.

Left after this right after this right after this left after this.

It is all earlier.

And longer.

And after after it at all.

If the name name of wool if the woman and as much not alone that it is put there.

If at first here and there if she hears as the door door and more as a fact and never angry.

If not at all as soon as and it had for the best was she too to have heard all as well as all that.

When the same as it is when at first as well as when there is and it can when as much as it does and questioned.

How has he and not heard when he had and was left would it be and not for for them.

This is due to her sister.

Could it have have it had and the rest for its use to be seated and as much as leaning.

This and there for the noise by its use for the rest and as well when and how does she know any other.

In a way in their way in her way in a day in a day in the day time and at least.

The real and the ideal the one who finding fault does not

cause more than imitation and the other who in consequence looks again. The one who has every wish and all wishes the other who has wishes and every wish. There is no difference between two years and one year in each case they can be induced either to leave or to stay.

Part of the time.

Copy cold and copy colder copy and cold and as cold and yet fortunately it is economical and not insufficient.

In this way we say how much is there and not at all unwillingly.

A description of standard weights and measures.

Should squares which are divided in two have eight and seven which makes fifteen or can there be some other arrangement.

She came in with what. She came in with what. With what did she come in.

And then as if with cress. Cress having in itself the necessary ingredient instead of being reminded there has been more and less. And for this and as this and when if again or, can a place be made by adding places to it. Places which are added are those in which beauty is repeated. Finally and wished and succeeded. Having no doubt, no doubt having to have had an example of it.

This makes their agreement so important.

When this is heard.

Come Tuesday come Tuesday and come.

Wednesday.

Thursday.

Thursday is the day arranged.

Thursday is the day arranged seriously. For and because it is as much meant.

As a sound.

Name, his name.

Fortunately by his name.

Like that.

It will be like that.

Fortunately by her name.

Name, her name.

Fortunately by her name.

It will be like that.

Fortunately by her name.

A different occasion to-morrow, a different occasion to-morrow a different occasion, a different occasion, a different occasion, occasionally, to-morrow.

Should and no.

Having had one, one at a time, having had one one at a time having had one at a time having had one one at a time.

More than plainly.

As much more and plainly and plainly as much more.

Changing hats hats change.

Changing doors doors change.

Changing chairs chairs change.

Changing.

The next time like that.

Any more.

And any more like that.

There are not there will not there will not be any more.

There will not be any more like that just now.

As much like that.

If coming and come and to come.

When you are out how do you get in.

The thirtieth of May in the morning she had three sisters and one brother the thirtieth of may in the morning there had been another brother, who would have been older, the thirtieth of May in the morning the brother who was younger than any sister was not at all concerned with the fact that his sister being older would certainly be going farther away than any other sister. She would be satisfied.

On the thirtieth of May in the morning and there were four sisters one brother a father a grandfather and a mother. It is not at all likely that the others would be returning before the middle of July to spend the time with the others who concerned themselves with the work of the summer. The emotion would not last long.

In no sense can happiness be encouraged.

Payments.

Pointing to many places.

Obviously.

Partial payments.

Partly to her.

Let it be remembered that if and there is let it be remembered that there is to be conscientiousness.

Let it be remembered that if and there is augmentation let it be remembered that there is to be conscientiousness.

Once not.

Once and not.

Let it be remembered that at once and once.

Let it be remembered.

It is not remembered.

Let it be remembered that without its being good enough, let it as it is not good enough to let it as it is good enough to let it be remembered at once.

They took every advantage.

EARLY AND LATE (*1925*) *"starts with the rhythm of Saint-Rémy and ends up with something else." It is "Gertrude Stein amusing herself" and "trying to get out of the Saint-Rémy period." It is full of jokes and personal references. The names refer to people.*

V.T.

EARLY AND LATE

Early and late earlier and later, earlier and later too late and later, and as late.

Was it Celestine.

At once.

Was it Eugene.

At once

Was it Paul

At once

Was it Odile or a stranger.

Was it Esther

At once.

Was it at once.

He was hindered.
How many are sold.
As many as that.
How many are told.
As many as all that.
How many more are expected.
As many more.
How many more.
Very many more.
To settle down carefully and receive it all at once.
At once.
At least.
To be very much impressed by it at all.
Four and of the four three.
Four and of the four two.
Four and of the four three and two.
Four and of the four one and one.
Of the four one is seventeen one is nineteen one is fifty one one is forty-four. Which are the three of the four. Which are the two of the four. Which are the one and one of the four.
At once.
None at once.
At once and yesterday.
And between.
Not easily and at once and none at once.
Following one another before hand.
Expect expect to and not as seen. She saw.
Four-four and not to use does anybody after all does anybody does anybody does anybody after all.
Just like Esther only reddened her hair reddened a black and white fur coat and long nose and thin.
Just like Celestine only dark and fat and and accompanied.
Just like Eugene
Just like Celestine
Just like Esther.
And in between
This is better.

Why do they let their mind dwell upon it.
Questions and questioned and rapidly at once.
Not in reminded.
And begin at once.
No
Second
No
The rapidly and approached, intended and reproached.

If in advancing the interests of one in whom she believed and by whom she was convinced would it be of any importance if at once and at one time, if and accountable and inauguration which makes other thoughts come and not to be administered. In connection with this and building by not as easily surrounding an entrance and prolonging. Is there any reason to doubt that they are both separately in their return extending what must further their peace. Peace at what.

Needing and known too.
And whether there or there is. There used to be.
As reminded.
Not a disappointment.
Who hopes it.
Who hopes it.
He has heard.
He has had it.
Bonnington is a name.
Beginning. To be beginning.
To be beginning.
Bonnington is a name.
Beginning. To be beginning.
Changed to when my wife came into my life.
Changed to Bonnington is a name.
Prices.
Prices and beginning. To be beginning. Prices and to be beginning. In exchange for a little one.
A little one and apology.
How do many do as much as they try to do.
Disturbed by and distributed in such a way that over here

two hundred over here and over there two hundred over there.

Delay does not does not delay does not and understood easily. And very interestingly.

Stop it and stop it.

And very interestingly.

He said and in advice fortunately the difference.

Gather it to be when and furthermore having decided not to see and furthermore not to see to it. As if it had to be in place of it and coming occasionally.

Indifferently.

In the morning she insisted that they cover it so that they would be able afterwards to have said, half said and practically, she as in that way it was quite apt to be carefully and as well done as won.

Won should never be used in connection with early and late.

And quietly.

It becomes more and more evident.

Who said that they should that they would never who said that they would that they never would who said that they never would undertake to have to have heard it. We hope for three successes.

Freight.

And remember.

Occupying, occupying, weighed and occupying, occupying and weighed.

Actually actually and connected with it too.

He said as many more as indifferently and to be referred to as in a chair.

It is difficult to mention objects and then and then, and then, the difficulty, difficultily with difficulty objects mentioned objects are mentioned and with difficulty.

To receive roast.

Two mentioned, deer and veal. Two mentioned, bread and butter, two mentioned at first and prepared, two mentioned coming at once and partly.

It was partly this.

Fortunes are lost just as easily.

Applicable.

City a city.

To tell all about it.

They made a fence a fence of trust, they made a fence a fence and must and must they, they made a fence they made a fence and who made a fence. Jo did. Why did Jo make a fence. Jo made a fence practically to prepare it.

In preparation always sounds, sounds and sounds, sounds are more than once those that they care for, care for should end as it is. She moved.

It was a pleasure not to see and to see to see and so, to see and so and it was a pleasure and she had had it heard, heard all that in all that all in that way.

Not as certainly as before.

How often they are alike, alike alike, and not to be three things heard but not too many.

To find it later.

To find it earlier.

To find it earlier.

To find it.

Was it what was wanted, what was wanted what was it that was wanted.

Teas and teas.

This connects with such such words as tease.

Tease and tease.

This connects with such words such and such words and as much and later and early and late, and later.

Persons and places and a novel.

It is very carefully, left left right and left, it is very carefully wholesome and perhaps, perhaps as much as in the voice. When the voices have higher and leave it to them.

Persons and places and regular and they need to have news and recitals. Recitals of the arrival of the boat.

Persons, to persons.

Places, to places.

Divided by twenty-two and then twenty-two, divided by seventy-five and then seventy-five. Twice.

Twice as early.

Twice two.

Twenty-two.

Early and late.

The nice way to sing to roses is this. Sing to roses.

The nice way to tell a story of festoons is this.

A bridge is made of what gives so much. A bridge is made by what gives what gives what gives what gives so much. A bridge is made as much as a bridge is made as much. It really is as much. As a bridge is made.

A nice way to tell the story of a table a small table a little table is to mention the part that in the morning, later in the morning, in the morning, the following morning earlier in the morning, and perhaps all the time it was easy to imagine an opening. Who fills openings. Who fills four and one opening. What fills it. It is a self filler. Please yourself.

The useful and necessary at once.

Who knows how many eagles there are.

Who knows how many there are.

Carefully taking care of one another.

Please do.

Early and late or please do.

Actually in paint.

Who sees who sees who sees and not having decided.

Decide deceive deceive distress distress, deny deny declare declare does it do does it do to ask more for it than that does it do to refuse what has been arranged does it do to have ear-rings to have to have ear-rings valuably valuably and differently and differently and an advantage.

Once or twice and numbers too, numbers at once numbers for you, a number for you a number of what a number a nice number a very nice number a number of very nice numbers. The first number that was attractive was forgotten. The second number that was as attractive was the one that eighty-two carried away and the third number that was attractive that was attractive that was attractive the third number that was attractive to be sure at length at most. Most and best, at length at most at best. Eight.

Why don't they have him. Why don't they take him. Why

don't they ask him. Why don't they like him, why don't they like him, why don't they ask him why don't they want him, why don't they find him, why don't they call him, why don't they try him, why don't they change to him why aren't they to have him, why aren't they to choose him, why aren't they likely to wait for him, why don't they need him, why don't they return to him, why don't they why does it matter to him why does it change it at once and later. In a minute when they say in a minute as all day and better.

Every one eats butter and here she is at last.

Habits and markets all at once or twice more.

Habits and markets and all at once or twice more. He asked and he asked and he asked to asked to asked to asked to as to what. Twice more. Markets and habits. Twice and twice more.

First and last only. Only ought to be only. Excuse me for having introduced it at all.

FINIS.

PATRIARCHAL POETRY

PATRIARCHAL POETRY. *In 1927 Miss Stein remarked to me that she was writing a long piece to be called "Patriarchal Poetry." "There are all these emotions lying around; no reason why we shouldn't use them," she said. Using emotion as the subject matter of art had since the turn of the century been discouraged by the modern movement. Nevertheless, she had been impressed with the work of certain nonabstract painters who had been shown for the first time in 1926 at the Galerie Druet. These were Christian Bérard, Pavel Tchelitchew, Léonid Berman, and Kristians Tonny. Pierre Charbonier and Thérèse Debains were also shown. She had bought pictures by Tchelitchew and Tonny and become their close friend. I had also become a friend in 1926 and had set various of her texts to music. In the spring of 1927 she composed for me an opera libretto on a Spanish subject,* Four Saints in Three Acts. *She also knew, through me, the French poet Georges Hugnet. There is no question but that she was immersed in the neo-Romantic movement, a movement of which the chief originality lay in the restoration of personal sentiment, of emotion, to a major place in art's overt subject matter.*

Miss Stein had begun right after World War I to search for a "new painter," or for another movement in painting capable of offering her a stimulus comparable to that which certain painters had provided before the war. She did not find another Picasso (though she did become devoted, after 1930, to the work of Francis Rose). What she found was a new range, for her, of literary expression.

She was also working constantly during the 1920's at grammar and rhetoric. In 1927 she was still worried about the paragraph; her studies of the sentence had not yet begun. "Paragraphs are emotional," she would say later; and she would discard the paragraph as a form. But "Patriarchal Poetry" is all paragraphs, all grammar, all emotion. "Patriarchal Poetry" is the first of Gertrude Stein's long works in the neo-Romantic vein. Lucy Church Amiably, *which incorporates emotion with landscape, is probably the most celebrated of these. "Patriarchal Poetry" is significant for its research into the paragraph both as a literary form and as a carrier of pure emotion. The structure of emotion is its theme.*

It is hermetic writing; direct communication of ideas is not its purpose. Its purpose is the description of emotion and, in the neo-Romantic manner, the communication of emotion. Like "As a Wife Has a Cow. A Love Story," which Miss Stein liked to refer to as her Tristan and Isolde, *it counts on repetition, subtle and exhaustive, for much of its power, just as Romantic music does. It also avoids picture-words—the nouns of image and the verbs of motion. It is full of prepositions and pronouns, of adverbs and auxiliaries, of all the kinds of words that express connection.*

Between Tender Buttons *and "Patriarchal Poetry" there were fifteen years. These years included for Miss Stein much travel, her motorization, a major war, and a revolution in esthetics. Also growth in artistic mastery. Before* Tender Buttons *there had been mostly narration. Then came description—visual, bright-colored, explosive. After that, love poetry, the daily life, grammar, and how to write. And through them all Miss Stein arrived at something new, something completely different from* Tender Buttons, *though equally hermetic. "Patriarchal Poetry" is not cubistic at all, not angular or explosive or in any way visual. It is rounded, romantic, visceral, auditory, vastly structured, developed like a symphony.*

After 1927 emotion is rarely absent from Miss Stein's poetic production. Also, little by little her hermeticism disappears. The next two decades show an elaborate and massive, if somewhat slow and certainly elliptical, return to straightforward communication. She had mastered writing in all its forms and revealed by means of obscurity and hermeticism vast reaches hitherto little explored of language and of "the human mind." But at the end of her life, as at the beginning of her writing career, it was "human nature," as expressed through language, that interested her most. Brewsie and Willie *is a picture of American manhood and of the American language in 1945, a summation of her friendship with the new American Army, and a book thoroughly translucent as to mean-*

ing. Her last complete work, The Mother of Us All *(1946), a study of American nineteenth-century political life and also of American feminism, has a plainness of language and an emotional impact of almost biblical grandeur. At its very end Susan B. Anthony pronounces unequivocally her own funeral oration, and Gertrude Stein hers:*

> We cannot retrace our steps, going forward may be the same as going backwards. We cannot retrace our steps, retrace our steps. All my long life, all my life, we do not retrace our steps, all my long life, but.
> (*A silence a long silence*)
> But—we do not retrace our steps, all my long life, and here, here we are here, in marble and gold, did I say gold, yes I said gold, in marble and gold and where—
> (*A silence*)
> Where is where. In my long life of effort and strife, dear life, life is strife, in my long life, it will not come and go, I tell you so, it will stay it will pay but
> (*A long silence*)
> But do I want what we have got, has it not gone, what made it live, has it not gone because now it is had, in my long life in my long life
> (*Silence*)
> Life is strife, I was a martyr all my life not to what I won but to what was done.
> (*Silence*)
> Do you know because I tell you so, or do you know, do you know.
> (*Silence*)
> My long life, my long life.
> *Curtain* *

V.T.

* Reprinted from *Last Operas and Plays* (New York, Rinehart & Co., 1949), by permission of the publisher.

PATRIARCHAL POETRY

As long as it took fasten it back to a place where after all he would be carried away, he would be carried away as long as it took fasten it back to a place where he would be carried away as long as it took.

For before let it before to be before spell to be before to be before to have to be to be for before to be tell to be to having held to be to be for before to call to be for to be before to till until to be till before to be for before to be until to be for before to for to be for before will for before to be shall to be to be for to be for to be before still to be will before to be before for to be to be for before to be before such to be for to be much before to be for before will be for to be for before to be well to be well before to be before for before might while to be might before to be might while to be might before while to be might to be while before for might to be for before to for while to be while for before while before to for which as for before had for before had for before to for to before.

Hire hire let it have to have to hire representative to hire to representative to representative hire to representative to hire wire to representative to hire representative to hire.

There never was a mistake in addition.

Ought ought my prize my ought ought prize with a denies with a denies to be ought ought to denies with a to ought to ought ought with a denies plainly detained practically to be next. With a with a would it last with a with a have it passed come to be with this and theirs there is a million of it shares and stairs and stairs to right about. How can you change from their to be sad to sat. Coming again yesterday.

Once to be when once to be when once to be having an advantage all the time.

Little pieces of their leaving which makes it put it there to be theirs for the beginning of left altogether practically for the sake of relieving it partly.

As your as to your as to your able to be told too much as to your as to as able to receive their measure of rather whether intermediary and left to the might it be letting having when win. When win makes it dark when win makes it dark to held to beheld behold be as particularly in respect to not letting half of it be by. Be by in this away.

To lay when in please and letting it be known to be come to this not in not in not in nightingale in which is not in land in hand there is it leaving light out out in this or this or this beside which may it for it to be in it lest and louder louder to be known which is could might this near special have near nearly reconcile oblige and indestructible and mainly in this use.

Mainly will fill remaining sad had which is to be following dukedom duke in their use say to amount with a part let it go as if with should it might my makes it a leader.

Feels which is there.

To change a boy with a cross from there to there.

Let him have him have him heard let him have him heard him third let him have him have him intend let him have him have him defend let him have him have him third let him have him have him heard let him have him have him occurred let him have him have him third.

Forty-nine Clive as well forty-nine Clive as well forty-nine sixty-nine seventy-nine eighty-nine one hundred and nine Clive as well forty-nine Clive as well which is that it presses it to be or to be stay or to be twenty a day or to be next to be or to be twenty to stay or to be which never separates two more two women.

Fairly letting it see that the change is as to be did Nelly and Lily love to be did Nelly and Lily went to see and to see which is if could it be that so little is known was known if so little was known shone stone come bestow bestown so little as was known could which that for them recognisably.

Wishing for Patriarchal Poetry.

Once threes letting two sees letting two three threes letting it be after these two these threes can be two near threes in threes twos letting two in two twos slower twos choose twos threes never came twos two twos relieve threes twos threes. Threes twos relieves twos to twos to twos to twos relieve to twos to relieve two threes to relieves two relieves threes twos two to relieve threes relieves threes relieve twos relieves threes two twos

slowly twos relieve threes threes to twos relieve relieve two to
relieve threes twos twos relieves twos threes threes relieves twos
two relieve twos relieves relieve twos relieves threes relieve twos
slowly twos to relieves relieve threes relieve threes twos two
relieve twos threes relieves relieve relieves twos two twos threes
relieves threes two twos relieve relieves relieves threes relieve
relieves threes relieves as two so threes twos relieves twos relieve.

Who hears whom once once to snow they might if they
trained fruit-trees they might if they leaned over there they might
look like it which when it could if it as if when it left to them to
their use of pansies and daisies use of them use of them of use of
pansies and daisies use of pansies and daisies use of them use of
them of use use of pansies and use of pansies and use of pansies
and use use of them use of pansies and daisies use of use of them
which is what they which is what they they do they which is
what they do there out and out and leave it to the meaning of
their by their with their allowance making allowed what is it.

They have it with it reconsider it with it they with it reconsider it with it they have it with it reconsider it have it they with it
reconsider it they have it they with it reconsider it they with it
they reconsider it have it they have it reconsider it with it have it
reconsider it have it with it. She said an older sister not an older
sister she said an older sister not an older sister she said an older
sister have it with it reconsider it with it reconsider it have it
an older sister have it with it. She said she had followed flowers
she had said she had said she had followed she had said she had said
she had followed she had said with it have it reconsider it have it
with it she had said have followed have said have had have followed have said followed had followed had said followed flowers
which she had had will it reconsider it with it have it had said followed had followed had followed flowers had said had with it
had followed flowers had have had with it had said had have had
with it.

Is no gain.

Is no gain.

To is no gain.

Is to to is no gain.

Is to is to to is no gain.

Is to is no is to is no gain.

Is no gain.

Is to is no gain.

Is to is to is no gain.

Is no gain.

Is to is no gain.

With it which it as it if it is to be to be to come to in which to do in that place.

As much as if it was like as if might be coming to see me.

What comes to be the same as lilies. An ostrich egg and their after lines.

It made that be alike and with it an indefinable reconciliation with roads and better to be not as much as felt to be as well very well as the looking like not only little pieces there. Comparing with it.

Not easily very much very easily, wish to be wish to be rest to be like not easily rest to be not like not like rest to be not like it rest to not like rest to be not like it.

How is it to be rest to be receiving rest to be how like it rest to be receiving to be like it. Compare something else to something else. To be rose.

Such a pretty bird.

Not to such a pretty bird. Not to not to not to not to such a pretty bird.

Not to such a pretty bird.

Not to such a pretty bird.

As to as such a pretty bird. As to as to as such a pretty bird.

To and such a pretty bird.

And to and such a pretty bird.

And to as to not to as to and such a pretty bird.

As to and to not to as to and such a pretty bird and to as such a pretty bird and to not to as such a pretty bird and to as to not to and to and such a pretty bird as to and such a pretty bird and to and such a pretty bird not to and to as such a pretty bird as to as such a pretty bird and to as such a pretty bird and to as to and to not to and to as to as such a pretty bird and to as such a pretty bird and to as to not to as to and to and such a pretty bird and to and

such a pretty bird as to and such a pretty bird not to and such a
pretty bird not to and such a pretty bird as to and such a pretty
bird and to and such a pretty bird as to and to and such a pretty
bird not to as to and such a pretty bird and to not as to and to not
to as such as pretty bird and such a pretty bird not to and such
a pretty bird as to and such a pretty bird as such a pretty bird and
to as such a pretty bird and to and such a pretty bird not to and
such a pretty bird as to and such a pretty bird not to as such a
pretty bird not to and such a pretty bird as to and such a pretty
bird not to as to and to not to as such a pretty bird and to not
to and to and such a pretty bird as to and such a pretty bird
and to as such a pretty bird as to as such a pretty bird not to
and to as to and such a pretty bird as to and to and to as to
as such a pretty bird as such a pretty bird and to as such a pretty
bird and to and such a pretty bird and to and such and to and to
and such a pretty bird and to and to and such a pretty bird and
to and such a pretty bird and to and such a pretty bird and to
and such a pretty bird and to and such a pretty bird and to as to
and to and such a pretty bird and to as to as such a pretty bird
and to and to and such a pretty bird and such a pretty bird and to
and such a pretty bird and to and to and such a pretty bird and
to and such a pretty bird.

Was it a fish was heard was it a bird was it a cow was stirred
was it a third was it a cow was stirred was it a third was it a bird
was heard was it a third was it a fish was heard was it a third.
Fishes a bird cows were stirred a bird fishes were heard a bird
cows were stirred a third. A third is all. Come too.

Patriarchal means suppose patriarchal means and close patriarchal means and chose chose Monday Patriarchal means in close
some day patriarchal means and chose chose Sunday patriarchal
means and chose chose one day patriarchal means and close close
Tuesday. Tuesday is around Friday and welcomes as welcomes
not only a cow but introductory. This aways patriarchal as sweet.

Patriarchal make it ready.

Patriarchal in investigation and renewing of an intermediate
rectification of the initial boundary between cows and fishes.
Both are admittedly not inferior in which case they may be obtained as the result of organisation industry concentration as-

sistance and matter of fact and by this this is their chance and to appear and to reunite as to their date and their estate. They have been in no need of stretches stretches of their especial and apart and here now.

Favored by the by favored by let it by the by favored by the by. Patriarchal poetry and not meat on Monday patriarchal poetry and meat on Tuesday. Patriarchal poetry and venison on Wednesday Patriarchal poetry and fish on Friday Patriarchal poetry and birds on Sunday Patriarchal poetry and chickens on Tuesday patriarchal poetry and beef on Thursday. Patriarchal poetry and ham on Monday patriarchal poetry and pork on Thursday patriarchal poetry and beef on Tuesday patriarchal poetry and fish on Wednesday Patriarchal poetry and eggs on Thursday patriarchal poetry and carrots on Friday patriarchal poetry and extras on Saturday patriarchal poetry and venison on Sunday Patriarchal poetry and lamb on Tuesday patriarchal poetry and jellies on Friday patriarchal poetry and turkeys on Tuesday.

They made hitherto be by and by.

It can easily be returned ten when this, two might it be too just inside, not as if chosen that not as if chosen, withal if it had been known to be going to be here and this needed to be as as green. This is what has been brought here.

Once or two makes that be not at all practically their choice practically their choice.

Might a bit of it be all the would be might be if a bit of it be all they would be if it if it would be all be if it would be a bit of all of it would be, a very great difference between making money peaceably and making money peaceably a great difference between making money making money peaceably making money peaceably making money peaceably.

Reject rejoice rejuvenate rejuvenate rejoice reject rejoice rejuvenate reject rejuvenate reject rejoice. Not as if it was tried. How kindly they receive the the then there this at all.

In change.

Might it be while it is not as it is undid undone to be theirs awhile yet. Not in their mistake which is why it is not after or not further in at all to their cause. Patriarchal poetry partly. In an as much to be in exactly their measure. Patriarchal poetry partly.

Made to be precisely this which is as she is to be connectedly leave it when it is to be admittedly continued to be which is which is to be that it is which it is as she connectedly to be which is as she continued as to this to be continuously not to be connected to be which to be admittedly continued to be which is which is which it is to be. They might change it as it can be made to be which is which is the next left out of it in this and this occasionally settled to the same as the left of it to the undertaking of the regular regulation of it which is which which is which is which is what it is when it is needed to be left about to this when to this and they have been undetermined and as likely as it is which it is which it is which is it which is it not as in time and at a time when it is not to be certain certain makes it to be makes it to be makes it to be makes it to be makes it to be that there is not in that in consideration of the preparation of the change which is their chance inestimably.

Let it be as likely why that they have it as they try to manage. Follow. If any one decides that a year is a year beginning and end if any one decides that a year is a year beginning if any one decides that a year is a year if any one decides that a year simultaneously recognised. In recognition.

Once when if the land was there beside once when if the land was there beside.

Once when if the land was there beside.

Once when if the land was there beside.

If any one decided that a year was a year when once if any one decided that a year was a year if when once if once if any one when once if any one decided that a year was a year beside.

Patriarchal poetry includes when it is Wednesday and patriarchal includes when it is Wednesday and patriarchal poetry includes when it is Wednesday.

Never like to bother to be sure never like to bother to be sure never like to bother to be sure never like never like to never like to bother to be sure never like to bother never like to bother to be sure.

Three things which are when they are prepared. Three

things which are when they are prepared. Let it alone to be let it alone to be let it alone to be to be sure. Let it alone to be sure.

Three things which are when they had had this to their best arrangement meaning never having had it here as soon.

She might be let it be let it be here as soon. She might be let it be let it be let it be here as soon. She might be let it be here as soon. She might be let it be let it be she might be she might be let it be she might be let it be she might be let it be here as soon. Theirs which way marguerites. Theirs might be let it there as soon.

When is and thank and is and and and is when is when is and when thank when is and when and thank. When is and when is and thank. This when is and when thank and thank. When is and when thank and this when is and thank.

Have hear which have hear which have hear which leave and leave her have hear which have hear which leave her hear which leave her hear she leave her hear which. They might by by they might by by which might by which they might by which they by which they might which they might by which they by which they might by which. In face of it.

Let it be which is it be which is it be which is it let it let it which is it let it which let it which is it let it be which is it be which let it be which let it which is it which is it let it let it which is it let it. Near which with it which with near which with which with near which with near which with near which with it near which near which with near which near which with which with it.

Leave it with it let it go able to be shiny so with it can be is it near let it have it as it may come well be. This is why after all at a time that is which is why after all at the time this is why it is after all at the time this is why this is why this is after all after why this is after all at the time. This is why this is why this is after all this is why this is after all at the time.

Not a piece of which is why a wedding left have wedding left which is why which is why not which is why not a piece of why a a wedding having why a wedding left. Which is what is why is why is why which is what is why is why is why a wedding left.

Leaving left which is why they might be here be here be here. Be here be here. Which is why is why is why is why is which is why is why is why which is here. Not commence to to to be to leave to come to see to let it be to be to be at once mind it mind timely always change timely to kindly kindly to timely timely to kindly timely to kindly always to change kindly to timely kindly to timely always to change timely to kindly.

If he is not used to it he is not used to it, this is the beginning of their singling singling makes Africa shortly if he is not used to it he is not used to it this makes oriole shortly if he is not used to it if he is not used to it if he is not used to it if he is not used if he is not used to it if he is not used to it if he is not used to it he if he is not used to it he is not used to it and this makes an after either after it. She might be likely as to renew prune and see prune. This is what order does.

Next to vast which is which is it.

Next to vast which is why do I be behind the chair because of a chimney fire and higher why do I beside belie what is it when is it which is it well all to be tell all to be well all to be never do do the difference between effort and be in be in within be mine be in be within be within in.

To be we to be to be we to be to be to be we to be we to be to be to be to be to be to be to be we we to be to be to be we to be. Once. To be we to be to be to be we to be. Once. To be to be to be to be to be we to be. Once. To be we to be to be to be.

We to be. Once. We to be. Once. We to be be to be we to be. Once. We to be.

Once. We to be we to be. Once. To be. Once. We to be. Once. To be. Once. To be we to be. Once. To be. Once. To be we to be. We to be. Once. To be. We to be. Once.

To be we to be. Once. To be. Once. To be. Once. To be. Once. To be. Once. We to be. To be we to be. We to be. To be we to be. We to be. Once. To be to be to be. We to be. We to be. To be. Once. We to be.

Once. We to be.

Once. We to be. We to be. Once. To be we to be. Once. To be. Once. To be we to be. Once. We to be. To be. We to be. Once. Once. To be. Once. To be. Once. We to be. Once. We

to be. We to be. Once. To be. Once. We to be. We to be. We
to be. To be. Once. To be. We to be.

Their origin and their history patriarchal poetry their origin
and their history patriarchal poetry their origin and their history.

Patriarchal Poetry.

Their origin and their history.

Patriarchal Poetry their origin and their history their history
patriarchal poetry their origin patriarchal poetry their history
their origin patriarchal poetry their history patriarchal poetry
their origin patriarchal poetry their history their origin.

That is one case.

Able sweet and in a seat.

Patriarchal poetry their origin their history their origin. Patriarchal poetry their history their origin.

Two make it do three make it five four make it more five
make it arrive and sundries.

Letters and leaves tables and plainly restive and recover and
bide away, away to say regularly.

Never to mention patriarchal poetry altogether.

Two two two occasionally two two as you say two two two
not in their explanation two two must you be very well apprised
that it had had such an effect that only one out of a great many
and there were a great many believe in three relatively and moreover were you aware of the fact that interchangeable and interchangeable was it while they were if not avoided. She knew that
is to say she had really informed herself. Patriarchal poetry makes
no mistake.

Never to have followed farther there and knitting, is knitting
knitting if it is only what is described as called that they should
not come to say and how do you do every new year Saturday.
Every new year Saturday is likely to bring pleasure is likely to
give pleasure is likely to bring pleasure every new year Saturday
is likely to bring pleasure.

Day which is what is which is what is day which is what is day
which is which is what is which is what is day.

I double you, of course you do. You double me, very likely
to be. You double I double I double you double. I double you
double me I double you you double me.

When this you see remarkably.
Patriarchal poetry needs rectification and there about it.
Come to a distance and it still bears their name.
Prosperity and theirs prosperity left to it.
To be told to be harsh to be told to be harsh to be to them.
One.
To be told to be harsh to be told to be harsh to them.
None.
To be told to be harsh to be told to be harsh to them.
When.
To be told to be harsh to be told to be harsh to them.
Then.
What is the result.

The result is that they know the difference between instead and instead and made and made and said and said.

The result is that they might be as very well two and as soon three and to be sure, four and which is why they might not be.

Elegant replaced by delicate and tender, delicate and tender replaced by one from there instead of five from there, there is not there this is what has happened evidently.

Why while while why while why why identity identity why while while why. Why while while while while identity.

Patriarchal Poetry is the same as Patriotic poetry is the same as patriarchal poetry is the same as Patriotic poetry is the same as patriarchal poetry is the same.

Patriarchal poetry is the same.

If in in crossing there is a if in crossing if in in crossing nearly there is a distance if in crossing there is a distance between measurement and exact if in in crossing if in in crossing there is a measurement between and in in exact she says I must be careful and I will.

If in in crossing there is an opportunity not only but also and in in looking in looking in regarding if in in looking if in in regarding if in in regarding there is an opportunty if in in looking there is an opportunity if in in regarding there is an opportunity to verify verify sometimes as more sometimes as more sometimes as more.

Fish eggs commonly fish eggs. Architects commonly fortunately indicatively architects indicatively architects. Elaborated at a time with it with it at a time with it at a time attentively to-day.

Does she know how to ask her brother is there any difference between turning it again again and again and again or turning it again and again. In resembling two brothers.

That makes patriarchal poetry apart.

Intermediate or patriarchal poetry.

If at once sixty-five have come one by one if at once sixty five have come one by one if at once sixty-five have come one by one. This took two and two have been added to by Jenny. Never to name Jenny. Have been added to by two. Never have named Helen Jenny never have named Agnes Helen never have named Helen Jenny. There is no difference between having been born in Brittany and having been born in Algeria.

These words containing as they do neither reproaches nor satisfaction may be finally very nearly rearranged and why, because they mean to be partly left alone. Patriarchal poetry and kindly, it would be very kind in him in him of him of him to be as much obliged as that. Patriotic poetry. It would be as plainly an advantage if not only but altogether repeatedly it should be left not only to them but for them but for them. Explain to them by for them. Explain shall it be explain will it be explain can it be explain as it is to be explain letting it be had as if he had had more than wishes. More than wishes.

Patriarchal poetry more than wishes.

Assigned to Patriarchal Poetry.

Assigned to patriarchal poetry too sue sue sue sue shall sue sell and magnificent can as coming let the same shall shall shall shall let it share is share is share shall shall shall shall shell shell shall share is share shell can shell be shell be shell moving in in in inner moving move inner in in inner in meant meant might might may collect collected recollected to refuse what it is is it.

Having started at once at once.

Put it with it with it and it and it come to ten.

Put it with it with it and it and it for it for it made to be extra.

With it put it put it prepare it prepare it add it add it or it or it would it would it and make it all at once.

Put it with it with it and it and it in it in it add it add it at it at it with it with it put it put it to this to understand.

Put it with it with it add it add it at it at it or it or it to be placed intend.

Put it with it with it in it in it at it at it add it add it or it or it letting it be while it is left as it might could do their danger.

Could it with it with it put it put it place it place it stand it stand it two doors or two doors two tables or two tables two let two let two let two to be sure.

Put it with it with it and it and it in it in it add it add it or it or it to it to be added to it.

There is no doubt about it.

Actually.

To be sure.

Left to the rest if to be sure that to be sent come to be had in to be known or to be liked and to be to be to be to be to be mine.

It always can be one two three it can be always can can always be one two three. It can always be one two three.

It is very trying to have him have it have it have him. have it as she said the last was very very much and very much to distance to distance them.

Every time there is a wish wish it. Every time there is a wish wish it. Every time there is a wish wish it.

Every time there is a wish wish it.

Dedicated to all the way through. Dedicated to all the way through.

Dedicated too all the way through. Dedicated too all the way through.

Apples and fishes day-light and wishes apples and fishes day-light and wishes day-light at seven.

All the way through dedicated to you.

Day-light and wishes apples and fishes, dedicated to you all the way through day-light and fishes apples and wishes dedicated to all the way through dedicated to you dedicated to you all the way through day-light and fishes apples and fishes day-light and wishes apples and fishes dedicated to you all the way through day-light and fishes apples and wishes apples and fishes day-light and wishes dedicated to dedicated through all the way through dedicated to.

Not at once Tuesday.

They might be finally their name name same came came came came or share sharer article entreat coming in letting this be there letting this be there.

Patriarchal poetry come too.

When with patriarchal poetry when with patriarchal poetry come too.

There must be more french in France there must be more French in France patriarchal poetry come too.

Patriarchal poetry come too there must be more french in France patriarchal come too there must be more french in France.

Patriarchal Poetry come to.

There must be more french in France.

Helen greatly relieves Alice patriarchal poetry come too there must be patriarchal poetry come too.

In a way second first in a way first second in a way in a way first second in a way.

Rearrangement is nearly rearrangement. Finally nearly rearrangement is finally nearly rearrangement nearly not now finally nearly nearly finally rearrangement nearly rearrangement and not now how nearly finally rearrangement. If two tables are near together finally nearly not now.

Finally nearly not now.

Able able nearly nearly nearly nearly able able finally nearly able nearly not now finally finally nearly able.

They make it be very well three or nearly three at a time.

Splendid confidence in the one addressed and equal distrust of the one who has done everything that is necessary. Finally nearly able not now able finally nearly not now.

Rearrangement is a rearrangement a rearrangement is widely known a rearrangement is widely known. A rearrangement is widely known. As a rearrangement is widely known.

As a rearrangement is widely known.

So can a rearrangement which is widely known be a rearrangement which is widely known which is widely known.

Let her be to be to be to be let her be to be to be let her to be let her to be let her be to be when is it that they are shy.

Very well to try.

Let her be that is to be let her be that is to be let her be let her try.

Let her be let her be let her be to be to be shy let her be to be let her be to be let her try.

Let her try.

Let her be let her be let her be let her be to be to be let her be let her try.

To be shy.

Let her be.

Let her try.

Let her be let her let her let her be let her be let her be let her be shy let her be let her be let her try.

Let her try.

Let her be.

Let her be shy.

Let her be.

Let her be let her be let her let her try.

Let her try to be let her try to be let her be shy let her try to be let her try to be let her be let her be let her try.

Let her be shy.

Let her try.

Let her try.

Let her be

Let her let her be shy.

Let her try.

Let her be.

Let her let her be shy.

Let her be let her let her be shy

Let her let her let her let her try.

Let her try.

Let her try.

Let her try.

Let her be.

Let her be let her

Let her try.

Let her be let her.
Let her be let her let her try.
Let her try.
Let her
Let her try.
Let her be shy.
Let her
Let her
Let her be.
Let her be shy.
Let her be let her try.
Let her try.
Let her try.
Let her try.
Let her let her try
Let her be shy.
Let her try
Let her let her try to be let her try.
Let her try.
Just let her try.
Let her try.
Never to be what he said.
Never to be what he said.
Never to be what he said.
Let her to be what he said.
Let her to be what he said.

Not to let her to be what he said not to let her to be what he said.

Never to be let her to be never let her to be what he said. Never let her to be what he said.

Never to let her to be what he said. Never to let her to be let her to be let her to be let her what he said.

Near near near nearly pink near nearly pink nearly near near nearly pink. Wet inside and pink outside. Pink outside and wet inside wet inside and pink outside latterly nearly near near pink near near nearly three three pink two gentle one strong three pink all medium medium as medium as medium sized as sized. One as one not mistaken but interrupted. One regularly better adapted if readily readily to-day. This is this this readily. Thursday.

This part the part the part of it.

And let to be coming to have it known.

As a difference.

By two by one by and by.

A hyacinth resembles a rose. A rose resembles a blossom a blossom resembles a calla lily a calla lily resembles a jonquil and a jonquil resembles a marguerite a marguerite resembles a rose in bloom a rose in bloom resembles a lily of the valley a lily of the valley resembles a violet and a violet resembles a bird.

What is the difference between right away and a pearl there is this difference between right away and a pearl a pearl is milk white and right away is at once. This is indeed an explanation.

Patriarchal poetry or indeed an explanation.

Try to be at night try to be to be at night try to be at night try to be at night try to be to try to be to try to be to try to be at night.

Never which when where to be sent to be sent to be sent to be never which when where never to be sent to be sent to be sent never which when where to be sent never to be sent never to be sent never which when where to be sent never to be sent never to be sent which when where never to be sent which when where never which when where never which to be sent never which when where to be sent never which when where to be sent which when where to be sent never to be sent never which when where to be sent never which when which when where to be sent never which when where never which when where which when where never to be sent which when where.

Never to be sent which when where.

As fair as fair to them.

It was not without some difficulty.

Five thousand every year.

Three thousand divided by five three thousand divided as five.

Happily very happily.

They happily very happily.

Happily very happily.

In consequence consequently.

Extra extremely additionally.

Intend or intend or intend or intend or intend additionally.

Returning retaining relatively.

This makes no difference between to be told so admittedly.

Patriarchal Poetry connectedly.

Sentence sent once patriarchal poetry sentence sent once.

Patriarchal poetry sentence sent once.

Patriarchal Poetry.

Patriarchal Poetry sentence sent once.

Patriarchal Poetry is used with a spoon.

Patriarchal poetry is used with a spoon with a spoon.

Patriarchal poetry is used with a spoon.

Patriarchal poetry used with a spoon.

Patriarchal poetry in and for the relating of now and ably.

Patriarchal poetry in preferring needless needless needlessly patriarchal poetry precluding needlessly but it can.

How often do we tell tell tell tale tell tale tell tale tell tale might be tell tale.

Supposing never never never never supposing never never in supposed widening.

Remember all of it too.

Patriarchal poetry reasonably.

Patriarchal poetry administratedly.

Patriarchal poetry with them too.

Patriarchal poetry as to mind.

Patriarchal poetry reserved.

Patriarchal poetry interdiminished.

Patriarchal poetry in regular places largely in regular places placed regularly as if it were as if it were placed regularly.

Patriarchal poetry in regular places placed regularly as if it were placed regularly regularly placed regularly as if it were.

Patriarchal poetry every little while. Not once twenty-five not once twenty-five not once slower not once twenty not once twenty-five. Patriarchal poetry every little while not every little while once every little while once every little while once every twenty once every little while once every twenty-five once every little while once every little while every once twenty-five once.

Make it a mistake.

Patriarchal she said what is it I know what it is it is I know I know so that I know what it is I know so I know so I know so I know what it is. Very slowly. I know what it is it is on the one side a to be her to be his to be their to be in an and to be I know what it is it is he who was an known not known was he was at first it was the grandfather then it was not that in that the father not of that grandfather and then she to be to be sure to be sure to be I know to be sure to be I know to be sure to be not as good as that. To be sure not to be sure to be sure correctly saying to be sure to be that. It was that. She was right. It was that.

Patriarchal Poetry.

A SONNET

To the wife of my bosom
All happiness from everything
And her husband.
May he be good and considerate
Gay and cheerful and restful.
And make her the best wife
In the world
The happiest and the most content
With reason.
To the wife of my bosom
Whose transcendent virtues
Are those to be most admired
Loved and adored and indeed
Her virtues are all inclusive
Her virtues her beauty and her beauties
Her charms her qualities her joyous nature
All of it makes of her husband
A proud and happy man.

Patriarchal poetry makes no mistake makes no mistake in estimating the value to be placed upon the best and most arranged of considerations of this in as apt to be not only to be partially and as cautiously considered as in allowance which is one at a time. At a chance at a chance encounter it can be very well as appointed as appointed not only considerately but as it as use.

Patriarchal poetry to be sure to be sure to be sure candidly

candidly and aroused patriarchal to be sure and candidly and aroused once in a while and as a circumstance within that arranged within that arranged to be not only not only not only not not secretive but as one at a time not in not to include cautiously cautiously cautiously at one in not to be finally prepared. Patriarchal poetry may be mistaken may be undivided may be usefully to be sure settled and they would be after a while as establish in relatively understanding a promise of not in time but at a time wholly reconciled to feel that as well by an instance of escaped and interrelated choice. That makes it even.

Patriarchal poetry may seem misplaced at one time.

Patriarchal poetry might be what they wanted.

Patriarchal poetry shall be as much as if it was counted from one to one hundred.

From one to one hundred.

From one to one hundred.

From one to one hundred.

Counted from one to one hundred.

Nobody says soften as often.

From one to one hundred.

Has to say happen as often.

Laying while it was while it was while it was. While it was.

Patriarchal poetry while it was just as close as when they were then being used not only in here but also out there which is what was the thing that was not only requested but also desired which when there is not as much as if they could be while it can shall have and this was what was all when it was not used just for that but simply can be not what is it like when they use it.

As much as that patriarchal poetry as much as that.

Patriarchal poetry as much as that.

To like patriarchal poetry as much as that.

To like patriarchal poetry as much as that is what she did.

Patriarchal poetry usually.

In finally finding this out out and out out and about to find it out when it is neither there nor by that time by the time it is not why they had it.

Why they had it.

What is the difference between a glass pen and a pen what is the difference between a glass pen and a pen what is the difference between a glass pen and a pen to smile at the difference between a glass pen and a pen.

To smile at the difference between a glass pen and a pen is what he did.

Patriarchal poetry makes it as usual.

Patriarchal poetry one two three.

Patriarchal poetry accountably.

Patriarchal poetry as much.

Patriarchal Poetry reasonably.

Patriarchal Poetry which is what they did.

One Patriarchal Poetry.

Two Patriarchal Poetry.

Three Patriarchal Poetry.

One two three.

One two three.

One Patriarchal Poetry.

Two Patriarchal Poetry.

Three Patriarchal Poetry.

When she might be what it was to be left to be what they had as they could.

Patriarchal Poetry as if as if it made it be a choice beside.

The Patriarchal Poetry.

At the time that they were sure surely certain certainly aroused arousing laid lessening let letting be it as if it as if it were to be to be as if it were to be letting let it nearly all it could be not be nearly should be which is there which is it there.

Once more a sign.

Signed by them.

Signed by him.

Signed it.

Signed it as it was.

Patriarchal Poetry and rushing Patriarchal Poetry and rushing.

Having had having had having had who having had who had having having had and not five not four not three not one not three not two not four not one not one done.

Patriarchal poetry recollected.

Putting three together all the time two together all the time

two together all the time two together two together two together
all the time putting five together three together all the time. Never
to think of Patriarchal Poetry at one time.

Patriarchal poetry at one time.

Allowed allowed allowed makes it be theirs once once as they
had had it have having have have having having is the same.

Patriarchal Poetry is the same.

Patriarchal Poetry.

It is very well and nicely done in Patriarchal Poetry which is
begun to be begun and this was why if when if when when did
they please themselves indeed. When he did not say leave it to that
but rather indeed as it might be that it was not expressed simultaneously was expressed to be no more as it is very well to trouble
him. He will attend to it in time. Be very well accustomed to this
in that and plan. There is not only no accounting for tastes but
very well identified extra coming out very well identified as repeated verdure and so established as more than for it.

She asked as she came down should she and at that moment
there was no answer but if leaving it alone meant all by it out of
it all by it very truly and could be used to plainly plainly expressed. She will be determined determined not by but on account
of implication implication re-entered which means entered again
and upon.

This could be illustrated and is and is and is. There makes more
than contain contained mine too. Very well to please please.

Once in a while.

Patriarchal poetry once in a while.

Patriarchal Poetry out of pink once in a while.

Patriarchal Poetry out of pink to be bird once in a while.

Patriarchal Poetry out of pink to be bird left and three once
in a while.

Patriarchal Poetry handles once in a while.

Patriarchal Poetry once in a while.

Patriarchal Poetry once in a while.

Patriarchal Poetry to be added.

Patriarchal Poetry reconciled.

Patriarchal Poetry left alone.

Patriarchal Poetry and left of it left of it Patriarchal Poetry left of it Patriarchal Poetry left of it as many twice as many patriarchal poetry left to it twice as many once as it was once it was once every once in a while patriarchal poetry every once in a while.

Patriarchal Poetry might have been in two. Patriarchal Poetry added to added to to once to be once in two Patriarchal poetry to be added to once to add to to add to patriarchal poetry to add to to be to be to add to to add to patriarchal poetry to add to.

One little two little one little two little one little at one time one little one little two little two little two little at one at a time.

One little one little two little two little one little two little as to two little as to two little as to one little as to one two little as to two two little two. Two little two little two little one little two one two one two little two. One little one little one little two little two little one little two one little two.

Need which need which as it is need which need which as it is very need which need which it is very warm here is it.

Need which need which need need in need need which need which is it need in need which need which need which is it.

Need in need need which is it.

What is the difference between a fig and an apple. One comes before the other. What is the difference between a fig and an apple one comes before the other what is the difference between a fig and an apple one comes before the other.

When they are here they are here too here too they are here too. When they are here they are here too when they are here they are here too.

As out in it there.

As not out not out in it there as out in it out in it there as out in it there as not out in it there as out in as out in it as out in it there.

Next to next next to Saturday next to next next to Saturday next to next next to Saturday.

This shows it all.

This shows it all next to next next to Saturday this shows it all.

Once or twice or once or twice once or twice or once or twice this shows it all or next to next this shows it all or once or

twice or once or twice or once or twice this shows it all or next
to next this shows it all or next to next or Saturday or next to next
this shows it all or next to next or next to next or Saturday or
next to next or once or twice this shows it all or next to next or
once or twice this shows it all or Saturday or next to next this
shows it all or once or twice this shows it all or Saturday or next
to next or once or twice this shows it all or once or twice this
shows it all or next to next this shows it all or once or twice
this shows it all or next to next or once or twice or once or twice
this shows it all or next to next this shows it all or once or twice this
shows it all or next to next or once or twice this shows it all or
next to next or next to next or next to next or once or twice or
once or twice or next to next or next to next or once or twice
this shows it all this shows it all or once or twice or next to next
this shows it all or next to next this shows it all or next to next
this shows it all or next to next this shows it all or once or twice
or once or twice this shows it all or once or twice or next to next
this shows it all this shows it all or next to next or shows it
all or once or twice this shows it all or shows it all or next to next
or once or twice or shows it all or once or twice or next to next
or next to next or once or twice or next to next or next to next
or shows it all or shows it all or next to next or once or twice or
shows it all or next to next or shows it all or next to next or shows
it all or once or twice or next to next or next to next or next to
next or next or next or next or next or shows it all or next or next
or next to next or shows it all or next to next to next to next to
next.
Not needed near nearest.
Settle it pink with pink.
Pinkily.
Find it a time at most.
Time it at most at most.
Every differs from Avery Avery differs from every within.
As it is as it is as it is as it is in line as it is in line with it.
Next to be with it next to be with it with it with with with it
next to it with it with it. Return with it.
Even if it did not touch it would you like to give it would
you like to give it give me my even if it did not touch it would

you like to give me my. Even if you like to give it if you did not touch it would you like to give me my.

One divided into into what what is it.

As left to left left to it here left to it here which is not queer which is not queer where when when most when most and best what is the difference between breakfast lunch supper and dinner what is the difference between breakfast and lunch and supper and dinner.

She had it here who to who to she had it here who to she had it here who to she had it here who to she had it here who to who to she had it here who to. Who to she had it here who to.

Not and is added added is and not added added is not and added added is and not added added added is not and added added not and is added added is and is added added and is not and added added and is not and added added is and is not added added is and not and added added is and not and added.

Let leave it out be out let leave it out be out be out let leave it out be out let leave it out be out. Let leave it out be out let leave it out be out. Let leave it out be out. Let leave it out. Let leave it out. Let. Let leave it out. Let leave it out. Let leave it out.

Eighty eighty one which is why to be after one one two Seattle blue and feathers they change which is why to blame it once or twice singly to be sure.

A day as to say a day two to say to say a day a day to say to say to say to say a day as to-day to say as to say to-day. To dates dates different from here and there from here and there.

Let it be arranged for them.

What is the difference between Elizabeth and Edith. She knows. There is no difference between Elizabeth and Edith that she knows. What is the difference. She knows. There is no difference as she knows. What is the difference between Elizabeth and Edith that she knows. There is the difference between Elizabeth and Edith which she knows. There is she knows a difference between Elizabeth and Edith which she knows. Elizabeth and Edith as she knows.

Contained in time forty makes forty-nine. Contained in time as forty makes forty-nine contained in time contained in time

as forty makes forty-nine contained in time as forty makes forty-
nine.

Forty-nine more or at the door.

Forty-nine or more or as before. Forty-nine or forty-nine or
forty-nine.

I wish to sit with Elizabeth who is sitting. I wish to sit with
Elizabeth who is sitting I wish to sit with Elizabeth who is sitting.
I wish to sit with Elizabeth who is sitting.

Forty-nine or four attached to them more more than they
were as well as they were as often as they are once or twice before.

As peculiarly mine in time.

Reform the past and not the future this is what the past can
teach her reform the past and not the future which can be left
to be here now here now as it is made to be made to be here now
here now.

Reform the future not the past as fast as last as first as third
as had as hand it as it happened to be why they did. Did two too
two were sent one at once and one afterwards.

Afterwards.

How can patriarchal poetry be often praised often praised.

To get away from me.

She came in.

Wishes.

She went in

Fishes.

She sat in the room

Yes she did.

Patriarchal poetry.

She was where they had it be nearly as nicely in arrangement.

In arrangement.

To be sure.

What is the difference between ardent and ardently.

Leave it alone.

If one does not care to eat if one does not care to eat oysters
one has no interest in lambs.

That is as usual.

Everything described as in a way in a way in a way gradually.

Likes to be having it come.

Likes to be.

Having it come.

Have not had that.

Around.

One two three one two three one two three one two three four.

Find it again.

When you said when.

When you said

When you said

When you said when.

Find it again.

Find it again

When you said when.

They said they said.

They said they said they said when they said men.

Men many men many how many many many many men men men said many here.

Many here said many many said many which frequently allowed later in recollection many many said when as naturally to be sure.

Very many as to that which which which one which which which which one.

Patriarchal poetry relined.

It is at least last let letting letting letting letting it be theirs.

Theirs at least letting at least letting it be theirs.

Letting it be at least be letting it be theirs.

Letting it be theirs at least letting it be theirs.

When she was as was she was as was she was not yet neither pronounced so and tempted.

Not this this is the way that they make it theirs not they.

Not they.

Patriarchal Poetry makes mistakes.

One two one two my baby is who one two one two one two

my baby or two one two. One two one one or two one one one
one one one one one one or two. Are to.

It is very nearly a pleasure to be warm.

It is very nearly a pleasure to be warm.

It is very nearly a pleasure to be warm.

A line a day book.

One which is mine.

Two in time

Let it alone

Theirs as well

Having it now

Letting it be their share.

Settled it at once.

Liking it or not

How do you do.

It.

Very well very well seriously.

Patriarchal Poetry defined.

Patriarchal Poetry should be this without which and organisation. It should be defined as once leaving once leaving it here having been placed in that way at once letting this be with them after
all. Patriarchal Poetry makes it a master piece like this makes it
which which alone makes like it like it previously to know that
it that that might that might be all very well patriarchal poetry
might be resumed.

How do you do it.

Patriarchal Poetry might be withstood.

Patriarchal Poetry at peace.

Patriarchal Poetry a piece.

Patriarchal Poetry in peace.

Patriarchal Poetry in pieces.

Patriarchal Poetry as peace to return to Patriarchal Poetry
at peace.

Patriarchal Poetry or peace to return to Patriarchal Poetry
or pieces of Patriarchal Poetry.

Very pretty very prettily very prettily very pretty very
prettily.

To never blame them for the mischance of eradicating this and that by then.

Not at the time not at that time not in time to do it. Not a time to do it. Patriarchal Poetry or not a time to do it.

Patriarchal Poetry or made a way patriarchal Poetry tenderly.

Patriarchal Poetry or made a way patriarchal poetry or made a way patriarchal poetry as well as even seen even seen clearly even seen clearly and under and over overtake overtaken by it now. Patriarchal Poetry and replace. Patriarchal Poetry and enough. Patriarchal Poetry and at pains to allow them this and that that it would be plentifully as aroused and leaving leaving it exactly as they might with it all be be careful carefully in that and arranging arrangement adapted adapting in regulating regulate and see seat seating send sent by nearly as withstand precluded in this instance veritably in reunion reunion attached to intermediate remarked remarking plentiful and theirs at once. Patriarchal Poetry has that return.

Patriarchal Poetry might be what is left.

Indifferently.

In differently undertaking their being there there to them there to them with them with their pleasure pleasurable recondite and really really relieve relieving remain remade to be sure certainly and in and and on on account account to be nestled and nestling as understood which with regard to it if when and more leave leaving lying where it was as when when in in this this to be in finally to see so so that that should always be refused refusing refusing makes it have have it having having hinted hindered and implicated resist resist was to be exchanged as to be for for it in never having as there can be shared sharing letting it land lie lie to adjacent to see me. When it goes quickly they must choose Patriarchal Poetry originally originate as originating believe believing repudiate repudiating an impulse. It is not left to right to-day to stay. When this you see remember me should never be added to that.

Patriarchal Poetry and remind reminding clearly come came and left instantly with their entire consenting to be enclosed within what is exacting which might and might and partaking of mentioning much of it to be to be this is mine left to them in

place of how very nicely it can be planted so as to be productive
even if necessarily there is no effort left to them by their having
previously made it be nearly able to be found finding where where
it is when it is very likely to be this in the demand of remaining.
Patriarchal Poetry intimately and intimating that it is to be so
as plead. Plead can have to do with room. Room noon and
nicely.

    Even what was gay.
    Easier in left.
    Easier in an left.
    Easier an left.
    Easier in an left.
    Horticulturally.
    Easier in august.
    Easier an august.
    Easier an in august
    Howard.
    Easier how housed.
    Ivory
    Ivoried.
    Less
    Lest.
    Like it can be used in joining gs.
    By principally.
    Led
    Leaden haul
    Leaden haul if it hails
    Let them you see
    Useful makes buttercup buttercup hyacinth too makes it be
lilied by water and you.
    That is the way they ended.
    It.
    It was was it.
    You jump in the dark, when it is very bright very bright very
bright now.
    Very bright now.
    Might might tell me.
    Withstand.

In second second time time to be next next which is not convincing convincing inhabitable that much that much there.

As one to go.

Letting it letting it letting it alone.

Finally as to be sure.

Selecting that that to that selecting that to that to that all that. All and and and and and and it it is very well thought out.

What is it.

Aim less.

What is it.

Aim less.

Sword less.

What is it

Sword less

What is it

Aim less

What is it.

What is it aim less what is it.

It did so.

It did so.

Said so

Said it did so.

Said it did so did so said so said it did so just as any one might.

Said it did so just as any one might said it did so said so just as any one might.

If water is softened who softened water.

Patriarchal Poetry means in return for that.

Patriarchal poetry means in return.

Nettles nettles her.

Nettle nettle her.

Nettle nettle nettle her nettles nettles nettles her nettle nettle nettle her nettles nettles nettles her. It nettles her to nettle her to nettle her exchange it nettles her exchange to nettle her exchange it nettles her.

Made a mark remarkable made a remarkable interpretation made a remarkable made a remarkable made a remarkable interpretation made a remarkable interpretation now and made a remarkable made a remarkable interpretation made a mark made a remarkable made a remarkable interpretation made a remarkable interpretation now and here here out here out here. The more to change. Hours and hours. The more to change hours and hours the more to change hours and hours.

It was a pleasant hour however however it was a pleasant hour, it was a pleasant hour however it was a pleasant hour resemble hour however it was a pleasant however it was a pleasant hour resemble hour assemble however hour it was a pleasant hour however.

Patriarchal Poetry in assemble.

Assemble Patriarchal Poetry in assemble it would be assemble assemble Patriarchal Poetry in assemble.

It would be Patriarchal Poetry in assemble.

Assemble Patriarchal Poetry resign resign Patriarchal Poetry to believe in trees.

Early trees.

Assemble moss roses and to try.

Assemble Patriarchal Poetry moss roses resemble Patriarchal poetry assign assign to it assemble Patriarchal Poetry resemble moss roses to try.

Patriarchal Poetry resemble to try.

Moss roses assemble Patriarchal Poetry resign lost a lost to try. Resemble Patriarchal Poetry to love to.

To wish to does.

Patriarchal Poetry to why.

Patriarchal Poetry ally.

Patriarchal Poetry with to try to all ally to ally to wish to why to. Why did it seem originally look as well as very nearly pronounceably satisfy lining.

To by to by that by by a while any any stay stationary.

Stationary has been invalidated.

And not as surprised.

Patriarchal Poetry surprised supposed.

Patriarchal Poetry she did she did.

Did she Patriarchal Poetry.

Is to be periwinkle which she met which is when it is astounded and come yet as she did with this in this and this let in their to be sure it wishes it for them an instance in this as this allows allows it to to be sure now when it is as well as it is and has ever been outlined.

There are three things that are different pillow pleasure pre-pare and after while. There are two things that they prepare maidenly see it and ask it as it if has been where they went. There are enough to go. One thing altogether altogether as he might. Might he.

Never to do never to do never to do to do to do never to do never to do never to do to do to do to do never to do never never to do to do it as if it were an anemone an anemone an anemone to be an anemone to be to be certain to let to let it to let it alone.

What is the difference between two spoonfuls and three. None.

Patriarchal Poetry as signed.

Patriarchal Poetry might which it is very well very well leave it to me very well patriarchal poetry leave it to me leave it to me leave it to leave it to me naturally to see the second and third first naturally first naturally to see naturally to first see the second and third first to see to see the second and third to see the second and third naturally to see it first.

Not as well said as she said regret that regret that not as well said as she said Patriarchal Poetry as well said as she said it Patri-archal Poetry untied. Patriarchal Poetry.

Do we.

What is the difference between Mary and May. What is the difference between May and day. What is the difference between day and daughter what is the difference between daughter and there what is the difference between there and day-light what is the difference between day-light and let what is the difference between let and letting what is the difference between letting and to see what is the difference between to see immediately patriarchal poetry and rejoice.

Patriarchal Poetry made and made.

Patriarchal Poetry makes a land a lamb. There is no use at all in reorganising in reorganising. There is no use at all in reorganis-ing chocolate as a dainty.

Patriarchal Poetry reheard.

Patriarchal Poetry to be filled to be filled to be filled to be

filled to method method who hears method method who hears
who hears who hears method method method who hears who
hears who hears and method and method and method and who
hears and who who hears and method method is delightful and
who and who who hears method is method is method is delightful
is who hears is delightful who hears method is who hears method
is method is method is delightful is delightful who hears who
hears of of delightful who hears of method of delightful who of
whom of whom of of who hears of method method is delightful. Unified in their expanse. Unified in letting there there there
one two one two three there in a chain a chain how do you
laterally in relation to auditors and obliged obliged currently.

Patriarchal Poetry is the same.

Patriarchal Poetry thirteen.

With or with willing with willing mean.

I mean I mean.

Patriarchal Poetry connected with mean.

Queen with willing.

With willing.

Patriarchal Poetry obtained with seize.

Willing.

Patriarchal Poetry in chance to be found.

Patriarchal Poetry obliged as mint to be mint to be mint
to be obliged as mint to be.

Mint may be come to be as well as cloud and best.

Patriarchal Poetry deny why.

Patriarchal Poetry come by the way to go.

Patriarchal Poetry interdicted.

Patriarchal Poetry at best.

Best and Most.

Long and Short.

Left and Right.

There and More.

Near and Far.

Gone and Come.

Light and Fair.

Here and There.

This and Now.

Felt and How
Next and Near.
In and On.
New and Try
In and This.
Which and Felt.
Come and Leave.
By and Well.
Returned.
Patriarchal Poetry indeed.
Patriarchal Poetry which is let it be come from having a mild
and came and same and with it all.
Near.
To be shelled from almond.
Return Patriarchal Poetry at this time.
Begin with a little ruff a little ruffle.
Return with all that.
Returned with all that four and all that returned with four
with all that.
How many daisies are there in it.
How many daisies are there in it.
How many daisies are there in it.
How many daisies are there in it.
A line a day book.
How many daisies are there in it.
Patriarchal Poetry a line a day book.
Patriarchal Poetry.
A line a day book.
Patriarchal Poetry.
When there is in it.
When there is in it.
A line a day book.
When there is in it.
Patriarchal Poetry a line a day book when there is in it.
By that time lands lands there.
By that time lands there a line a day book when there is that
in it.
Patriarchal Poetry reclaimed renamed replaced and gathered

together as they went in and left it more where it is in when it
pleased when it was pleased when it can be pleased to be gone
over carefully and letting it be a chance for them to lead to lead
to lead not only by left but by leaves.

They made it be obstinately in their change and with it with
it let it let it leave it in the opportunity. Who comes to be with
a glance with a glance at it at it in palms and palms too orderly
to orderly in changes of plates and places and beguiled beguiled
with a restless impression of having come to be all of it as might
as might as might and she encouraged. Patriarchal Poetry might
be as useless. With a with a with a won and delay. With a with a
with a won and delay.

He might object to it not being there as they were left to them
all around. As we went out by the same way we came back again
after a detour.

That is one account on one account.

Having found anemones and a very few different shelves we
were for a long time just staying by the time that it could have
been as desirable. Desirable makes it be left to them.

Patriarchal Poetry includes not being received.

Patriarchal Poetry comes suddenly as around.

And now.

There is no difference between spring and summer none at all.

And wishes.

Patriarchal Poetry there is no difference between spring and
summer not at all and wishes.

There is no difference between spring and summer not at all
and wishes.

There is no difference not at all between spring and summer
not at all and wishes.

Yes as well.

And how many times.

Yes as well and how many times yes as well.

How many times yes as well ordinarily.

Having marked yes as well ordinarily having marked yes as
well.

It was to be which is theirs left in this which can have all their
thinking it as fine.

It was to be which is theirs left in this which is which is which can which can which may which may which will which will which in which in which are they know they know to care for it having come back without and it would be better if there had not been any at all to find to find to find. It is not desirable to mix what he did with adding adding to choose to choose. Very well part of her part of her very well part of her. Very well part of her. Patriarchal Poetry in pears. There is no choice of cherries.

Will he do.

Patriarchal Poetry in coins.

Not what it is.

Patriarchal Poetry net in it pleases. Patriarchal Poetry surplus if rather admittedly in repercussion instance and glance separating letting dwindling be in knife to be which is not wound wound entirely as white wool white will white change white see white settle white understand white in the way white be lighten lighten let letting bear this neatly nearly made in vain.

Patriarchal Poetry who seats seasons patriarchal poetry in gather meanders patriarchal poetry engaging this in their place their place their allow. Patriarchal Poetry. If he has no farther no farther no farther to no farther to no farther to no to no to farther to not to be right to be known to be even as a chance. Is it best to support Allan Allan will Allan Allan is it best to support Allan Allan patriarchal poetry patriarchal poetry is it best to support Allan Allan will Allan best to support Allan will patriarchal poetry Allan will patriarchal poetry Allan will patriarchal poetry is it best to support Allan patriarchal poetry Allan will is it best Allan will is it best to support Allan patriarchal poetry Allan will best to support patriarchal poetry Allan will is it best Allan will to support patriarchal poetry patriarchal poetry Allan will patriarchal poetry Allan will.

Is it best to support patriarchal poetry Allan will patriarchal poetry.

Patriarchal Poetry makes it incumbent to know on what day races will take place and where otherwise there would be much inconvenience everywhere.

Patriarchal Poetry erases what is eventually their purpose

and their inclination and their reception and their without their
being beset. Patriarchal poetry an entity.

What is the difference between their charm and to charm.

Patriarchal Poetry in negligence.

Patriarchal Poetry they do not follow that they do not follow
that this does not follow that this does not follow that theirs does
not follow that theirs does not follow that the not following
that the not following that having decided not to abandon a sister
for another. This makes patriarchal poetry in their place in their
places in their places in the place in the place of is it in the next
to it as much as aroused feeling so feeling it feeling at once to be
in the wish and what is it of theirs. Suspiciously. Patriarchal poetry for instance. Patriarchal poetry not minded not minded it.
In now. Patriarchal poetry left to renown. Renown.

It is very certainly better not to be what is it when it is in the
afternoon.

Patriarchal poetry which is it. Which is it after it is after it is
after it is after before soon when it is by the time that when they
make let it be not only because why should why should why
should it all be fine.

Patriarchal poetry they do not do it right.

Patriarchal poetry letting it be alright.

Patriarchal Poetry having it placed where it is.

Patriarchal Poetry might have it.

Might have it.

Patriarchal Poetry a choice.

Patriarchal poetry because of it.

Patriarchal Poetry replaced.

Patriarchal Poetry withstood and placated.

Patriarchal Poetry in arrangement.

Patriarchal Poetry that day.

Patriarchal Poetry might it be very likely which is it as it
can be very precisely unified as tries.

Patriarchal poetry with them lest they be stated.

Patriarchal poetry. He might be he might he he might be he
might be.

Patriarchal poetry a while a way.

Patriarchal poetry if patriarchal poetry is what you say why do you delight in never having positively made it choose.

Patriarchal poetry never linking patriarchal poetry.

Sometime not a thing.

Patriarchal Poetry sometimes not anything.

Patriarchal Poetry which which which which is it.

Patriarchal Poetry left to them.

Patriarchal poetry left together.

Patriarchal Poetry does not like to be allowed after a while to be what is more formidably forget me nots anemones china lilies plants articles chances printing pears and likely meant very likely meant to be given to him.

Patriarchal Poetry would concern itself with when it is in their happening to be left about left about now.

There is no interest in resemblances.

Patriarchal poetry one at a time.

This can be so.

To by any way.

Patriarchal poetry in requesting in request in request best patriarchal poetry leave that alone.

Patriarchal poetry noise noiselessly.

Patriarchal poetry not in fact in fact.

After patriarchal poetry.

I defy any one to turn a better heel than that while reading.

Patriarchal poetry reminded.

Patriarchal poetry reminded of it.

Patriarchal Poetry reminded of it too.

Patriarchal Poetry reminded of it too to be sure.

Patriarchal Poetry reminded of it too to be sure really. Really left.

Patriarchal Poetry and crackers in that case.

Patriarchal Poetry and left bread in that case.

Patriarchal Poetry and might in that case.

Patriarchal Poetry connected in that case with it.

Patriarchal Poetry make it do a day.

Is he fond of him.

If he is fond of him if he is fond of him is he fond of his birthday the next day. If he is fond of his birthday the next day is he fond of the birthday trimming if he is fond of the birthday the day is he fond of the day before the day before the day of the day before the birthday. Every day is a birthday the day before. Patriarchal Poetry the day before.

Patriarchal Poetry the day that it might.

Patriarchal Poetry does not make it never made it will not have been making it be that way in their behalf.

Patriarchal Poetry insistance.

Insist.

Patriarchal Poetry insist insistance.

Patriarchal Poetry which is which is it.

Patriarchal Poetry and left it left it by left it by left it. Patriarchal Poetry what is the difference Patriarchal Poetry.

Patriarchal Poetry.

Not patriarchal poetry all at a time.

To find patriarchal poetry about.

Patriarchal Poetry is named patriarchal poetry.

If patriarchal poetry is nearly by nearly means it to be to be so.

Patriarchal Poetry and for them then.

Patriarchal Poetry did he leave his son.

Patriarchal Poetry Gabrielle did her share.

Patriarchal poetry it is curious.

Patriarchal poetry please place better.

Patriarchal poetry in come I mean I mean.

Patriarchal poetry they do their best at once more once more once more once more to do to do would it be left to advise advise realise realise dismay dismay delighted with her pleasure.

Patriarchal poetry left to inundate them.

Patriarchal Poetry in pieces. Pieces which have left it as names which have left it as names to to all said all said as delight.

Patriarchal poetry the difference.

Patriarchal poetry needed with weeded with seeded with payed it with left it without it with me. When this you see give it to me.

Patriarchal poetry makes it be have you it here.

Patriarchal Poetry twice.

Patriarchal Poetry in time.

It should be left.

Patriarchal Poetry with him.

Patriarchal Poetry.

Patriarchal Poetry at a time.

Patriarchal Poetry not patriarchal poetry.

Patriarchal Poetry as wishes.

Patriarchal poetry might be found here.

Patriarchal poetry interested as that.

Patriarchal Poetry left.

Patriarchal Poetry left left.

Patriarchal poetry left left left right left.

Patriarchal poetry in justice.

Patriarchal poetry in sight.

Patriarchal poetry in what is what is what is what is what.

Patriarchal poetry might to-morrow.

Patriarchal Poetry might be finished to-morrow.

Dinky pinky dinky pinky dinky pinky dinky pinky once and try. Dinky pinky dinky pinky dinky pinky lullaby. Once sleepy one once does not once need a lullaby. Not to try.

Patriarchal Poetry not to try. Patriarchal Poetry and lullaby. Patriarchal Poetry not to try Patriarchal poetry at once and why patriarchal poetry at once and by by and by Patriarchal poetry has to be which is best for them at three which is best and will be be and why why patriarchal poetry is not to try try twice.

Patriarchal Poetry having patriarchal poetry. Having patriarchal poetry having patriarchal poetry. Having patriarchal poetry. Having patriarchal poetry and twice, patriarchal poetry.

He might have met.

Patriarchal poetry and twice patriarchal poetry.